Jessie let out an involuntary shriek as Boyce dove out of the bed to tackle the first figure into the room— a man with his hat pulled low and a dark bandanna across the lower half of his face.

Jessie, heedless of her nudity, kicked off the covers and yanked open the nightstand drawer and extracted her Colt.

"Go ahead and shoot, Miss Starbuck."

"I hit what I aim at," Jessie warned, bringing her gun around to bear on the outlaw trio.

"All that shooting will wake up your hands. So we'll have to shoot some of them as well. And when it's all over and done, you'll still be coming along with us.

"The question you got to answer is, do you want it *that* way, or *quietly,* with nobody getting hurt?"

WESLEY ELLIS

LONE STAR

AND THE WOLF PACK

JOVE BOOKS, NEW YORK

LONE STAR AND THE WOLF PACK

A Jove Book / published by arrangement with the author

PRINTING HISTORY
Jove edition / January 1993

ISBN: 0-515-11019-1

Jove Books are published by The Berkley Publishing Group,
200 Madison Avenue, New York, New York 10016.
The name "JOVE" and the "J" logo
are trademarks belonging to Jove Publications, Inc.

PRINTED IN THE UNITED STATES OF AMERICA

10 9 8 7 6 5 4 3 2 1

LONE STAR

AND THE
WOLF PACK

★
Chapter 1

Ki paused a moment, twisting around in his saddle to contemplate the sunrise breaking over the Texas plain. It was a cool spring dawn, the sun's first flush breaking pink, as radiant as a pleased woman's blush, before that rosy glow bled down into the gun-metal gray that truly marked morning's beginning.

It was five days into the annual roundup on the Starbuck spread. The Circle Star ranch hands were branding cattle prior to taking the beeves on the short drive to the railroad holding pens in the nearby town of Sarah. Ki was the acting ramrod. Custom had it that the job was more or less a supervisory position, but Ki believed in leading by example. Before even the wranglers in charge of the horses had crawled from their bedrolls, he'd saddled up to make a swing around the herd, to check for stragglers that might have wandered off during the night.

But now the rest of the hands were up and around. The smells of morning coffee and frying bacon wafting from the chuck wagon had been replaced by the pungent scent of burning oak as the cowboys stoked the branding fires.

Ki rode toward the herd and then let the reins of his mount go slack, granting his sturdy cow pony the freedom to do its job. The buckskin plunged into the roiling mass of cows

1

like a retriever splashing into water after a fallen duck. Ki's horse was the product of much mixed breeding; it had the exuberant, unspoiled spirit of an untamed mustang and the buckskin coloring—mustard tan, with black mane and tail—of its thoroughbred, noble Andalusian Arab lineage. As with the dog, Ki believed that it was the mongrel that usually proved to be exemplary, but, of course, since Ki had had a Japanese mother and an American father, he would always have within his heart a place for creatures of mixed ancestry.

Now Ki gently guided his mount with knee pressure along, practicing *Bajutsu,* the Japanese warrior's art of horsemanship that left one's hands free to handle weapons. Here on the Circle Star spread, during roundup, it amused Ki to see a "home-grown" variant of *Bajutsu* being practiced by almost all the cowboys. Any experienced hand knew enough to let his horse do most of the work, knew that the art of cutting a calf out of the herd for branding was an almost mystical dance between pony and cow. The thing for a cowboy to do was go along quietly for the ride, the better to admire the adroitness born of training and bloodlines in his horse.

Ki's buckskin, a veteran of previous roundups, swiftly, silently closed on an oblivious calf trotting alongside its mother. Again, Ki was pleased, for swift, silent movement was the samurai's way, taught to Ki during his childhood in Japan, along with all the other *bugei,* or techniques of the martial arts, by the master warrior Hirata, prior to the Great One's death.

The samurai readied his lasso as his mount singled out the calf and began to prod it gently toward the edge of the herd, and the closest branding station. The calf broke free of the herd and began to run, and then, perhaps smelling the fire, abruptly wheeled, intent upon regaining the security of its mother's side. Ki's buckskin swerved to block the calf, as he set his lasso twirling. Using a side-armed, underhanded cast, the samurai managed to slip the rope under the doggie's hind legs. A soft twitch of his mount's reins, and his horse came to a stop. Meanwhile, Ki had taken up the lasso's slack with a few quick dallies of the excess around his saddle horn, quickly toppling the calf.

Usually Ki went barefoot, for his feet were callused and tough from his years of martial arts training. During the

2

roundup, however, he wore boots because he often had to dig in his heels to reel tight an ornery roped steer. Except for his boots, his garb this morning was his usual working outfit: a pair of snug-fitting, broken-in denim jeans, a blousy, collarless pullover shirt of cotton twill, and a loose, many-pocketed leather vest. Ki went hatless, using a thin, rawhide thong to keep his thick, shiny, blue-black hair out of his eyes during the hot, dirty work of roundup. He wore no gun, but cached away in that innocent-seeming vest were all the weapons he usually required.

Now Ki watched as one cowboy on foot released his lasso from around the calf's legs and then effortlessly hogtied the writhing critter. Another hand took a properly heated branding iron from the smouldering charcoal embers, pulled the calf's hide tight, and pressed home the iron's cherry-red business end. The calf mewled, the acrid stench of burned hair briefly filled the air, and then it was over. The released calf, quickly regaining its wobbly legs, ambled off to rejoin its mother.

Ki coiled up his lasso and rode at an easy lope away from the herd. He headed in the direction of the chuck wagon and the wrangler's remuda, figuring on exchanging his winded buck for a fresh horse. The roundup was proceeding smoothly, he thought, but then a Circle Star roundup was always somewhat easier than the roundups on other ranches. For one thing, cowboys didn't have to worry about separating Circle Star cows from animals belonging to other spreads, as the Starbuck range was so vast, and its herd numbered over a hundred thousand. Almost a week ago the roundup had begun at the far end of the ranch; they were now about dead center of the Starbuck holdings, and they were still several days' ride from the main house and outbuildings.

"Boss! Yo! Boss!"

Ki reined in his buck as a rider broke through a clump of stunted hardwoods. As the hand drew closer, Ki recognized him: it was old Hank Tyson, the boss wrangler. Both Hank and his lathered horse, a big-boned bay, were covered with dust.

"Boss, I got something to talk to you about," the rider muttered, removing his face kerchief in order to spit.

"As I have told you before, Hank, you need not call me Boss," Ki said patiently and sighed. "My name will do fine."

3

"I'm jest ascared you won't want me call'n you anything at all after I tell you what I got to tell you . . ." Hank shrugged, seemingly unable to look Ki in the eye.

The boss wrangler was in his late sixties. He'd been a tall, barrel-chested man in his youth, Ki suspected, but the years had stooped him, settling all of his muscle into his belly, which now strained the buttons of his threadbare brown flannel shirt and protruded over the waistband of his baggy jeans.

Hank had a gray, close-cropped beard, more than likely meant to make up for the lack of hair on his head. He wore a canvas, leather-visored cap to protect his dome from the sun, well-worn cordovan boots, and what looked to be a .44 single-action Colt Peacemaker, with sweat-stained wooden grips, tucked into a plain, light tan holster cinched high on his right hip.

"Jest scared that when you find out what's happened you'll tell me to collect my belong'ns and turn me out."

"Hank, you know that could never happen," Ki said, thinking the old hand sounded close to tears. "Jessica Starbuck has told you as much herself."

"Yes, Boss—I mean, Ki." Hank hurried to correct himself. "I'm jest afraid that when Miss Jessie finds out . . ."

"Finds out what?" Ki tried to interrupt.

" . . . finds out what's happened she'll lose patience with me. Decide she's got no place for an old hand—"

"Hank, *I* am starting to lose patience," Ki fumed. "Jessie herself has told me that she couldn't imagine running the spread without you."

That last bit was something of a white lie, of course, but Ki, being half-Japanese, held to the creed of revering one's elders. What Jessica *had* told the samurai, well over a year ago when Hank had first arrived at the Circle Star, was that Hank Tyson and her father, Alex Starbuck, had been friends in the old days, when she'd been just a little girl. Hank had started out working as a hand for her father, then a ramrod, and eventually became foreman of the Circle Star. Then Alex further promoted his friend, asking Hank to head off to far-flung parts as his representative, to look after scattered Starbuck cattle interests. Hank had done a good job, roving far and wide, getting new cattle ranch holdings into shape. Unfortunately, he turned out to have little head for business.

4

He was the best at streamlining a cowpunching operation, but couldn't make hide nor hair out of ledgers and account books, which kept him from rising further in the Starbuck business empire. And Hank was just as bad at riding herd over his own money as he was at trying to rein in Alex Starbuck's finances. Jessie's father had handsomely paid the man for his work, but Hank had pissed it all away. Last year, when Hank had arrived at the Circle Star from a Starbuck cattle operation in Wyoming, too plain old busted-up and saddle-sprung to continue with his ranch manager duties, flat broke and worried about his future, Jessie had assured him that he had a home for life and no duties at all, except those he chose. Six months ago, when the job opened up, Hank had eagerly taken on the post of boss wrangler.

"You know that Jessie says you have a pension here," Ki assured Hank. "And Jessica Starbuck does not go back on her word."

"Fine girl, what a fine girl," Hank murmured in an emotional, trembling voice. He wiped away what seemed to be a tear glossing his old eyes, which were faded to the blue of a well-washed work shirt. "What a tussler she is!" he exclaimed in that hoarse tone of voice some men use when their feelings of love grow too strong. "Just like her daddy. What a tussler—"

"Hank, you had something to tell me?" Ki prodded, trying to get the conversation back on the right track.

"Oh, bejesus, yes!" Hank exclaimed, raising a cloud of trail dust as he slapped his thigh.

"Come on, then," Ki sighed wearily. "You can tell me what it is while we ride back to the remuda. I need a fresh mount."

The cow ponies were smart, and needed a minimum of water and feed, but they required a good deal of rest in order to thrive. The men made it a point to exchange their mounts several times during the workday.

"That's jest it, Ki," Hank blurted. "You can't change your horse 'cause there ain't none! Every blessed one of 'em has run off!"

"Tell me about it while we ride back to the remuda," Ki demanded. Or at least, he thought grimly, setting off, where the remuda was . . .

"There ain't much to tell," Hank remarked, spurring his bay into a canter alongside Ki's buck. "I sent that kid I got helping me—"

5

"Yes, Joady Cooper," Ki said and nodded impatiently.

"Yep, well, I sent Joady to take fresh mounts to some of the boys, and when I got back—"

"You were gone as well when the horses ran off?" Ki interrupted, frowning.

"Yeah." Hank blushed. "Ya see, I felt nature's call to take me my morning constitutional, and when you get to be my age, Ki, you take it while the takin's good. Anyway I went off to find me some privacy in them hickory trees over yonder, and when I got back, I found my rope corral chewed, and them horses skedaddled."

"Cook was near by. He saw nothing?" Ki asked.

"Ain't rightly asked 'im," Hank replied. "But you know Cookie. Once he's got his nose in his kettles, he don't rightly pay noth'n else no mind."

Ki nodded, not bothering to stop as they rode past the chuck wagon, where the cook was busy preparing the midday meal, and then through an island of hickory rising up from the lush green prairie.

"Here we be," Hank said. "But there ain't much to see, 'cept for where a dozen fine cow ponies *used* to be."

That depends on how you look, Ki thought as he quickly surveyed the perimeter bounded by Hank's makeshift corral: four wooden stakes pounded into the dirt and strung with rope.

"What are you looking for?" Hank asked as Ki dismounted and then got down on his hands and knees to study the ground.

"Boot prints," Ki replied.

"Whose?" Hank pushed back his cap to scratch at his scalp. "You mean mine and Joady's?"

Ki did not answer, concentrating his attention on the ground. The grass thereabouts had been grazed down to stubble and the ground pounded hard by the milling horses. An army could have come marching through there without leaving a trace heel mark.

"Hell, them nags bit through the ropes over *here*," Hank said, still watching Ki with a puzzled expression.

Ki walked over to where Hank was standing and picked up one of the frayed rope ends lying in the dirt. He looked at it closely and then shook his head.

"This rope was not gnawed apart, Hank. It was cut."

"How can you tell?"

"I have spent my life studying edged weapons," the samurai replied. "And even if I was wrong about the rope, there is something else . . ."

Ki gestured over his shoulder to where his buck and Hank's mare were standing, waiting. Hank looked confused for a moment, but then what Ki was getting at finally dawned on him.

"Right . . ." the boss wrangler mused. "Starbuck mounts are trained not to wander when their reins touch the ground." He shook his head. "But these nags weren't bridled. I still say that they gnawed the rope for the salt from the dried sweat soaked into the hemp, and then lit off for some fool reason."

"And do you not find it odd that a remuda full of horses should be so clever as to pick the moment when both their handlers were absent to make their break?" Ki remarked.

"You say'n somethin' spooked 'em?"

"I think we are finally starting to agree." Ki's sardonic smile quickly faded. "But where is Joady?"

"I sent him off to track down them nags," Hank said, and then frowned. "What's the matter? Why you look'n so worried all of a sudden?"

"Come, we will ride after him," Ki said, starting for his buck. "The trail the runaway horses have left is clear enough. But first I must stop at the chuck wagon to get my bow."

"So you *do* think a coyote spooked 'em?" Hank demanded as they mounted up. "That's why you're fetch'n your bow, right?"

"Perhaps," Ki murmured. He knew what Hank was getting at: A well-placed arrow could make short work of a coyote, and do it quietly. Ki had issued strict orders to the men not to use their guns against predators, as he was worried that a gunshot might provoke a stampede.

"But coyotes are not the only would-be predators of the herd," Ki told the boss wrangler. "Roundup time draws cattle—and horse—thieves the way honey does flies."

Ki and Hank pushed their already winded mounts as hard as they dared for the better part of an hour, following the trail left by the horses. Eventually the flat pastures gave

7

way to granite outcroppings, the land broken by shallow creeks, arroyos that would soon flood, and knolls covered with scraggly clumps of post-oak and blackjack. And above it all was a mid-morning sky as blue as cornflowers.

Ki concentrated on his riding, coaxing his roan to run along the narrow spine of a ridge, to climb a steep, rocky foothill, and then slide skittering on its haunches down the far side. It vexed him mightily that he had to physically stretch the already tired buckskin to its utmost, but there was no help for it. The samurai suspected horse thieves. He hoped he was somehow wrong, but that cut rope back at the remuda made him fear the worst for young Joady Cooper, who even now might be riding into danger by chasing after the mounts.

" . . . so then I told Big Bob 'Wake up and smell the coffee!' " Hank was saying. " 'It's 1880,' I says. 'The cowboys' days is numbered . . . ' "

Sensing his agitation, Ki let the old wrangler chatter on. Hank knew as well as anyone that if Ki were right about it being horse thieves at the bottom of all this, then poor Joady didn't stand a chance.

"Yep, that's what I told old Bob," Hank continued as they began to pick their way up a gradually steepening rise of crumbly sandstone. "I told him, 'All the old Texas cattle trails—Chisholm, the Shawnee, the Goodnight-Loving—are going the way of the buffalo, 'cause there ain't no sense in cattlemen walk'n the profits off of their cattle, when their beef can arrive fat and tender, ride'n the iron horse, cause—' "

He stopped short as they heard the shots. There were not just one or two reports, which might signify a hunter, but a steady, rattling series, like dry kindling crackling.

"Goddamn! I reckon you was right, Ki!" Hank fretted. "That's likely poor Joady, up against who knows what."

They mercilessly kneed their winded mounts into a hard run over the crest of the sandstone rise. Down below was a series of granite outcroppings that turned the trail they'd been following into a switchback maze. They could see gray clouds of gunsmoke drifting lazily on a breeze that carried the stink of spent gunpowder.

"There's Joady," Hank exclaimed, pointing to a young wrangler crouched behind one of the boulders. Joady had his revolver gripped in both hands and steadied on top of the rock, and he was firing as fast as he could thumb back the hammer. From their vantage point on the rise, Ki and Hank could see gun barrels poking out from the rocks to return Joady's fire. Whoever the young wrangler was shooting at had decided to make their stand about fifty yards from where Joady was crouched.

"As I feared, it seems Joady rode into an ambush," Ki muttered.

"Damn right," Hank spat. "No-account bastards must have shot the kid's horse right out from under him."

Ki nodded. About ten yards into the boulder-studded no-man's-land between the two positions lay a roan gelding, its side ripped open by bullets. One leg still kicked feebly in the air. "Joady was lucky to make it to the safety of the rocks."

"We've got to help him!" Hank had already drawn his Peacemaker, but before he could ride off, Ki grabbed hold of his mount's reins. The wrangler's mare, confused by the contradictory commands, and already very frightened by the noise of the battle down below, showed the whites of its eyes as it snorted and bucked.

"What are you up to?" Hank demanded of Ki as he struggled to bring his mount back under his control. The animal quieted, to stand trembling and pawing at the ground. "We've got to get down there and lend a hand!"

"Listen to me," Ki ordered sternly. "It will not help us to have those horse thieves shoot our mounts the way they shot Joady's."

Hank nodded meekly. "Dammit, you're right, of course. What should we do, then?"

"I want you to tether our mounts in that stand of aspens we passed at the base of this rise. There they will be safe and calm." Ki had already dismounted and drawn his Japanese bow from its specially designed saddle boot. The bow was a crookedly shaped weapon, about four feet long. He strapped his quiver of arrows about his waist, resting it behind his right hip, as if it were a gun holster. "Once you've seen to the horses, join Joady and me down below, but be careful."

As Hank led their horses back down the rise, Ki scurried to join the badly outnumbered young wrangler. The men hiding in the rocks were no longer returning Joady's fire. Ki considered that a bad omen. It meant these outlaws were

9

professionals who were not easily panicked. Most likely they were waiting for Joady to use up all his ammunition. Then they could attack with no risk to themselves.

Joady whirled around as Ki approached. "What the hell—?" the frightened young cowboy gasped, bringing his pistol to bear.

Ki was close enough to grab the revolver's hot barrel, slipping his thumb between the cocked hammer and the firing pin, to keep Joady from squeezing off a shot. He wrenched it easily from the boy's grasp.

"Sorry, sir!" Joady blurted. He was a redheaded, freckle-faced, skinny kid, no more than sixteen or seventeen years old. But the boy was tall for his age, and looked older in his working cowboy's outfit of cracked, worn chaps, ancient canvas trousers, and a dark green flannel shirt patched in a dozen places. His flat-crowned, black Stetson was battered, brim-broken, and stained with sweat. "Guess I'm a mite spooked," the boy continued, looking embarrassed.

"Understandable, considering the circumstances," Ki murmured, handing Joady back his gun. The boy's Colt Peacemaker had had its bluing rubbed pretty much off, and its black rubber grips were held in place with several dingy twists of rope. Ki noticed that Joady wore his holster on a smooth belt, but the bellows pocket of his shirt contained extra cartridges.

Just then, Hank joined the two men. He had a couple of canteens slung over his shoulder.

"I sure could use a drink of water," Joady said, licking his dry lips.

"*I* sure could use a *rifle*," Hank muttered as he handed Joady one of the canteens, watching as the kid took several long swallows.

"We might as well wish for the cavalry, while we are at it," Ki said and shrugged. He'd never yet run across an honest, working cowboy who owned a rifle. Long guns, beside being expensive, got in the way when strapped to a saddle during a hand's riding and roping chores. Single-action handguns, used more as makeshift hammers than as weapons, were the rule, since most cowboys lived out their lives never drawing on anything but coyotes.

"What happened, son?" Hank asked as Joady handed back the canteen.

"I was follow'n the trail after them horses we lost when I found myself in the midst of an ambush. There's a whole bunch of owlhoots over yonder, and they've got a dozen Circle Star horses tethered along with their own horses behind some rocks over to our left."

From the horse thieves' position came a shot. The round ricocheted off the boulder the three were crouched behind, dusting them with pulverized granite.

It was a rifle shot, Ki thought broodingly. The outlaws would be well armed. For them, as for a samurai, weapons were the tools of the trade . . .

"Joady, what in tarnation do you think you were up to try'n to hold off these hard men all by your lonesome?" Hank scolded.

"I've got to say that wasn't my plan," Joady admitted sheepishly. "Like I told you, I rode right into 'em before I knew it. And before I could ride out of range they shot my horse out from under me. I scrambled behind this here rock, and it's been a Mexican standoff ever since."

"Maybe now that we're here, they'll just ride off," Hank offered.

"We cannot let them go with Starbuck horses," Ki interjected.

His words were drowned out by gunfire erupting from the horse thieves' position. Rounds struck their boulder and whined off. Joady ducked out of sight, while Ki and Hank took up positions on either side of the rock. One of the thieves made a zigzag run toward the horses, firing his pistol as he did so. The other outlaws kept firing, trying to cover their man.

Hank thumbed back the hammer of his Colt, took aim, and squeezed the trigger. His gun spat fire and smoke, its report echoing off the surrounding rocks. Ki saw the outlaw Hank had been aiming at spin to the ground.

"Still got my touch," Hank said smugly. "A man shoots enough tin cans off enough fence rails it stands to reason that when push comes to shove he's gonna have what it takes to—"

"Hank, how much ammunition do you have?" Ki demanded.

The boss wrangler felt the cartridge loops stitched onto his gunbelt. "Oh, hell, Ki. I only got six on my belt, and the four

11

left in my gun. Don't believe in keeping one under my firing pin, you know."

"I only got seven left," Joady said and moped.

"It will not do," Ki declared. "I am certain the men we are up against have plenty of ammo. We are likely badly outnumbered, and while it is clear that they are just as adamant about keeping the stolen horses as we are about getting them back, we cannot count on a repetition of that last desperate ploy on their part. I also suspect that they are already spreading out among these rocks," Ki continued, causing the two wranglers to look around them uneasily. "Joady," the samurai said, "you must get away to bring help."

"No, sir!" Joady hotly began to argue. "I mean, no disrespect, sir, but this is no time for us to split up—"

"It is precisely the time." Ki cut the boy off, his calm, even tone overriding Joady's emotional outburst. "You must ride back to the roundup for help."

"That's over an hour from here," Joady exclaimed. "Over two hours there and back. You can't hold out that long."

"We've got no choice, son," Hank said. "I agree with Ki. Hell, them owlhoots will be able to see you get away, but by then you'll be out of rifle range. Maybe then they'll give it up and vamoose without them horses. Knowing that they got a time limit—even if it is over two hours—might just spook them into running."

Joady glanced skeptically at the two older men. "Don't tell me you both believe that."

"Somebody has got to go for help," Ki said.

"Then it ought to be Hank," Joady said stubbornly.

"That don't make any sense, son, when you're the better rider," the old wrangler pointed out. "My rheumatism is such that I just can't ride hell-bent for leather for more than a mile or so before my tailbone gives out . . . Now you know that for a fact, boy . . ."

"Yessir," Joady mumbled.

"It'd take me twice as long to get back to the herd as it would you, and you know that, too!"

"Maybe we all ought to go," Joady suddenly said.

"Three men on two horses?" Hank scowled. "Them hardtacks would catch us, for sure!"

"And there is another reason," Ki softly interjected. "You are likely thinking, So what if a few Circle Star horses are lost? Jessie Starbuck has plenty more . . . To me, however, the question of whether she might miss a few horses is irrelevant. I have long ago sworn an oath to the late Alex Starbuck, Jessie's father, to protect Starbuck life and property. For that reason I would fight for one horse as if it were a thousand. To do anything less would betray my samurai tradition."

"Sir?" Joady looked puzzled. "Your Sam Rye Who?"

Ki smiled. "What I meant was, to do anything less would not be honorable."

Ki, watching the young wrangler's face, could see that his words had struck home.

"Sir, I didn't really mean that we should give up them horses," Joady earnestly said. "That's why I stayed here in the first place—"

"I know that, Joady—" Ki began.

"I mean, as a Circle Star wrangler, it's my *job* to take care of Miss Starbuck's horses. I feel just as strongly about doin' my job as you," the boy insisted.

"And you done a fine job of it, son," Hank said.

"Joady, there is no doubt in my mind that you are a brave and honorable young man," Ki said. "But sometimes, the bravest thing a warrior can do is to turn away from a fight."

The boy pondered it. "I'll leave you my gun and extra ammo," he murmured, handing his Peacemaker and spare cartridges to Hank.

"You'll find our horses down the far side of the rise," Ki instructed. "Take them both and switch from one to the other. You'll make better time."

"Now git a move on," Hank growled. He peeked over the top of the boulder, his revolvers at the ready. "No tell'n where those thieves are. The longer you wait, the more risk you'll be take'n until you reach your horses."

"I'll be back as quick as I can, I promise," Joady fervently swore, and then sprinted off.

"Keep an eye on him, Hank," Ki murmured. He himself did not look back, but concentrated on scanning the area before him as he drew an arrow from his lacquered quiver and nocked it into his bowstring. "Let me know when he is out of their range," he muttered. "A good man with a rifle could pick him off until he gets over that crest."

"Not much chance of that happen'n," Hank said and chuckled. "That boy's run'n like a jackrabbit with his cotton tail on

13

fire. He's scrabblin' on all fours up the rise. He's halfway up already. I'm glad we talked him into go'n. Boy that age has got his whole life in front of him. He's got no business trade'n lead with hardcases—" He stopped abruptly. "Oh, no! Ki! I'm sure I saw the sun glint off of a gun barrel! They must have a man up there!"

It is as I feared, Ki thought. They are professionals. He spun around in time to see Joady, still on all fours, make the crest of the rise. The boy straightened up to start down the far side, but then stood frozen, silhouetted against the blue sky. The young wrangler was staring transfixed at something. Ki, following his gaze, saw an outlaw appear from the rocks. The man held what looked to be a stubby, double-barreled shotgun. Joady put up his hands. Ki aimed at the shotgunner, drawing back his arrow, even as he despaired, knowing the range was too great. Before he could let fly his shaft, the outlaw shouldered his own weapon and cut loose with both barrels, then quickly ducked back behind cover.

"Christ! The boy's been gut shot!" Hank moaned as Joady tottered backward, clutching at his belly. Then he fell, pinwheeling back down the near side of the slope, coming to rest in that awful, still position that only a corpse can assume.

"They killed 'im!" Hank leapt to his feet.

"Hank! Get down!" Ki commanded, but it was no use. The old wrangler was in a rage, worse than a grizzly rousted out of his cave. He fanned off several shots up the crest, aiming at nothing, lost in his fury, screaming out, "You murdering bastard!"

Ki moved quickly to tackle the old man and get him safely back under cover, but he was too late. He heard the shots coming from the main grouping of outlaws, glimpsed the muzzle flashes out of the corner of his eye. Ricochets glanced off the rock as Hank dropped his gun and sagged to the ground, his legs straight out in front of him, a bitter look of disbelief twisting his features as he pressed his hand against the spreading bloodstain on his side.

"Goddamn . . ." Hank cursed. "Damn this fool temper of mine. It's gotten me into scrapes before, but nothin ever as bad as this . . . I'm sorry, Ki, but when I saw young Joady shot down like a dog I jest went plumb loco . . ."

14

"I understand," Ki said. "But the way to avenge Joady is to stay in control of your emotions so as to be able to strike at the proper time."

"You're a cold one, you are, Ki," Hank chided.

Ki began to answer, but then thought better of it. It was hard to follow a warrior's path, and harder still to make others see the way. Instead, as gently as he could, he untucked the bottom flap of Hank's shirt to examine the wound. "You are fortunate," he told the wrangler. "The wound is not serious. The bullet passed clear through, back to front, just beneath your rib. There is nothing broken."

"But I sure am bleed'n . . . ," Hank muttered weakly.

"We can put a stop to that." Ki shrugged off his vest and then removed his shirt. He tore the shirt into halves and folded the cotton cloth into absorbent compresses. "Give me your trousers belt," the samurai ordered. When Hank complied, Ki placed the cloth compresses over the bullet's entrance and exit wounds and cinched them tightly in place with Hank's belt, stanching the blood flow.

"God, I feel weak as a kitten," Hank complained.

Ki nodded, frowning. "This changes things," he sighed. "I must now go on the offensive. There is enough cover between ourselves and the enemy so that if I keep my head down, I will not be seen. Or, at least I won't be seen until it is too late for the sight of me to do them any good," the samurai added as he took up his bow and put on his vest.

"Dammit, Ki, you're just one man—"

"In this situation that is all for the better," Ki said shucking his boots so as to move quicker and more quietly. "It will be myself against them in a maze, and the advantage will be mine, for I can kill anything I come across, while they will first have to ascertain whether their target is friend or foe."

"You're a strange one, but you got balls, I'll give you that much," Hank said and nodded. His eyes happened onto the weapons in Ki's hands. "What the hell kind of arrowhead is that, anyway?"

"This is one of the twenty-four different types of war arrows," Ki explained. "The twenty-four are called *nakazashi*. This particular arrow is called the 'belly-cutter.' "

At first, Hank seemed puzzled, but as he stared at the twisting, corkscrew shape of the arrowhead, the meaning of

15

its name became clear to him. "You shoot that thing into a man's belly?" he asked, and when Ki nodded, the wrangler shuddered.

"Well, at least I can back up your play." Hank tried to sit up, but he winced, turning pale.

Ki gently pushed him back down. "You can be of greatest service by staying right here," the samurai began. "If you should get a shot at any of them, take it, but under no account should you expose yourself to their fire."

"Course not," Hank grumbled. "I may be short-tempered, but I ain't a fool."

Ki, staring at Hank, just sighed. The old wrangler was as stalwart as they came, but not much for keeping a level head on his shoulders. "Remember to keep that belt around your middle cinched tight," the samurai muttered, and slipped away toward the horse thieves' encampment.

It was indeed an ominous situation he was getting himself into, Ki realized, but he was optimistic that as long as he kept himself lower than the tops of the many boulders in the field, he could hunt in relative safety. He kept his bow at the ready, which was a fortunate thing, for he met his first outlaw head-on.

The man was crouched fifteen feet away. As he brought up his revolver, the samurai pulled back on the bowstring and let the shaft fly. The arrow hissed across the five-yard distance to puncture the outlaw's sternum. The man cried out, dropping his gun and toppling forward on his knees. His fall forced the arrow's shaft deeper into his body. The corkscrew point ripped through the man's back, tearing a jagged hole in his plaid shirt.

The horse thief's death cry would attract others to the scene. Ki fitted another arrow to his bowstring and waited. This shaft had a traditional arrowhead, but a ceramic bulb was fitted just aft of its business end. Holes in the bulb were designed to catch the wind as the arrow flew.

Ki let it fly at the first outlaw he saw, a man about twenty yards away. The air rushing through the bulb created a high-pitched keening sound. The horse thief looked sideways and up at the sky, his revolver wavering uncertainly. He was still trying to figure out what the noise was and where it was coming from when the "death's song" arrow took him through the neck.

16

Ki did not wait to watch his target fall. He slipped away, weaving between the boulders the way a cougar stalks the tall grass.

"What the hell was that noise?" Ki heard one of the outlaws call anxiously. "Some kind of bird?"

"Jack's dead!" hissed a new voice coming from a different direction. "Another one of those damn arrows!"

"What are we up against? An Injun?"

Ki heard shots being fired from behind. He glanced in that direction and caught a glimpse of Hank squeezing off rounds from his Peacemaker at a pair of outlaws rushing toward his position. First one outlaw and then the other went down under the grizzled old wrangler's fire.

Good for you, Ki thought. Hank had just landed two strikes toward avenging Joady.

Ki began to move back toward where he'd left Hank, and away from those gathered voices. There were now too many horse thieves in one place. It was better to bide his time. Ki was beginning to think they were going to get out of this alive. Hank was showing admirable sense—

As Ki came around a boulder, he literally bumped into one of the horse thieves. The man grabbed Ki's bow at the same time that the samurai locked his fingers about the wrist of the outlaw's gun hand.

"I got him," shouted the horse thief. He was a big, strong man and knew how to wrestle. He launched himself backward, planting his boots against Ki's chest as he did so. The samurai's bow fell as he was propelled forward and up into the air by his opponent's jackknifing legs. No time for this, Ki thought desperately as he was somersaulted over the horse thief's head, to land jarringly upon the ground.

Throughout his fall, Ki had held onto the man's wrist, immobilizing it so that the horse thief could not aim his pistol. Now Ki executed a wrist-twist that caused the revolver to slip from the horse thief's fingers. Ki flipped over on his belly and swatted the gun away with the back of his hand. The pistol was out of reach, but Ki's sending it there had given his adversary time to rise up on his knees and twist around, getting behind the samurai. The man locked his thick forearm across Ki's windpipe.

The two struggled like that, on their knees, for some seconds. Ki had to drive his elbow into the man's rock-hard belly three times before the horse thief's choke-hold loosened. A shot ricocheted off of granite, sending stinging chips of stone against Ki's cheek as he wrenched free of the other man's grasp.

"Hurry up!" the horse thief groaned, looking past Ki, and rubbing at his bruised belly. He pulled a hunting knife from its sheath on his gunbelt and lunged toward the samurai.

Ki glanced over his shoulder and faltered as he reached inside his vest for a *shuriken* throwing blade. Another horse thief was joining the fray, gripping his Winchester by the barrel as if it were a club, to swing it at Ki. The samurai barely aimed, flicking the *shuriken* underhanded at this new assailant, but luckily the blade found its target. The Winchester fell from the man's hands as he cried out in agony, staring in horror at the steel embedded in his chest, and then slumped backward, his last breath wheezing out of him as his body settled into death.

There was no time to reach for a second *shuriken*. The first horse thief's long knife was being thrust toward Ki's gut. The samurai sidestepped to the left, beginning to counter the man's knife attack with a downward block. As Ki moved sideways, he brought his right fist up across his own chest. Then, as the horse thief extended his knife hand, Ki snapped his fist downward and to the right, to catch the outside of the man's hand. Now that the horse thief's blade was deflected, Ki could counter with a forward snap-kick to the man's solar plexus, causing his opponent to double over, the wind knocked out of him.

Ki slammed the edge of his hand hard against the man's neck, snapping it, finishing him off—and realized too late that that had been a bad move. Now that the horse thief had fallen away, his companions could open fire. The horse thieves had come out from around the rocks they'd been hiding behind and were now rushing toward Ki. The samurai counted five of them, and all were firing their guns. The air was filled with the sound of shots and the singsong whine of lead richocheting off rock. Ki leapt into the air like a trout on a hook, twisting his body in an attempt to make himself a more difficult target. Behind him he heard Hank bellowing curses as he emptied his brace of Peacemakers at the outlaws. The rounds kicking up dust around the outlaws momentarily

18

spoiled their aim, giving Ki a reprieve, and two more badmen ultimately went down under the old wrangler's fusillade, but then Hank's guns were empty, and there were still three horse thieves left.

"Leave the old man out of it for the time being. Now that his guns are empty, he's harmless," one of the outlaws growled. "Get the Injun."

All three were aiming point-blank at Ki. Even as he reached for his *shuriken* throwing blades, he knew it was pointless. There were too many—

The shots that suddenly began to rain down from up on the rise behind Ki and Hank took everyone by surprise. At first Ki thought the shooter was the outlaw who'd killed Joady, anxious to join in the fray, because the figure was armed with what looked to be the same stubby shoulder weapon, but then the samurai remembered that Joady's killer had been armed with a *shotgun*—this new shooter was working some sort of squat-barreled lever-action *rifle*. What's more the shooter was aiming at the outlaws!

"Holy shit!" Hank croaked, peering over his shoulder. "Who the hell *is* that?"

Ki was wondering the same. The figure was short and slightly built, dressed in oversized denims and a baggy, tan canvas range jacket with an upturned, dark brown corduroy collar. He wore his hat tugged low and had a red bandanna covering the lower half of his face. The way he moved as he crabbed sideways to avoid the outlaws' returning fire made Ki think of a colt. Here was someone still a little too long of leg, sleek and agile and fluid of movement, but presently endowed with only a hint of the grace that was to come.

It's a boy, no older than Joady, up there, Ki thought. It has to be.

But there was nothing boyish about the way the figure up on the ridge was handling his midget rifle. The shooter stood in a crouch, the stock of his weapon wedged tight against his hip, and quickly levered off shots as he swept the barrel of his strange gun back and forth. Whoever the newcomer was, the whining staccato of his rapidly firing weapon was an awesome sound, and its effect on the remaining three horse thieves was terrible to see.

19

The outlaw trio backpedaled away, trying to retreat to the shelter of the rocks, snapping off shots up the ridge as they ran, but it was no use. The rifleman's rounds kicked up dust around the outlaws, and suddenly the badmen were flailing the air, trying to bat away the bullets peppering their bodies, as if they'd stumbled into a hornet's nest. Ki heard thin laughter wafting down from the ridge as the three outlaws crumpled to the ground and lay still.

And then the shooting ended. The silence was overwhelming. There was just the anxious whickering of the nearby stolen horses and the creak of gunbelts and boot leather as the newly fallen corpses settled. The air stank of cordite and the sweet, coppery scent of blood.

"Damn, I seen a lot," Hank breathed. "But I never seen nobody handle a rifle like that."

"He levered off shots faster than most men could work a double-action Colt," Ki agreed, watching as the rifleman sauntered down the rise while thumbing fresh rounds into his weapon's magazine.

"Hey, mister!" Hank started up toward the rise, his brace of Peacemakers still grasped loosely in his hands. "That was some shooting—"

"Hold it!" the rifleman called out. The metallic, rolling click as he levered a round into his weapon's chamber sounded awesome. "Drop those guns, old man, or I'll drop you!"

"What, these?" Hank asked, sounding bemused. "Take it easy, son, they're empty!"

"Do as he says, Hank," Ki quickly said. Unlike Hank, he realized how volatile the situation was, because he remembered the way the newcomer had laughed as his rounds had cut down the outlaws. This one enjoys killing, Ki thought.

"Old man, you're a second away from dying," the rifleman warned.

His voice, while muffled by the bandanna across his mouth, sounded high-pitched, reed-thin. A boy, surely, Ki decided.

"Easy, son . . ." The old wrangler let his pistols fall to the ground.

"Smart of you," the rifleman said.

Yes, a boy, Ki mused. Skillful in battle, but rash, and full of arrogance. His warrior's spirit not yet fully harnessed, which made him as unpredictable as a stick of dynamite with a short fuse.

"You saved our lives," the samurai said, trying to placate the boy. "We are in your debt."

"That's right, Injun, I did save your lives," the boy said, only his dark eyes visible beneath his hat's brim and above the masking bandanna. He brought his sawed-off rifle to bear on Ki. "I saved your lives, and I can take them away just as easy, so you just move away from that bow of yours and get set to do exactly as I tell you!"

★

Chapter 2

"Either one of you move, and I'll cut you down."

Ki stared at the boy, who now stood ten feet away, and at the squat barrel of the sawed-off rifle pointed unwaveringly at his middle. Killing him would be a simple matter, Ki thought, feeling the weight of the *shuriken* throwing blades inside his vest. But it would not be honorable to take the life of an impetuous boy, especially since this youngster had just saved them from the horse thieves. The trick will be to neutralize him without doing him serious injury . . .

"What's gotten into you?" Hank sputtered. "You can't think we're also outlaws."

"All I know is there's a bunch of dead outlaws here, and you two," the boy said in that same reedy tone, muffled by the red bandanna across his mouth. With that hat of his pulled down so low, the kid still seemed nothing put a pair of big eyes, the color of tobacco. "Maybe you two are honest, or maybe you're cut from the same cloth as those others."

When the boy momentarily gestured with his gun toward the corpses littering the ground, Ki almost made his move, but then he stopped himself. I must wait for exactly the right time, he thought. I must be as certain as possible that I can succeed in disarming the boy without putting myself in a position where I must kill him to save my own life. Anything less would be dishonorable . . .

"Before I decide anything about you and the Injun," the boy said, still addressing Hank, "I've got some questions I intend to ask, and you'd best answer."

"There was another man up on the ridge," Ki said. "He killed a young man who was with us."

"The hombre with the shotgun?" the boy asked. When Ki nodded, the boy laughed. "I got him first off. I knew that with all the shooting going on down here, nobody was going to pay any mind to my squeezing off one shot."

"Then Joady's death is avenged, after all," Hank muttered, sounding satisfied. But then he began to sway on his feet.

"Mister?" the boy asked sharply. "You all right? You look pale."

"Feel'n dizzy . . . I . . ." Hank trailed off, shaking his head as if he were punch-drunk.

"He has been shot, and he lost a lot of blood," Ki said, tensing. He sensed that his opportunity to act was close at hand.

"Hell, I'm okay," Hank announced, and then fainted dead away, slumping lifelessly to the ground. It was to the boy's credit that he instinctively moved toward Hank's prone figure, lowering his rifle.

Ki dove forward, somersaulting toward the boy. The youngster, spotting Ki coming at him, instinctively swung his gun around and fired. The kid is fast, Ki thought as he tumbled. The boy managed to lever off two more rapid-fire shots. The sound of his rifle was like thunder as the rounds nipped after Ki, pelting him with dirt. The samurai was tumbling as fast as he could, trying desperately to stay below the boy's angle of fire.

His third somersault put him at the boy's boot tips. Ki balanced himself on his hands, his back to the shooter. Before the boy could fire a fourth time, Ki swung his legs up and over, the way a scorpion will whip its tail up over its back to bring its stinger into play. The samurai's powerful ankles locked about the boy's torso, pinning his arms. The sawed-off rifle fell from the boy's grasp as Ki twisted his hips, putting everything he had into the spin.

Yelping, the boy was wrenched off his feet. He hit the ground hard, his hat flew off, and out tumbled a shoulder-length mane of auburn curls. Ki momentarily loosened his scissors hold—this *was* just a boy, after all—to give the kid a chance to breathe, and the boy took advantage of the respite to squirm free. Snarling, he hurled himself at the samurai, sitting squarely on Ki's stomach. Ki bucked him off, but not before realizing that the fellow he was bucking was a *her*—he'd had enough womanly bottoms straddling his belly to know another when he felt it!

The girl was crawling rapidly on all fours toward her little rifle, but Hank, who'd evidently miraculously recovered from his "faint," beat her to it. The old wrangler snatched it up and away just as her fingers touched it. Seeing she was licked, she gave up in disgust, settling into a cross-legged sitting position in the dust.

Her bandanna, as well, had slipped during the tussle, so that Ki had ample opportunity to see how lovely she was. She was no more than twenty, he guessed.

"You're pretty fast, Injun." Her dark eyes shot daggers Ki's way.

"So are you." Ki returned the compliment.

She shrugged, looking sullen. "Not fast enough, though. Not *this* time," she added meaningfully.

"That was a very clever ruse on your part," Ki told Hank.

"Thank you," the wrangler replied, smiling weakly. "Only trouble is, all that jumping around must have jarred someth'n loose." He knelt to the ground, clutching his side.

"Your friend doesn't look too good," the girl said evenly.

"No, he does not," Ki murmured, going over to Hank. Kneeling beside him, the samurai loosened Hank's bandages and examined the wounds.

"How bad?" Hank asked.

"The bleeding has begun again," Ki somberly told the worried wrangler. The samurai paused, to look at the girl still sitting cross-legged on the ground. "What is your name?"

At first she hesitated to reply. "It's Annie . . . ," she reluctantly said. "Annie Slade."

"Annie Slade, my name is Ki, and this is Hank, and I assure you, we are not outlaws."

"Then what are you doing with the likes of them that was?" she shot back.

25

"Those horses you hear whickering over yonder belong to the Circle Star ranch." Quickly, Ki recounted to Annie all that had taken place prior to her dramatic arrival on the scene. " . . . So, you see, you have nothing to fear from us," he concluded.

"I've heard of Jessie Starbuck, of course," Annie said thoughtfully.

"Imagine her take'n us for horse thieves," Hank snorted.

"And I do seem to remember something about some kind of half-breed riding with her."

Ki let that last part slide. "How did *you* happen to be here?" he asked her.

Again she seemed to hesitate, but this time she shrugged, as if deciding to herself that what she had to say would make no difference. "This band of deceased desperadoes belonged to Wolf Martyn."

"Wolf Martyn!" Hank echoed, shuddering. "He rides with twenty hard men! God preserve us if he's in these parts."

"He is. I just don't know *where,* exactly," Annie replied. "And his gang is down some, after today," she added, sounding satisfied. "I've been on the trail of these bandits for close to a week in the hopes that they would lead me back to Wolf's hideout."

"Your horse and gear?" Ki asked.

"Somewhere close by is all I'm saying," Annie said, her eyes narrowing.

"And why would a purty little thing like you want to go mess'n about with the likes of Wolf Martyn?" Hank demanded.

Annie Slade's dark eyes were as unwavering as twin gun barrels as she replied, "Because Wolf Martyn murdered my mama and my daddy, and I intend to send him straight to hell for his trouble!"

The story she told was brief, and she recited it in calm, unemotional tones, which only increased the horrible impact of what she had to say. Six months ago she'd been living with her parents just outside the town of Spindle Creek, on the near side of the Texas-Oklahoma border. The Slades ran the stage relay depot. Annie, their only child, was engaged to be married. Everything was wonderful—until the day Wolf Martyn and his band of lieutenants rode in.

26

"They said all they wanted was food, whiskey, and to water their horses," Annie told Ki and Hank. She spoke softly, with eyes downcast, her finger idly tracing circles in the dust. "Daddy believed them, or else he just wanted to." She shrugged. "Anyway, he told mama and me just to do as Wolf Martyn and his four men said. My daddy, he didn't keep a handgun, but he had a Winchester .44-40 stashed behind the bar. He and I used to take it hunting together—" Her voice broke, and she squeezed her eyes shut, hard, as if to hold back the tears. "Anyway, Daddy and I locked eyes early on, and I knew that he didn't want me to make a move for that rifle, so I didn't, and he didn't either, and we treated Wolf Martyn and his seconds-in-command to our finest food and drink. Things went tolerable, if you know what I mean, until Wolf got himself a mite too liquored up, and made a grab for my mama. Lucky I was out at the well fetching water, or else he might have put his hands on me . . ." She shuddered. "Daddy couldn't hold with Wolf touching my mother, of course," she said quickly, the pride evident in her quavering voice. "I was back from the well and looking in the window, so I saw it all: He went after Wolf with his fists, and knocked that bastard down, too, but then one of Wolf's men shot my daddy in the back, and then Wolf himself, in a rage, drew his pistol and shot down Mama."

"How'd you survive?" Hank asked, sounding awestruck.

"As soon as the shooting started, I turned tail and ran to hide in the stables," she explained. "Wolf and his men searched for me, but they were only five, and there were several outbuildings to the depot, and they knew they had to skedaddle before the next stage pulled in . . ."

"And so all by your lonesome you decided to set out to track down Wolf Martyn," Hank said, his voice full of admiration.

"Track him down, and shoot him dead," Annie agreed.

"If that ain't the spunkiest thing I ever heard . . ." Hank chuckled, and then winced. "Damn, it hurts to laugh."

Ki addressed Annie. "There are some things I can do to make Hank more comfortable. It would be helpful if I could trust you while I was doing them. What do you say?"

Annie shrugged, her big, brown eyes intent upon Ki. "You two are the ones with Li'l Pete."

"Excuse me?" Ki asked.

"Li'l Pete." She gestured toward her gun.

Ki picked up the midget rifle and examined it. It was a Winchester .44-40, its barrel sawed off to what looked to be an eighteen-inch length. "Is this your father's rifle?" the samurai asked. "The one he had stashed behind the bar?"

"It is," Annie nodded. "My daddy used to call it Big Pete. Taught me to shoot with it, too. I had a gunsmith take off some of the barrel to make it a mite more handy to keep close by in all types of situations."

"You lost some range doin' that," Hank pointed out.

"That's okay," Annie said matter-of-factly. "I intend to shoot Wolf close-up. I want him to see who's hand-delivered his rotten soul to the devil."

"Lordy," Hank breathed.

"So now it is Li'l Pete?" Ki asked, mostly to change the subject.

"Yep." She opened her range jacket to reveal a scabbard suspended from a shoulder harness dangling down on her left side. "I carry him in this here cross-draw rig I had a leathersmith work up for me."

Ki nodded. "Annie, we have told you who we are. Do you believe us?"

"Like I said, you got Li'l Pete," she repeated defiantly.

"In that case . . ." Ki tossed her the rifle. Surprised, she had to scramble to catch it. "There, now you have Li'l Pete back again," the samurai told her.

"Damn, Ki," Hank whispered. "Sure, she's purty, but she's hard as nails. You can't trust her."

Ki said nothing. He trusted his instincts in these matters.

Annie looked at the gun in her hands, and than back at Ki for a long moment. Then she tucked Li'l Pete into her shoulder rig. "Mama taught me a fair amount of doctoring," she said, getting to her feet. "Let me have a look at that wound."

Ki fetched the canteens as Annie gingerly removed the blood-sticky compresses from Hank's wound and peered at it. "Looks like you won't be dying, today," she told the wincing wrangler.

"Course I ain't gonna die," Hank muttered, gratefully accepting a canteen from Ki and sipping at it. "It just smarts a bit, is all, and has got me feel'n all rubbery."

"That's due to the loss of blood," Ki said, placing the extra canteen within easy reach. "You need liquid. Drink sparingly, but often."

"Rather be drink'n whiskey," Hank said and sulked.

"Too bad we can't make him a poultice to draw out some of that sting," Annie murmured, pressing Hank's bandage back into place.

"Perhaps we can," Ki said. "There is a certain combination of mosses and ferns that is effective in this regard . . ."

"Injun medicine?" Annie asked.

Ki sighed, not taking offense. He knew that thanks to his almond-shaped brown eyes, tawny skin color, and straight, nearly blue-black hair, many people took him for an Indian. "Annie, I am of Japanese ancestry."

"That's like a Chinaman, right?" Annie looked up at him.

"Not from my perspective." Ki smiled. "Anyway, my mother was Japanese, and my father was an American. And I am a samurai, a professional warrior in the Starbuck employ."

"You mean, like a hired gunslick?"

"Quite so," Ki replied. "Like a gunslick, a samurai pledges his professional services to a family pursuing a cause or course that he believes in. Long ago, I pledged myself to Alex Starbuck, Jessie's father. Jessie and I were mere youngsters in those days, but Alex, having lived in the Orient, knew that a young samurai might be lacking in experience, but not in prowess. I was entrusted with the task of guarding Jessie, keeping her safe from harm." He paused. "And so, to this day, my duties continue."

"Well, you're sure good at what you do," Annie said. "I saw you throw that little silver knife of yours, and then duking it out with those outlaws . . . Hell, you never even made a fist!"

"It is called *te*," Ki explained. "In English, the word roughly translates as 'hand.' *Te* is the art of empty-hand fighting."

"Well, whatever it is, it's something! I still can't believe how you outraced my bullets when you took me on!"

"Coming from a worthy opponent such as yourself, that is indeed a compliment," Ki said, and was rewarded by Annie's blushing rose-pink.

"Go on with you, now," she scolded, but her smile was a mile wide, and startlingly white against her tanned skin. "To think a girl could sink so low that the only compliment she

29

can draw is on how good she is in a fight . . ." She shook her head, rolling her big brown eyes in mock despair.

"Oh, there is *plenty* more to compliment you on," Ki said, enjoying the flirtation. Now that they'd called a truce, he couldn't help wondering if this sleek little wildcat would be as worthy an opponent in love as in war . . .

But then Annie seemed to catch herself, as if she'd thought twice about what she was getting into. "This warrior training of yours, it taught you the art of healing as well as killing?" she asked

"Yes," Ki replied. "During my years of apprenticeship I learned a great deal about medicine in addition to the martial arts." Specifically, it had been his training in *atemi*—the art of striking with little force but devastating effect against a foe's pressure points—that had taught him the various nerve centers of the body. Along with that knowledge came his understanding of human anatomy and related subjects. A warrior had to know how to treat injuries sustained in battle. "I know, for example, the properties of various herbs and plants, and how they can be used either to poison or to cure."

"Like I said, my mama taught me a little something about herb healing, too," Annie said. "The plants you're likely talking about grow in and near water, and we aren't near any."

"You are wrong about that," Ki said. "I smell water."

She looked at him skeptically. "That's powerful odd," she said. "You can *smell* water? I don't believe it!"

"It's true, but not for you, if you don't believe."

"What?" She stared, and then covered her mouth to hide her giggle. "You're powerful odd," she repeated.

"And you are a lovely young woman when you laugh."

"Well." Annie swiftly regained her composure. "Seeing's believing. If there's water, why don't you just show me?"

"First let us see if we can make Hank more comfortable in the meantime," the samurai said. "You wait here with him. I will be right back."

He ran quickly into the rocks where the outlaws had been ensconced, smiling as his keen hearing picking up Annie asking, "Does he always go barefoot?" and Hank replying, "You called it right the first time—he's powerful odd . . ."

As Ki had hoped, the outlaws, prepared to wait out poor young Joady, had brought their bedrolls and saddlebags with them into the rocks. Ki scooped up blankets, and some hard-tack and jerky to help replenish Hank's strength, and then returned to where the wrangler and Annie were waiting.

"Hell, this is more like it." Hank chuckled as he settled into the blankets and then began to contentedly munch on the meat and crackers, washing down the food with sips from the canteen. "Don't reckon you came up with a bottle of rye," he said hopefully.

"Even if I had, you could not have any in your condition," Ki replied. "Annie, would you like to come with me, or would you prefer to keep Hank company?"

"I'll go with you," she said. "I could do with washing some of this blood off my hands. *If* you're right about the water."

"I am," Ki said.

"Anyway," she pointed to Hank, who'd tucked himself in and now had his eyes closed, "I think he's going to be snoring away in a few seconds."

"The sleep will do much to restore him," Ki said, pleased. "Come on, then." He sniffed the air. "The water is this way."

The samurai followed his nose, angling off through the boulders, past scrubby clumps of post-oak and blackjack. Grasshoppers, churned up by the day's warmth, hurled themselves across the walkers' path, sounding like crumpled paper as they bounced off the rocks. They walked through a grove of walnut trees, where they found the stolen horses along with the outlaws' mounts, loosely tethered with braided, leather hobbles. The horses seemed content to whinny softly to each other as they grazed upon the sweet grass carpeting the secluded grove.

"Gee, I don't *see* any water . . ." Annie said sarcastically.

"Do not be such a brat," Ki absently scolded. He stood still, closing his eyes and sniffing. "Somewhere over there." He led her past a tall oak tree, and then they saw the brook of pure, sweet water bubbling up from the ground. It cascaded over mossy rocks to feed a small, shallow pool encircled with bulrushes. The sun turned the surface of the water to molten silver. Above the pool, dragonflies the color of jewels hovered and darted.

"Well I'll be . . . ," Annie said, incredulous. She looked at Ki and shook her head.

Ki watched as she hurried to the pool, stripping off her jacket and shrugging out of her shoulder rig, then rolling up the sleeves of her too-large, pale blue work shirt. She knelt on the pond's bank and leaned forward in order to wash Hank's dried blood from her hands and upper arms. "Oh, damn!" she cursed as her sleeves flopped down into the water. She eyed Ki, then shrugged and began to unbutton her shirt. "Don't you go getting any ideas, mister!" she warned.

"I cannot answer to my ideas, only my actions," Ki pointed out.

"You'll answer to Li'l Pete, if you don't behave," she warned, shedding her shirt.

Ki gazed in appreciation at the strong, graceful curve of her delicate back, and at her fine, round breasts swaying from side to side as she washed herself. She was so thin— likely due to her hard time spent on the trail chasing after Wolf Martyn—that her ribs showed. But that only made her adorable breasts, with their splendid, nut-brown aureoles and nipples, the more breathtaking. Ki watched her straining rump as she leaned out over the water. Her previously baggy pants were now pulled tautly as she knelt forward, fitting every delicious curve like a second skin. Droplets of perspiration rolled down her spine's deep furrow, to pool where the waistband of her trousers gaped. Ki glimpsed a teasing hint of the beginning swell of her buttocks whenever she leaned especially far forward.

"You seem very calm, considering that you are half-undressed in front of me," he observed.

Annie shrugged. "You get to learn what's really important and what ain't when you've been out in rough country as long as I have," she said. "Anyway, I told you I was engaged to be married once, right? Well, me and my beau, we took more than our share of long walks under a full moon, if you get my drift . . . And I'm not afraid of no man nor beast when I've got my Li'l Pete."

"Watching you wash yourself has given me a 'peter' of my own." Ki couldn't help laughing. "Only he is just now not so *little*!"

"Then you'd better let me cool him off!" Annie giggled, scooping up a double handful of water and sending it Ki's way, soaking the front of his jeans. "Oh, how clumsy of me!" she mocked.

"Indeed," Ki muttered wryly. "Annie, it seems you have made me wet."

She swallowed hard. "Well, why don't you take them off, and let them dry in the sun?"

Ki's almond eyes narrowed. He had engaged in light-hearted flirtation with this attractive young woman because he admired her warrior's spirit. Now, the flirtation was taking a new and serious turn. As attracted as he was to her, he wished to pursue the honorable course of action . . .

"Well," Annie demanded. "Aren't you going to?"

"I think it would be best if I kept my pants on."

"What's wrong?" she asked. "I already told you I was once engaged to be married."

"Why didn't you marry?" Ki asked, thinking to buy himself some time to decide how to go about handling this delicate situation.

"Well . . ." Annie appeared reluctant to talk. "I guess I can tell you. There's something about you that makes me think you'd understand . . . You see, when word went around town what happened out at my folks' place, gossip had it that Wolf Martyn and his crew all had their turns with me. That's not true, of course," she added quickly.

Ki held up his hand to stop her. "It would not matter to me even if it were true," he said. "Our honor comes from our conduct toward others, not from how others treat us."

Annie smiled. "Like I said, I knew you'd understand. Anyway, when my fiancé heard those dirty rumors about me, it changed things between us. He swore that he believed me about what really happened, but explained that his family's respected position in town—his people came from money—required that he take a wife whose reputation was pure . . ." Her voice faded as she shrugged wistfully over lost opportunities. "Oh, well . . . The short of it was that he asked if I'd let him out of our engagement, and, of course, I did. I'm not about to marry any man who doesn't want me."

"He was a fool," Ki said, feeling incredibly moved. The burdens this lovely young woman was so steadfastly shouldering! "He lost himself a treasure."

"Do you really think so?" She got to her feet and came around the edge of the pool, toward him. "It's been so long since I've heard tender words."

Ki gently tilted up her chin and kissed her. Her mouth was cool and sweetly wet from the spring water.

"Mmm . . ." She swooned against him. "And it's been so long since I've been held by anyone. Let's both get in the pond and do it," she breathed, stroking the swelling between his legs.

Ki shucked off his jeans and vest, taking the time to palm one of his *shuriken* throwing blades.

Annie quickly kicked off her boots and stepped out of her pants, then turned to face him. "Lord, you are the most handsome man!" She ran her fingers along Ki's sloping shoulders, the wiry muscles of his arms, and the cords of his calves and thighs. She giggled as she patted his rippling stomach muscles. "Your belly's got more ridges than these here badlands!"

Ki feasted his eyes on the rest of her, so newly exposed. Her legs, so long and well turned; her high, round, deeply clefted bottom as smooth as satin; her belly, curving seductively to the moist juncture of her thighs, beneath her glossy, dark pubic fur.

"To think such tantalizing curves were hiding in those baggy clothes," Ki murmured. "And to think I thought you were a *boy*."

Annie giggled. "It *is* a great disguise. When I'm dressed like that, with my hat pulled low and my bandanna high, there ain't no place Li'l Pete and I can't go."

Trembling in anticipation, she quickly twisted her long, dark hair into a topknot to keep it dry, and then she hopped into the pool. "Come on in, the water's just right." Annie grinned happily as she splashed about.

She looked altogether irresistible, and Ki did not hesitate to join her. The water was just warmed enough by the sun to be soothing. Ki settled himself, and was reaching out for Annie when she suddenly shook her head.

"Wait! I forgot something!" She clambered out of the pond, her breasts bouncing, and her luscious bottom spraying droplets as her hips wagged. "Ki?" Annie glanced over her shoulder.

"What?"

"While we're doing it, I'll need to keep Li'l Pete nearby," she said apologetically. "It's hard to explain, but—"

"No need to." Ki smiled, showing her the *shuriken* he'd palmed, the one he'd nestled on a flat rock, close by. "I am going to keep this within easy reach, as well. One of the first lessons a warrior learns is never to be unprepared to confront

34

an enemy. You and I are a lot alike, Annie."

"Kindred spirits!" she agreed happily, scooping up her holstered midget rifle and returning with it to the pond. She hung the weapon by its shoulder harness from a nearby branch on the bank of the pond and then threw herself into Ki's arms.

They enjoyed a long, wet kiss as the tips of her breasts rubbed against Ki's chest. He stretched out full-length on his back in the shallow water, comfortable upon the pool's smooth sandy bottom, sighing in contentment as he palmed the curves of Annie's twitching rump. Her nipples had swelled so brazenly that he couldn't resist giving them both a teasing nibble.

Annie laughed throatily as she stroked Ki's hardness, bobbing in the warm water. "What a nice fish I've caught." She giggled as her fingers lightly danced across the entire swollen, throbbing length of him. "Hmmm, it's a big fish. More like an eel . . ."

She began to nibble kisses across Ki's muscular chest. Her soft lips and velvety tongue licked and sucked at his sensitive nipples. "Hmmm, you taste so sweet . . ."

"And now it is my turn to taste," Ki said, sitting up. His hands encircled her slim waist to lift her up out of the water. He easily held her aloft, telling her to rest the backs of her legs on his shoulders, and then he used his head to burrow between her thighs, his tongue parting her glistening folds to lap up the sweetness coating her the way a morning's dew will coat spring grass.

"Oh, that feels so good," Annie cried out in ecstasy. Her back arched, and her body began to spasm as low, animal-like grunts of pleasure escaped her lips.

Ki waited for her pleasure to subside, and then carefully lowered her back into the water.

"I want you inside me!" she cooed. "Just for a little while, I want you to make me forget everything, and to feel safe . . ."

Ki rose up on his knees, at the same time spinning her around so that she was also on her knees, her back to him. He gently guided her forward so that she was supporting herself on her elbows. Her splayed, curvaceous rump, glistening with water droplets, and hued with just a hint of pink from rubbing against the pool's sandy bottom, was jutting out at him. Ki reached between her legs to press a finger against the core of her sex. Annie moaned, and arched her supple spine

35

to present more of her adorable backside to him.

"Take me now!" she begged. "I can't stand it another moment!"

Ki entered her from behind. As delightful as the warm water had been, it was nothing compared to the buttery softness that was Annie's silken furnace as she gripped and stroked his shaft.

"Oh, oh, I'm coming again already!" she cried out. Her hands formed fists that beat the surface of the pond, sending splashes geysering. What she was experiencing must have been truly overpowering, for as Ki pressed ever deeper, she attempted to pull away, rocking her hips and tilting her pelvis until just the tip of him was inside of her. Chuckling, he patted her damp, satiny haunches. Annie's hips began to churn the water. She thrust back, and in her haste to envelop every inch of Ki, she sank below the surface, getting her hair wet after all. The samurai hauled her up, a soaked and thoroughly tamed wildcat, sputtering and on the brink on orgasm, and then reached around with his free hand to fondle her nipples. By spreading his fingers, he could just span the distance between both crinkly-hard nuggets of delectable flesh.

Annie was coming continuously now; her hips bobbed and her head lolled as she emitted a series of guttural moans. Ki felt her powerful internal muscles convulse uncontrollably.

He began to pump within her like a steam piston, all the while stroking and massaging her lithe torso. She wiggled like a water moccasin. It was all Ki could do to hang on for the ride as he came.

After a few moments, he pulled free of Annie's molten center and fell back, sliding completely under the water. He popped up like a seal, shaking his head, sending droplets flying everwhere as his long, raven-black hair whipped around his head.

"Wouldn't it be nice to just stay here, forever?" Annie languorously mused.

"Yes, it would," Ki truthfully replied. "But duty calls."

"For the both of us," Annie agreed softly, and then stood up.

Ki watched her take Li'l Pete from its branch and exit the pool to get dressed. Duty calls, he thought ruefully. And followed her.

The samurai gathered up the necessary mosses and herbs to make Hank's poultice, and then they returned the way they had come. He pretty much expected the usual awkwardness a couple experiences after their first time making love, but Annie surprised him by being totally at ease. She ponders before she acts, he concluded, and thus lives with the consequences with no regrets. Truly she is a warrior . . .

When they got back, they found Hank still snoring raucously. "Let us try and administer to him while he is still asleep, to spare him the pain," Ki said.

"Then let me do it," Annie replied. "A woman's touch is even lighter than a samurai's."

"Who says?" Ki asked jokingly.

She responded by giving him a peck on the cheek. "That's my thanks," she said softly. "Later, think of it as my farewell."

Ki was watching her apply the poultice to the still-slumbering old man's wounds when a trio of Circle Star cowhands from the roundup appeared on horseback upon the crest of the ridge. Ki went to meet them, explained to them what had happened, and gave hurried orders for two of the men to see to the stolen Circle Star mounts, and the remaining cowboy to cut a couple of poles and gather the blankets to make a litter upon which to transport Hank and Joady. When Ki returned to the snoring wrangler, he found the poultice neatly applied, the bandages replaced—and Annie Slade gone.

" . . . think of it as my farewell . . ." she had said to him. Ki could still feel the cool imprint of her lips on his cheek. The samurai imagined the girl on her lonely quest to bring a notorious desperado to justice.

"Good hunting, Annie," he murmured, which was the best one warrior could wish for another.

★

Chapter 3

Jessie Starbuck was meeting with the president of the Cattleman's Trust when the bank robbery took place.

As soon as Jessie had come through the door, a teller had left his post in order fetch Lloyd Bondell, the president of the Trust. As Jessie waited, she thought that she was perfectly willing to let one of the junior officers see to her business, but she guessed that when your late daddy had founded the bank—which meant you pretty much owned the place lock, stock, and barrel—you had to get used to having the royal carpet rolled out every time you set foot inside.

The Trust had been established in the town of Sarah by Jessie's father the year she was born. In those days there had been banks ready to do business with the biggest and wealthiest cattle barons, but Alex Starbuck had felt there was a need for a financial institution willing to cater to the needs of smaller ranchers. Since then, the Cattleman's Trust had prospered by helping cattlemen of modest means to thrive, and helping the Lone Star State to become the cow capital of the world.

The Cattleman's Trust was located in a trim, two-story, white clapboard building on Sarah's wide main street. Let the big banks have their intimidating, cathedral-like vaulted ceilings, elaborate woodwork, and vast expanses of marble. Alex Starbuck had decreed that the Trust be an unassuming, welcoming place to smaller ranchers.

The Trust's ground floor was one big room. There was a line of tellers' posts behind a counter of polished oak, and behind the tellers a pair of enormous black safes with spit-polished brass combination dials. The second floor had an open balcony overlooking the banking area. The rooms behind the railing were the offices of the officials who supervised the Trust.

At this hour of the morning the Trust wasn't very busy. There were only three customers in the bank. Two were conducting their financial transactions with tellers, and Jessie knew both of them by name. The third man, however, was a stranger. He looked to be in his early thirties and was leaning on his elbows at the green baize writing stand, hunched over some papers.

Jessie studied him carefully. There was something about this jasper that set him apart from other men. Maybe it was his clothing. His gray tweed trousers, frock coat, light blue flannel shirt, and black ribbon tie all looked expensive, and fit him well, but his garb was dusty, as if he'd just finished a long, arduous ride. The man was clean-shaven, though, and quite good-looking, Jessie had to admit, as she watched him absently thumb back his gray Stetson to scratch at his tousled mass of brown curls. The more she studied him, the more she felt that it was his manner that had caught her attention. He had an air about him of a man who would be equally at home in a cutthroat poker game, a highfalutin dinner party, or out on the range, riding hard, intent on roping a steer. Jessie, gazing at him, decided that he was a well-to-do rancher here in Sarah to purchase himself some breeding stock.

The stranger must have felt Jessie's eyes upon him, for he suddenly looked up. The corners of his widely set hazel eyes seemed to crinkle in pleasure at the sight of her. His smile was easygoing . . .

But as he turned to more fully regard her, his frock coat gaped open. There was nothing easygoing about the revolver on his left hip, worn butt forward in a high-ride black holster. A well-to-do rancher? Jessie pondered. Then why was he wearing his shooting rig like a gunslick?

"Jessica, my dear girl!"

Jessie looked up to see Lloyd Bondell standing in the door-way of his second-floor office, at the head of the stairs.

"Jessica, my dear," Bondell repeated, hurrying down the stairs. He was a middle-aged man, with muttonchop whiskers and thinning blond hair, dressed in a blue suit and a red satin vest. "You're looking wonderful!"

Jessie, blushing, self-consciously ran her fingers through her spun-gold tresses, kissed with coppery highlights from her time spent beneath the strong Texas sun. She couldn't help wondering if that handsome stranger over at the writing stand was still looking at her. She didn't dare sneak a peek. Nonetheless, she was glad she'd decided to wear her dark green tweed skirt and matching hacking jacket; she knew the color brought out the emerald of her eyes. Cordovan riding boots and a brown Stetson, just now dangling on her back by its leather chin thong, completed her outfit.

"What a pleasure it is to see you, my dear," Bondell enthused. As he gave her a fatherly embrace, Jessie felt the small revolver in its shoulder holster under his left arm.

She'd left her own firearm at home, knowing from experi-ence that nothing riled some men more than seeing a female with a six-shooter strapped across her hips. And her daddy had taught her that there was a world of difference between being ready for trouble and going looking for it. Of course, she knew how to shoot; her father had taught her just as soon as she was big enough to hold a gun, and now she could out-do most of the gunslicks who thought they were something. Her revolver had been a gift from her father on her eighteenth birthday; he'd had it commissioned at the Colt factory during one of his Eastern business trips. It was a .38, but built on a double-action .44 frame to diminish the recoil in Jessie's slen-der hand. The Colt was finished in slate gray and had grips of polished peachwood.

But just because her Colt was stashed at home didn't mean that Jessie was going about defenseless. Her ivory-gripped, double-barreled .38-caliber derringer was just now tucked discreetly out of sight in her boot top.

"Now, then," Bondell said. "What can I do for you, Jessica?"

She glanced over at the stranger, to see that he'd gone back to his papers, and then pushed the intriguing fellow out of her mind as she turned her attention to her own business affairs.

41

"Lloyd, I'd like to arrange for a stipend to be paid on an ongoing basis to the parents of a late employee of mine."

Bondell frowned. "For how long, my dear?"

"Perpetuity," Jessie replied.

"My dear girl!" Bondell laughed lightly. "I don't think you're aware just how expensive that could be—"

"I'm exactly aware, Lloyd," Jessie said. She intended to set up the stipend for Joady Cooper's folks, who lived in Nebraska. Ki had told her what had occurred last week during the roundup, how outlaws had stolen some Circle Star horses, and how Joady had sacrificed his life in pursuit of his duties as wrangler. At first, Jessie had been angry that a boy's life had been ended over a few mounts, but Ki had quietly but firmly pointed out that the test of courage that Joady had faced had been unavoidable—the boy had either to do his utmost to meet his responsibilities, or rue his failure for the rest of his life. As to the danger, well, the West was a hard place, and when young Joady left Nebraska in pursuit of his future, the boy knew full well the potential dangers as well as the potential rewards of his endeavors.

Nevertheless, Joady had left a mother and a father back home in the Nebraska flatlands. And parents depended on a son for support during their sunset years. Now, there are some things that money can't buy, and so it was beyond the power of even a Texas princess like Jessie Starbuck to restore a boy to the loving embrace of his parents, but she could see to it that for the rest of their days those grieving parents would want for nothing that money could buy. The monthly stipend she would institute on the Coopers' behalf would amply see them through their retirement. It was the least Jessie could do to honor the memory of a brave young man who had given his life to defend the sanctity of the Circle Star brand.

"I know this stipend will be costly, but my mind is set on it," she now explained to Bondell. "Can we see to it, please?" she asked sweetly.

"Hmmm, well . . ." Bondell colored. "Yes, of course, Jessie . . . You're the boss."

Yes, that's true, Jessie thought. But there's no need to rub the man's nose in it . . .

"And perhaps you could advise me on the best way to go about setting it up," Jessie added, sensing Bondell's embarrassment, and wanting to ease his discomfort. Sooner or later, she got things done to her satisfaction, but she took pride in delicately, subtly wielding her authority over the wide-ranging Starbuck business empire that had prospered under her guidance since her father's death. Aspiring to an elegance in all things, the disagreeable as well as the pleasant, was something Ki had taught her, by example, of course . . .

And Bondell did seem mollified by her gesture. "If you'd join me upstairs in my office, Jessica, we can structure the stipend to your satisfaction," he was saying, ushering her to the foot of the staircase.

Jessie was about to start upstairs when the door into the Trust flew open and three hard-looking men barged in.

"All of you, this is a robbery," said one of the men, who was wearing a tan-fringed buckskin shirt and matching leather pants. He drew a glittering, nickeled ivory-gripped Colt from his holster. "Keep your hands where I can see 'em." He had pale blue eyes, as unforgiving as the winter wind cutting across the prairie, and a long, reddish beard, into which he'd braided little bits of bone. He herded the two customers at the tellers' counter over to the writing stand where the stranger was still standing, then plucked their revolvers from their holsters, dropped the guns to the floor, and kicked them out of reach. "Now your turn," Buckskin told the stranger. "You carry'n iron?"

Jessie's heart fell as the stranger silently held open his frock coat in order for Buckskin to see the revolver on his left hip. Something had made her think that if anyone in the bank could put a stop to this, it was the stranger, but now he was being disarmed.

"Nice gun," Buckskin said, holding the stranger's gleaming blue revolver up to the light. Jessie thought it looked like a double-action .44 Colt Lightning. It had ebony grips and a barrel cut down to five inches. "I'm gonna keep this one," Buckskin said, sliding the stranger's Colt into his own holster.

Now Jessie felt that stopping the robbery was up to her. But how? All she had was her little peashooter of a double-shot derringer. And she was up against three armed men. How could she even get it out of her boot top before they blasted her?

43

The one thing she had going for her was that she was a woman. In her experience, men didn't expect a woman to know her way around a handgun. That was most likely the reason why the robbers hadn't searched her, or even bothered to order her to stand with the male customers.

Meanwhile, another of the trio, wearing a buffalo plaid jacket and a revolver in an elaborately tooled, silver-studded holster, had stationed himself by the door to keep a lookout on the street. The third man, wearing striped pants and a denim range jacket, his shoulder-length, stringy brown hair hanging down from underneath his hat, hoisted himself over the tellers' counter. He drew his gun, cocked it, and placed it against the head of a wincing teller.

"Now you just open up them safes if you want to live through this," Striped Pants hissed to the trembling teller.

"I-I don't have the combinations!" the teller began to blubber.

Snarling, Striped Pants roughly thrust his pistol into the teller's ear, causing the petrified man to cry out.

"Maybe if you shoot that one, the others will come up with the combinations," remarked Buckskin, his shiny pistol trained on the huddled customers. The robber's pale blue eyes were as cold as a badland morning as he added, "Nothing like spread'n a little blood and brains to get other folks to remember'n what they seem to have forgot—"

"Don't shoot anybody." Lloyd Bondell spoke up. He turned imploringly to Striped Pants. "That clerk's telling you the truth. He really doesn't have the combination."

"We got to get a move on," piped up the outlaw in plaid, standing watch by the door. He stood aside as a customer came in, then quickly relieved the startled man of his gun and sent him over to the writing stand, where the others were being held prisoner.

Buckskin nodded, nervously tugging at his beard. His blue eyes narrowed into glittering slits as he looked Bondell over. "And who might you be, Mr. Robin Red Vest?" he demanded of Bondell.

"I'm the president of the bank, and I know the combinations—"

"Then you'll do fine." Buckskin grinned like a dog, revealing a mouth full of mossy green teeth. He crooked his finger as Bondell. "Come over here, Mr. Red Vest."

Jessie watched as Bondell did as he was told. She'd been silently willing him not to try anything foolish, and so was almost relieved when Buckskin patted him down and found and took away the gun in Bondell's shoulder holster.

"Lookit this here belly gun," Buckskin said and laughed, showing his partners in crime what looked to Jessie to be a nickel-plated Smith & Wesson .32. "This here will come in handy in a poker game," Buckskin continued. "I'm get'n me quite a collection today." He stuck the .32 into the front waistband of his tan leather trousers. "All right, Mr. Red Vest. You open up them safes, or that vest is gonna be a different color red."

"The combinations are upstairs, in my desk," Bondell began.

"Son of a bitch," muttered the man by the door, shaking his head.

"He's ly'n!" spat Striped Pants, who was still covering the tellers.

"All right, everybody," Buckskin announced. "I got me a gun in this here gent's ribs. Now we ride with Wolf Martyn, and we mean business!"

Wolf Martyn! Jessie thought, startled. Ki had said that the would-be horse thieves who'd killed Joady and tried to rustle Circle Star mounts had belonged to Martyn's band.

"If we have to, we'll kill everybody in here, to prove that," Buckskin was threatening.

"That won't be necessary." Jessie spoke up, trying hard not to look at Bondell's gun jutting so invitingly from Buckskin's waistband. Men like this just don't think of women and guns in the same breath, she reminded herself, steeling her courage. "Just let him go upstairs to fetch the combination, take the money, and leave."

"Yeah, sure, girlie," Buckskin said and scowled. "Let him go upstairs and fetch himself a gun, you mean."

"You could go with him," Jessie suggested.

"And just leave two men guarding all these citizens?" Buckskin shook his head.

Jessie paused, trying to do a credible job of acting as if she'd just thought of what she was about to say next. "Well . . . You could take me as your hostage, and then send Mr. Bondell upstairs by himself."

"Jessica! No!" Bondell gasped, shocked.

"If Mr. Bondell tries anything, you can shoot me," Jessie finished.

Buckskin pondered it. "All right . . . Come over here," he said. "And you"—he gave Bondell a shove—"git your ass up there and fetch that combination. You try anything funny, anything at all, and this purty li'l thing's brains will be stain'n the floor of your bank till kingdom come. Unnerstand?"

"Yes, I understand! Please don't hurt her!" Bondell pleaded, starting for the stairs.

As Jessie approached the man in buckskin, Striped Pants swung himself up and over the tellers' counter. "I'll go with Red Vest after all, just in case." He gestured with his gun at the tellers. "Them mice ain't gonna try nuth'n while you got the girl covered."

"Come here, honey," Buckskin breathed, holding his left hand out to Jessie, while his right held his gun trained on the customers by the writing stand. "Such a purty li'l thing. Let's you and me get better acquainted . . ."

Jessie forced herself to smile, trying not to wrinkle her nose as she made herself get close to Buckskin, and smelled his body stench. She tried not to gag as she felt his fetid breath thudding against her face . . .

But most of all, she tried not to let her eyes fix on that gun jutting butt-forward from the waistband of his trousers!

Bondell was at the top of the stairs, and Striped Pants, following, was halfway up, when Buckskin abruptly reached out with his left hand to draw Jessie close, pressing himself against her. "Howzabout a li'l kiss to remember you by?"

Jessie, repelled, felt his erection through the fly of his trousers as he lewdly bucked his hips against her. "I'll give you something to remember me by," she vowed. With lightning speed she wrapped her fingers around the butt of Bondell's gun and pulled the trigger while it was still tucked into the front of Buckskin's pants. The little .32 sounded like a firecracker going off, and Buckskin screamed, lurching backward as the front of his tan trousers was suddenly splattered with red. Jessie backpedaled, jerking the pistol loose from Buckskin's waist and shooting him twice more. Buckskin's pearl-handled revolver fell as he clutched at his chest and then sagged away.

A bullet tore a splintery hold in the tellers' counter just to the right of Jessie. It had come from the man by the door.

Another round scarred the planking between her boots. Striped Pants, halfway up the staircase, was making his presence known.

But it was the man by the door who had the clearer shot at her, Jessie knew. She would have to deal with him first.

The man in plaid was about to snap off another shot when Jessie whirled, crabbing sideways, firing as she did so. Her first round took the outlaw in the belly. His knees sagged, but the lightly powered .32 slug did not drop him. Jessie shot him again, this time in the chest. He fell to his knees, and then facedown on the floor, his nose making a bone-cracking sound as it met the planking. Jessie doubted that the would-be bank robber had felt the damage done to his face. From the way he fell, Jessie guessed that the man had died before his nose met the floor.

As dead as I'm going to be, she thought as she turned to watch the one remaining man on the staircase—good old Mr. Striped Pants—take careful aim. She didn't have to pull her gun's trigger and hear the click of the firing pin coming down on a spent shell to know that she was out of ammo. The .32 only held five shots, and there was no time to go digging for the derringer tucked into her boot. Looking up, she caught sight of Lloyd Bondell standing on the second-floor balcony, looking pale as a ghost, staring horrified in her direction.

"You came close, girlie," Striped Pants muttered. "But not close enough . . ."

Drawing herself up to her full height, Jessie looked Striped Pants in the eye. Thinking of Ki, she vowed that she would die well.

The man on the staircase squeezed the trigger.

But Striped Pants's aim went wild as three shots in rapid succession slammed into him, making him dance like a marionette with jerked strings. His revolver went clattering down the staircase, and then his body followed, his striped legs turning to rubber as he danced down the stairs, tottering and falling the last couple of feet, to land spread-eagled on the floor.

Jessie turned to see the handsome stranger standing over the corpse of the man in buckskin. The blued, slender barrel of his Colt Lightning was still smoking. The stranger stared grimly at the man he'd just killed, lying at the foot of the stairs. His good-looking, craggy features softened as he turned his gaze to Jessie.

"You all right?" His baritone echoed loudly in the tomb-quiet bank.

"Yes, thanks to you," Jessie breathed.

"Somebody go fetch Marshal Farley!" Bondell thundered from the second-floor balcony. One of the tellers scooted around the counter and went flying out of the bank.

Jessie pointed to the stranger's gun. "Where'd that come from?"

"I took it back from this one." He nudged the buckskinned corpse with his boot. "Figured he wasn't going to be needing it, after all." He shrugged. "I was hoping that fellow on the staircase was so intent on killing you that he wouldn't notice. Turned out I was right."

Jessie nodded. She set Bondell's gun on the tellers' counter, then brought the back of her hand to her forehead. She was feeling a touch light-headed now that it was all over. Yes, she was feeling just a mite dizzy . . .

Her knees began to sag, her vision to purple. She realized that she was fainting. But before she could slump, the stranger, smoothly holstering his weapon, sprinted forward to catch her. Next thing she knew he'd nimbly, easily, scooped her up off her feet, cradling her in his arms as if she were a child.

Still feeling faint, she rested her head on his broad shoulder. The masculine scents of bay rum, tobacco, gun oil, and cowhide enveloped her. She breathed deeply, feeling her strength return, and with it came the strongest impulse to kiss this handsome stranger who'd saved her life—

But such behavior would be scandalous! Why, she didn't even know his name!

"I'm feeling better," Jessie murmured. "You can put me down, now, Mr . . . ?"

"Boyce. Dan Boyce," he replied. "And are you sure you're better, Miss Starbuck?"

"Yes, and how do you know my name?"

"A beautiful girl name Jessica who lives in Sarah, Texas, and who can shoot the whiskers off a cat at fifty paces . . ." Boyce trailed off, grinning. "Who else could she be but Jessie Starbuck?"

"I see." Jessie nodded demurely. She'd never quite gotten the knack of dealing with her fame. "But Mr. Boyce—"

"Please call me Dan."

"Dan, then," Jessie said and smiled. "You were going to put me down?"

"Well, now . . . I'm not rightly sure . . ." Boyce began to tease. "Maybe I ought to carry you around like this for a day or so, just to make sure there's no relapse, you understand."

"Sadly, that won't be necessary." Jessie laughed.

"Darn." Boyce pretended to mope, setting her lightly on her feet. "I was getting to like holding you, Miss Starbuck . . ."

"Perhaps another time," Jessie replied, feeling her heartbeat quicken as Boyce's hazel eyes looked deeply into hers.

"That's a rendezvous I intend to keep," he murmured.

"What in tarnation!?!"

Town Marshal Farley stood in the doorway. He was a big-bellied, thick-necked man, with sparse yellow hair worn close-cropped and a face seamed and roasted pink by the Texas sun. Today he was dressed in baggy gray pants and a brown flannel shirt. His badge glittered on his broad chest, and his hand rested on the grip of the battered Peacemaker on his hip.

"Marshal, the bank was being robbed," Lloyd Bondell began, coming down the stairs. "But thanks to Jessica and this gentleman, the robbers got their just desserts!"

The Marshal listened intently as Bondell recounted what had happened, and then he turned his stern gaze on Dan Boyce.

"I've got just one question, Mr. Boyce," Farley muttered. "What was a stranger like you doing in my town—and the Cattleman's Trust—while a robbery was in progress?"

"Marshal, what are you suggesting?" Jessie asked.

"Just this, Jessie," Farley began, not taking his eyes off of Boyce while keeping his hand on the butt of his gun. "There's no way for us to know if Boyce here ain't one of them—"

"But Marshal," Jessie objected. "Those outlaws disarmed him, the same as they did everyone!"

"That's right. We saw the whole thing!" piped in the other customers who were still standing by the writing stand.

"That don't prove anything," Farley began.

"He's right, Miss Starbuck," Boyce added, to Jessie's consternation. "It's an old trick for a gang of bank robbers to send one of their own in early, and then pretend that he's just another honest bystander. They make a big show out of disarming their ringer, but of course he's carrying a second gun. That way they've got a man keeping his eye on the others, but nobody's keeping an eye on him."

"And in a situation like this—" Farley put in his two cents— "it ain't at all unheard of for that inside man, seeing that the robbery is going sour, to suddenly decide to switch sides."

"Exactly right," Boyce agreed as Farley scowled meaningfully at him.

"But now I got another question," Farley declared. "Just how do you happen to know so much about the tricks of the outlaw's trade?"

"Because you and I are more or less in the same business," Boyce replied. His right hand rose up, but then he hesitated. "May I take my wallet from my inside breast pocket?"

Farley nodded. "But just do it nice and slow like."

Boyce took out his wallet and flipped it open. Pinned inside was a six-pointed silver star.

" 'Special Agent, Texas & Pacific Railroad,' " Farley read, peering at the engraving on the star. He looked up at Boyce. "Well I'll be! A cinder dick!"

"I prefer the title railroad security man." Boyce chuckled.

"It's a relief to know you're on the right side of the law, after all," Jessie said and smiled. "But what's a railroad security agent doing in Sarah?"

"The railroad has been tipped off that Wolf Martyn's gang is in the vicinity," Boyce explained. "Our information is that Martyn plans a train robbery at the end of the month, when the train passes through carrying the government payroll to the Army station at Bent Hollow."

Jessie nodded. "We had some trouble with Wolf Martyn out on the Circle Star range." She went on to explain the circumstances of Joady Cooper's death. When she was done, she glanced apologetically at Farley. "I didn't burden you with the details before this, Marshal, since I know that your jurisdiction ends at the town limits."

Farley nodded. "And I wish these Wolf Martyn desperadoes had stayed outside my town." He stared morosely at the outlaws' corpses littering the Trust.

Boyce looked at Jessie. "What happened to your Circle Star horses corresponds with our information on how Wolf likes to operate," he told her. "Before he pulls a heist, he tries to get himself plenty of relief mounts, in case he and his boys have to make a sustained run for it." He turned to Farley. "The

50

reason I happened to be here when this attempted robbery took place is that I came to get a list of the ranches in the area. I figured to make the rounds asking folks if they've seen any suspicious-looking sorts lurking on their ranges."

"Well, I guess you found what you were looking for, then." Farley's sweeping gesture took in the dead outlaws.

"Not quite," Boyce remarked. "Between what happened on Starbuck land and what's happened here, Wolf's fangs have been pulled some, but he's still got teeth left. The fact of the matter is, until we nail Wolf Martyn's hide to the barn door, we've still got a mess of trouble on our hands."

"I reckon you're right, Boyce," Farley sighed.

"Marshal," Lloyd Bondell spoke up. "Do you think we could remove these bodies from my bank?"

"Oh, sure, Lloyd," Farley said. "I'll have one of my deputies fetch the undertaker."

"And I think I'm going to head over to the telegraph office to inform my superiors at the railroad as to what's happened." Boyce tipped his hat. "A pleasure to meet you, Miss Starbuck, even if the circumstances were a mite inopportune."

"Please call me Jessie."

"Jessie, then." Boyce smiled.

As Boyce exited the Trust, Farley spoke up. "Jessie, would you mind coming with me to my office? There's something I've been wanting to discuss with you, and now's as good a time as any, I reckon."

"Of course, Marshal." Jessie turned to Lloyd Bondell. "Perhaps we can discuss how to set up that stipend later this morning."

"If you don't mind, Jessica." Bondell looked inordinately grateful. "As you can see, I've got my hands full trying to get things back to normal."

Jessie let Farley take her arm as he escorted her out of the Trust. They strolled together down the raised wooden sidewalks that bordered Main Street, past several general stores, a bakery, two gunsmiths, another bank, and the telegraph office, where they saw Boyce through the window. Next they passed a magnificent, brightly painted three-story mansion. Above the wide golden-oak double doors there hung a sign painted in gilt script that read: "SARAH TOWNSHIP CATTLEMAN'S ASSOCIA-TION."

"You know it's funny," Farley said. "It's entirely natural that a man as rich as Midas, like Alex Starbuck was, would found an exclusive club like that Cattleman's Association. But there aren't many rich men who'd remember the little folk by also establishing something like the Cattleman's Trust."

"My father believed in giving back as much as he got," Jessie said quietly.

"And you feel the same way?" Farley asked, sounding both anxious and hopeful.

"Marshal, you know I do!" She stopped, digging in her heels, so that Farley, as well, had to come to a halt. "Now what's this about?"

Farley glanced around the crowded sidewalk, obviously worried about being overheard. "In my office, please, Jessie."

"Very well," she replied, thinking that the Marshal must have good reason for his secrecy.

Clustered together at the end of Main Street were several saloons and cafés, and on the same block, as if keeping watch like a stern parent, there was a combination jail and office labeled "TOWN MARSHAL." Farley held open the door for Jessie and then followed her in. A deputy was inside. "Be with you in a moment, Jessie," Farley explained, and proceeded to give his deputy instructions concerning getting the mess cleaned up inside the Cattleman's Trust.

While Jessie was waiting, she occupied herself looking around the office. A door to the rear, just behind the Marshal's desk, led to the cells. Along one wall was a rack of rifles and shotguns, all securely locked in place by a length of chain threaded through their trigger guards. On the opposite wall hung a motley assortment of Wanted flyers, from the federal government and neighboring territories, as well as from private organizations like the Pinkertons. Several straight-backed chairs stood scattered about.

"Jessie, please sit down," Farley said, as the deputy left the office. "Would you care for some coffee? I could make some."

"Now see here, Joe Farley!" Jessie stamped her foot. "You get whatever burr you got under your saddle out and done with! You've been an old family friend for years! Why, I remember how you used to bounce me on your knee so that

52

I could tell you my troubles! The least I can do is listen to yours for once!"

She waited, hoping that Farley would remember back to when she was a little girl. She knew how hard it was for people she'd grown up with to feel easy about discussing their troubles with her. After all, she was one of the richest, most powerful people in the United States.

And yet "Business is business, but friends are friends" was one of Jessie's favorite sayings. She didn't want Farley feeling timid just because she headed up the Starbuck empire, a mammoth chain of business holdings that stretched across the nation and abroad.

"Come on, now, Joe," she coaxed. "If there's something I can do for you, please allow me the pleasure of doing it."

Farley gazed at her lovingly. "How proud your daddy would be of you, girl . . . How proud." He turned red. "And I do have a favor to ask of you. It concerns my nephew, Tod Lane. He's my sister's boy, you see. Tod is going to be setting down roots in these parts in a couple of days . . . And I tole my sister I'd keep an eye on him . . . And he knows his way around a ranch, he does . . . And he could use a job . . . And so I thought maybe—"

"I think I see," Jessie cut him off. "You'd like me to find a place for him on the Circle Star. Is that it?"

"Yes, Jessie . . ."

She thought about it. "Well, if he's one quarter the man his uncle is, Tod Lane should be a fine worker." Jessie smiled. "You have him come around and see my foreman. We'll find him a bunk and a job to do."

"Uh, Jessie . . ." A perplexed look crossed Farley's beefy features. "There's something I haven't yet tole you about Tod. Something you need to know . . ."

"Well, what is it, Marshal? Spit it out," Jessie said lightly, trying to be encouraging.

Farley looked stricken. "It's hard to say, mostly because I'm ashamed, but—Ah, darn!" His shoulders slumped. "My nephew is an ex-convict, Jessie . . ."

"Oh . . ." Jessie couldn't help feeling shocked. Imagine, one of Joe Farley's family, a criminal! And then she realized how hard all of this must be for Farley, and her heart went out to the poor man.

"Tod isn't a bad sort!" Farley said quickly, his eyes anxiously searching Jessie's face for a clue to her reaction. "He just fell in with a bad crowd when he was no more than a boy, and for that, I tend to blame myself. You see, his daddy died when Tod was just knee-high to a grasshopper, so the boy grew up without a man's firm hand. Anyway, when he was fifteen, he ran away from home and hooked up with some outlaws. The boy got himself nabbed his first time out on the wrong side of the law."

"What did he do?" Jessie asked.

Farley rolled his eyes. "Bank robbery," he said softly.

"My word, Joe!" Jessie couldn't help gasping.

"All he did was wait outside the bank, holding the horses for the getaway." Farley tried to reassure her. "He got nabbed, and they gave him five years. Now he's served his time, and could use a chance to put his past behind him and go straight. I tole his mother to send him to me, that I'd find him something hereabouts and keep my eye on him. Seeing as to how he's got a record, I can't rightly make him a deputy, and he ain't got the education to get a job clerking, and so I reckoned that the Circle Star would be a good place for him, but I can see from your reaction that the notion makes you uncomfortable like, so I won't push—"

"Now see here, Joe Farley!" Jessie scolded. "Don't you go putting words in my mouth!" She shrugged. "Yes, I'll admit that the notion of hiring an ex-jailbird did take me by surprise, but I never said no to the idea, and I don't intend to!"

"You mean you'll take him on, knowing about his past?" Farley breathed.

"Of course, I will! He's your nephew, and that's what counts as far as I'm concerned," Jessie said kindly. "As far as that 'mistake' of his goes, everybody's entitled to one, and he sure has paid for his."

"Thank you, Jessie. Thank you!" Farley said happily. "Just one more thing. Could we keep Tod's past a secret between us? You know how folks can be. I reckon the boy has got enough adjusting to do without everyone hereabouts giving him the evil eye on account of his shady past."

Jessie, nodding, couldn't help thinking of Joady Cooper. One boy lost . . . but maybe another boy saved . . .

"If a fresh start is what your nephew wants," she told Farley, "then a fresh start is what he'll get, at the Circle Star."

★

Chapter 4

It was two weeks after the foiled robbery attempt at the Cattleman's Trust. Ki was in Sarah Township, watching as Tod Lane, the newest Circle Star employee, and several of the other Circle Star hands loaded up the supply wagon in front of Leland's Emporium, Sarah's largest general store.

Ki sat in the shade on the bench beneath the store's green canvas awning. He was waiting for Jessie, who had gone down the street to the dressmaker's shop to see about ordering some new clothes. As he waited, watching Tod and the others load sacks of flour into the buckboard, he thought about how pleased Jessie had been with the young man's work habits since he'd joined up with the Circle Star a fortnight ago.

The two hands working with Tod had both been with the ranch for years. Mikey was a grizzled old cowboy dressed in tattered black wool pants and a faded chambray work shirt. He doubled as the ranch's veterinarian. Jimmy Flame, so-called because of his bushy carrot-colored hair and matching handlebar mustache, was as handy with a hammer and saw as he was punching cows. Marshal Farley's nephew was a good-looking twenty-year-old, with long blond hair, widely set blue eyes, a dimpled chin, and an easygoing grin. He was a tireless worker, and as mild-mannered and courteous as a church deacon.

"Afternoon, Ki." It was Marshal Farley, making his rounds.

"Hi, there, Uncle Joe," Tod called out.

Farley waved. "How's the boy working out?" he quietly asked the samurai.

"Jessie wishes she had a dozen more like Tod," Ki replied.

"Ah, that's good to hear." Farley beamed. "It's caused me a few sleepless nights these past couple of weeks, worrying that I sent a fox into your chicken coop."

"You needn't worry," Ki assured him. "He is working out fine."

"What a difference a couple of weeks can make," Farley exclaimed. "Just look at that boy! I hardly recognize him!"

The Marshal had told both Jessie and Ki how the boy had arrived by train, looking pale and scrawny, wearing an ill-fitting suit of clothes and carrying his meager belongings in a paper sack. First thing Farley did was buy the kid a square meal, and then he took him right here to Leland's for some decent clothes.

"He looks like a tried and true cowhand in them jeans and boots," Farley said proudly. "He's put on about ten pounds, and he's gotten a fine tan working out-of-doors."

"Hello, Marshal," Jessie said, joining them. She stood easily in her low-heeled cordovan boots, resting one hand on her hip, her brown Stetson dangling on her back, held in place by its leather thong, revealing her tawny mane of honey-blond hair.

"We were talking about Tod," Ki said, standing up and smiling at Jessie. As he spoke, his almond eyes took in Jessie's form. Long-legged, she had high, full breasts, a slender waist, and a firm, plushly rounded bottom. None of her figure was in the least hidden by her denim jeans, white silk blouse, and wrangler's waist-length denim jacket. The clothes fit her like a second skin.

"Did you mention to the Marshal about Tod's new duties?" Jessie asked.

"I forgot," Ki said. "Tod, it turns out, has a way with horses," he now explained to Farley. "Old Hank Tyson, recuperating from his gunshot wound, needed someone to replace Joady Cooper, so we made Tod a wrangler. Since then Hank's taken quite a shine to Tod."

"That's just fine." The Marshal nodded. "Jessie, both Tod and I are in your debt for your kindness—"

"Nonsense," Jessie firmly said. "Let's hear no more about it."

Ki and Jessie watched as Farley continued on his rounds. Then Jessie said, "I'll settle up with Mr. Leland, and then we can head back to the ranch."

Ki nodded. They'd ridden in ahead of the buckboard. Their mounts were hitched up nearby.

Inside Leland's Emporium Ki wandered around the store while Jessie settled accounts with the rotund, whiskered proprietor. Most every foot of space was taken up with displays. One entire wall of the store was given over to tinned goods: ham, sardines, tomatoes, and the like. There were open sacks of coffee, flour, sugar, and salt propped against each other, and also bins of onions, apples, crackers, and dried beans. Children loved the store because of its fine stock of penny candy.

But Leland's sold hardware, leather goods, firearms, and clothing in addition to food. There were bins of nails, screws, nuts, and bolts, neatly stacked pyramids of soap, and shelves filled with patent medicines and toiletries. Belts, holsters, chaps, and tack gear hung from wall displays, as well as coils of new rope, stiff as wire, and clusters of canteens. Shelves of folded pants and shirts and stacks of hats kept the leather goods company. And behind Leland's counter were two racks of firearms. A chain snaked through the levers of the shiny new, expensive Winchester .44-40s, as well as through some lower-priced Henry repeaters. Chains were also laced through the trigger guards of the various Colt and Smith & Wesson pistols. Beneath the guns were stacked boxes of ammunition.

Ki studied his reflection in the full-length mirror hung on the wall near the shelves of new clothing. As much as he liked to go barefoot, today he was wearing black, rope-soled canvas slippers. He was in town, after all. The slippers allowed him the mobility to execute *te* foot strikes, but they were hard to come by. Leland's had had to special-order the slippers from San Francisco. The samurai was thinking that as long as he was here, he'd put in an order with Mr. Leland, when he glimpsed activity outside the store where the hands were finishing up loading the buckboard.

Ki went over to Leland's big plate-glass window for a better look.

Ki watched as the tall, muscular stranger dressed in a gray tweed, who'd been talking with the trio of Circle Star hands, turned away from Mikey and Jimmy Flame, to pay particular attention to Tod Lane. The other two hands went back to work, but Tod was prevented from doing so by the stranger, who nimbly sidestepped around the new hand to block his path. Ki couldn't hear what was being said, but it was clear that both voices and tempers were rising. Tod angrily tried to push past the stranger, who grabbed the young man by the arm, swung him around, and slammed him up against the side of the wagon.

That was all the samurai needed to see. He glanced back to where Jessie and Mr. Leland were bent over the storekeeper's account ledgers, settling up her tally. No need to disturb her, Ki thought, leaving the store. I can settle this by myself.

Outside, he could see that the stranger, who was taller than Tod, and outweighed him by at least twenty pounds, now had the young man pinned by the throat against the side of the buckboard.

"Let him go," Ki said loudly, stepping into the street and coming up behind the stranger.

"Who the hell are you?" the stranger demanded in a deep voice, turning his head to regard Ki, while still pinning poor, writhing Tod by the throat. "I asked you a question, fellow," the stranger crossly continued.

"I am your death, unless you release that boy right now," Ki said evenly. Meanwhile he inhaled deeply to calm his breathing, clear his mind, and center himself for the battle to come, for he had looked into the stranger's hazel eyes to see a warrior's soul.

Violence was imminent.

"What business is it of yours that this kid and I are having a discussion?" the stranger asked.

"The boy is with me—" Ki began.

"That's all I needed to know," the stranger interrupted. In a flash he'd released Tod and whirled to confront Ki, cross-drawing a revolver as he did so.

Ki's own fast reflexes saved him. Even as he was marveling at the stranger's speed, the samurai stepped in and swatted the man's gun with the edge of his right hand. The pistol went

58

flying off as the clearly surprised stranger, wincing, clasped his wrist.

The samurai expected the fight to be over, but once again the stranger surprised him by reaching out for Ki's shoulders and bringing up his knee, trying to draw Ki into a knee strike to his groin. Ki batted aside the stranger's outstretched arms with a circular block and then struck with a roundhouse kick. His torso bent sideways as his leg came up and around, catching the stranger on the side of the head. The man fell hard on his side, but in less time than it takes a rattler to strike, he'd scissored Ki's legs between his own and twisted his hips, dropping the samurai.

"I know me a few wrassling moves as well," the stranger said, grinning as if he were enjoying the tussel as he came around fast, rising up on his knees to snap out a left-right combination punch to Ki's head that had the samurai momentarily seeing stars.

Suddenly Tod Lane was trying his best to put a head-lock on the stranger, but the man in gray easily rose to his feet and shook Tod off as if he were a child. Tod threw a punch at the man's head, but the stranger ducked it, and retaliated with a solid uppercut to Tod's jaw that put the young hand flat on his back.

Ki noticed that Jimmy Flame and Mikey had stood back through all this. Most likely because they've seen me in action before, Ki thought. They now looked as if they were going to jump in.

"Stay out of it," Ki ordered them, and the two reluctantly nodded, going to the aid of the semiconscious Tod Lane.

While the stranger had been occupied with Tod, Ki had taken the opportunity to roll away and lightly rise to his feet. "You've got a good punch," he now told his adversary, shaking his head to get the cobwebs out.

"You haven't felt nothing yet," the stranger growled. He bounced in at Ki, looking agile, measuring distances, taking his time snapping out lefts and rights that Ki had to struggle to fend off. This one is an experienced street fighter, the samurai thought, blocking as his adversary feinted with a left and then quickly jabbed with a right. He has the potential to hurt me . . . Time to finish this . . .

He deftly sidestepped the next volley of punches to drive his elbow into the stranger's side. The man gasped in pain, his arms momentarily dropping, and Ki again punished the man's ribs with his elbow, at the same time delivering a side snap-kick to the man's leg. The stranger sagged to his knees, and Ki closed in, intent upon delivering with the side of his open hand a strike to the back of the man's neck that would put Ki's adversary out of the fight.

"*Ki, don't!*" the samurai heard Jessie cry out.

"*Ki, don't!*"

Jessie, horrified, stood in the doorway of Leland's Emporium. She'd been settling her bill with Sam Leland when both were distracted by the ruckus going on outside the store. She'd come outside to see Ki brawling with Dan Boyce, the railroad security agent. A crowd had gathered to watch the fight, and Jessie could see Marshal Farley lumbering up the street toward the scene.

"You don't understand, Ki," Jessie quickly called out as the samurai, looking bewildered, stood poised to deliver a coup de grace to Boyce. "That's—"

But before Jessie could finish her sentence, she saw that Boyce had recovered and was about to take advantage of Ki's distraction. "Dan, don't!"

Before the samurai could react, Boyce had locked his strong arms around Ki's neck and flipped him over his shoulder, sending him flying. Jessie was relieved to see Ki land as lightly as a bird on the soles of his feet.

"Son of a bitch, fellow, you've got more lives than a cat," Boyce breathed in wonderment, getting to his feet.

Jessie saw that Ki was getting ready to deliver one of his devastating kicks. "*That's enough!*" she bellowed. "*Both of you. Stop fighting right now!*"

"Yes, ma'am, Jessie," the stranger said and laughed, shaking his head. "I sure don't want to go any more rounds with this one."

"That's a wise decision, Dan," Jessie said.

"You mean, you two know each other?" Ki demanded, looking confused.

"We met two weeks ago, during the holdup," Jessie replied. "This is Dan Boyce, the railroad security agent I told you about."

"What?" Ki scowled at Boyce. "Why did you not say so?"

"Well, fellow, you didn't give me much of a chance, now, did you?" Boyce replied, dusting himself off and then retrieving his fallen hat and gun.

"You are the one who drew a weapon," Ki reminded him. "By the way, my name is Ki."

"Well, that's true, and I apologize for that, Ki."

"Ohhh . . . What hit me?" Tod Lane groaned, sitting up and rubbing his jaw.

"Easy there, Tod," Mikey soothed. "You get up nice and easy like."

"You got your butt kicked good, in case you don't know it, boy," Jimmy Flame said and chuckled, helping Tod to his feet.

Boyce walked over to sourly regard Tod, who was still gingerly rubbing his jaw. "Like I said, I apologize for that, Ki," the railroad agent continued loudly, "but when you said you rode with this bank robber—"

"Huh, bank robber?" gasped Jimmy Flame, lurching back in surprise and staring at Tod.

"Dan, please—Don't say any more!" Jessie said urgently. But she realized it was already too late.

Poor Tod's sordid past now stood revealed to everyone within earshot.

The young man looked crestfallen. His shoulders slumped and he stared at the ground, as if unable to meet anyone's gaze. Jessie's own heart fell as she saw the bystanders surrounding Tod murmuring among themselves, staring and pointing at him.

"Hell's bells!" Marshal Farley thundered, elbowing his way through the crowd to confront the railroad agent. "I've been told you poleaxed my nephew, here!"

"Your nephew!" Boyce shook his head, growing angry. "Well, if *that* doesn't beat all! Marshal, I was just doing my job. I was walking down the street when I spotted this jailbird kin of yours—"

Farley winced. "Keep that quiet, will you, man?"

"That cat's out of the bag, Uncle Joe," Tod said sadly, looking as if all he wanted to do was slink away.

Boyce, seeing Farley's accusing glare, grew defensive. "Like I said, I was just walking down the street when I saw this ex-con loading the wagon. He told me that he worked for the Circle Star, and those other two hands vouched for him,

61

but I figured he got the job without telling Jessie of his past. I didn't know he was your nephew, Farley."

"Dan, I *did* know about Tod's past," Jessie remarked.

"Well, I know that *now* . . . Jessie," Boyce said, shrugging. "But I didn't *then*, just as I didn't know the kid was your nephew, Farley." He shook his head, glancing ruefully at Ki. "Next thing I know, Ki is coming to the kid's defense. When Ki said he was with Tod, I wrongly jumped to the conclusion that they were fellow outlaws. The next thing I knew, I was in a wrassling match with a Texas Twister!"

"Hmmmph," the Marshal snorted, only slightly mollified. "What gives you the right to go strong-arming anybody, ex-con or no, in the *first* place, I'd like to know."

"What would *you* have done in my place, Marshal?" Boyce demanded, his hands on his hips. "You know *who* I am and *why* I'm here. Did you expect me to just stroll past, tipping my hat to an ex-con known to have ridden with Wolf Martyn?"

"Wolf Martyn!" Jessie exclaimed, shocked. Out of the corner of her eye she saw that Marshal Farley looked stricken.

"Sure, the kid rode with Wolf Martyn," Boyce insisted. "How do you think I recognized him? The railroad's got files complete with sketched likenesses on every outlaw who's ever linked up with the Wolf. Ever since I was given this assignment I've spent my evenings studying up on those likenesses, just in case I should happen to cross paths with one of Wolf's men." He paused, looking triumphant. "And now I *have* crossed paths with one. Am I right, young fellow?"

"Yes. I mean . . . No!" Tod stammered. "I mean, yeah, I was with Wolf Martyn's gang for a while, but not for very long. I was nabbed on my first robbery, you see . . . And I . . ."

Meanwhile, Jessie, too shaken to know what to think, noticed that Mikey and Jimmy Flame had now stepped away to glower along with most everyone else at the dejected-looking young hand. Uh-oh. There'll be trouble in the Circle Star bunkhouse when this gets around, she thought.

Marshal Farley had come over to stand next to her. "You should have told me, Joe," she said admonishingly.

Farley, looking miserable, hung his head. "I know I *should* have, but with all this stuff about Wolf Martyn being in the vicinity, I figured that you knowing young Tod there once

rode with the owlhoot would have set you against the boy."
He looked up, pleadingly. "It was *five years* ago, Jessie . . .
And the boy hardly had the time to meet Martyn before he was
nabbed."

"Goddamn, boy," Jimmy Flame muttered, and then quickly
looked toward Jessie. As he did, he blushed as scarlet as his
hair and mustache. "Excuse my language, ma'am, but it gets
my goat! I mean, the fact that the boy's a jailbird is one thing,
and bad enough. How's an honest hand supposed to sleep at
night know'n he's bunk'n with a fellow might steal the gold
out of his teeth while he's snor'n? But what's worse, how are
we supposed to cotton work'n with a man whose old gang
plugged that good boy, Joady Cooper?"

"*And* put a slug into old Hank Tyson," Mikey chimed in.

"But *I* didn't do it!" Tod cried out.

"Didn't say *you* did, boy," Mikey spat between Tod's
boots. "I *said* it was your *gang*."

Jessie shook her head. "You still should have told me
it was Martyn's gang, Joe, she murmured, more to herself
than to Farley. "Now I don't know what to do. I hate to
fire him, but I can't have trouble in the bunkhouse . . ."

"Jessie, if I may," Boyce spoke up loudly, putting his hand
on Tod's shoulder. "I think I might have been a little too rash
in rousting this young man here. Perhaps you could see your
way clear to keep him on? I'd hate to have the boy lose his
job, and with it, a fresh start in life, on account of me."

As Jessie listened to Boyce, she was surprised by his seem-
ing change of heart, and even more mystified to see him catch
her eye and then wink! He's got something up his sleeve, she
thought. But what? Oh well, since she was not at all happy
with the idea of firing Tod, she supposed she might as well
play along . . .

"Very well, Dan," she nodded. "Tod can stay on."

"Thank you, Miss Starbuck!" Tod called out happily.

"Galldarnit, Miss Jessie . . . ," Jimmy Flame began omi-
nously.

"For the time being, Tod will stay," she repeated firmly.

"Yes, ma'am," the old hand said in surrender. "But the other boys ain't going to like it."

"I believe Hank Tyson will accept that Tod has paid his
debt to society," Ki offered. "Why not ask him and see, Jimmy?"

"Maybe you're right, Ki," Jimmy muttered, turning away. "And then again, maybe you ain't . . ."

"Thank you, Jessie," Farley murmured.

"That's all right, Joe," she said. "You did what you thought was right, I guess."

Boyce was coming up to her as the crowd dispersed.

"Thanks for playing along with me, Jessie," the railroad agent whispered. "I've got a plan that just might nab us Wolf Martyn, *if* you'll play along—"

Jessie held up her hand to stop him. "You've got a lot of explaining to do, Dan Boyce, and this is neither the time nor place. Come to my ranch for dinner this evening. We can talk then."

Boyce cocked his thumb toward Ki. "Will *he* be there?"

"*Always,*" the samurai grumpily interjected.

Boyce, grinning, bowed at the waist and kissed Jessie's hand. "Not many opportunities for a man to break bread with both beauty *and* the beast. Dinner it is."

★
Chapter 5

Ki sipped at his scotch, neat. He was in the crowded bar next door to the hotel in Sarah, waiting for Dan Boyce, who had gone to his room to clean up after their brawl.

Jessie had accompanied the buckboard back to the ranch, to inform the housekeeper that there would be a guest for dinner. Ki had stayed behind to escort Boyce to the Circle Star. It was getting to be late afternoon, and the ranch was several hours from town. Jessie was concerned that Boyce, a stranger in these parts, might lose his way in the coming twilight.

Ki was standing at one end of the long, polished mahogany bar, watching as the bartenders were kept busy by the crowd. They drew mugs of draft from built-in taps decorated with ornate metal spigots, or poured shots from the extensive display of bottles on the backbar, beneath the wide, gleaming mirror.

Ki rested one slippered foot on the brass rail and stared into the mirror, feeling himself very much separate from the convivial goings-on. He was, of course, known in Sarah, and had been recognized by several men, but most tended not to say more than a few words to him. He was, after all, a half-breed, who truly belonged to no race, no country. He never would. To be ultimately alone was his destiny . . .

"What are you drinking?" Dan Boyce asked, sliding in at the bar beside Ki.

"Scotch," Ki replied. Over the years he'd developed a taste for the spirits imported from Scotland in exchange for Texas beef.

"Odd," Boyce said. "That's got to be hard to come by."

Ki shrugged. "Once, perhaps, but now imported foods and distilled spirits from Europe are becoming commonplace."

"Progress, I guess," Boyce observed. "Well, it keeps the railroads busy. Can I buy you another drink?" he asked as a bartender came over.

"Thank you." Ki nodded.

"Least I can do to make up for all that trouble I caused in front of the general store."

Boyce ordered another scotch for Ki and bourbon for himself, with a draft chaser. When the drinks arrived, he lifted his glass. "Here's to letting bygones be bygones, all right?"

The samurai touched his glass to Boyce's. The two men drank.

"That Jessie surely is quite a filly," Boyce said after a moment. "I suppose she's your girl?"

Ki took a deep breath, steeling himself for what he knew was coming. "No, she is not my girl."

Boyce shot him a skeptical look. "You telling me you got no claim on Jessie? No offense, my friend, but if that's the case, then I'd have to say you were telling me a mighty big fib. I'm a lawman, you see, and I take pride in my ability to read people. I saw how you looked at Jessie this afternoon—"

"Meaning what?" Ki asked sharply.

Boyce met the samurai's sharp gaze. "Meaning I'd be willing to wager a year's salary that you're head over heels in love with her."

Boyce paused, obviously waiting. Ki realized that he was going to have to say something if he wanted to put an end to this painful matter.

"I have pledged my services to Jessie. I would give my life for her if necessary—"

"There you go," Boyce murmured, his hazel eyes studying Ki from over the rim of his shot glass. "All the more reason for me to think that you love her."

"That is *your* concept of love, perhaps," Ki remarked. "But it is not a samurai's concept."

"I'm not following you." Boyce furrowed his brow.

"I could never have a love affair with Jessie," Ki said hesitatingly. "This is difficult for me, Boyce. I will only say that my . . . *love* . . . for Jessie must remain chaste. If I were to give in to my . . . *emotions* . . . concerning this matter, it would mean the lapse of my oath of total protection of her. That would be a stain on my honor that could only be erased by *seppuku*."

"And what's that, my friend?" Boyce asked.

"Suicide."

Boyce grimaced and gave a low whistle. "You sure are hard on yourself, Ki."

The samurai had to smile at that. "It is the only way I know. And now I must insist that we put an end to this conversation."

"I understand that you're a private kind of fellow," Boyce began. "I intend to respect your privacy. But I need to be perfectly clear on what you're saying, because I don't want to end up tussling with you again." He paused. "What I'm hearing is that you've got no objection to my courting her."

Ki saw that Boyce was watching him as if they were in a game of cutthroat poker for each other's bottom dollar. "Have I got that right?" the rail security man asked cautiously.

"Your desire for Jessie takes nothing from me, for I cannot lose what I can never have," Ki said evenly. "Now then!" he added brusquely. "The hour is getting late. I suggest we start for the ranch."

"Fine with me," Boyce replied, slapping down some money to cover their drinks. "I got that gelding I rented when I first arrived in town hitched up in front of the hotel."

Ki and Dan Boyce rode out of town via Main Street. About a mile beyond the town's limits the thoroughfare narrowed into a dirt trail that cut across a body of water known as Goat Creek, and for that reason, folks in this part of Texas had taken to calling it Goat Creek Road.

The sun was just setting, casting purple shadows across the land, when Ki and Boyce reached the halfway point of their ride, which was marked by a stand of dense woods that bracketed the trail.

Lost in his reveries, Ki was taken by surprise when Boyce reined in his mount, a chestnut gelding. "Somebody, or something, is up ahead," the railroad man said quietly.

"Yes, I see now," Ki murmured, slowing his own mount, a big roan, as he squinted against the gathering twilight. It appeared to be a buckboard, minus one wheel. It was angled across the trail, blocking passage. The buckboard's team, and its owner, were nowhere in sight.

For a brief moment in the fast-fading purple light, Ki thought the buckboard up ahead was the one that had earlier been in Sarah and belonged to the Circle Star. But as he and Boyce rode closer, they saw that this wagon was empty, whereas the Circle Star buckboard had been loaded down with supplies. And it would not be like Mikey or Jimmy Flame to leave Circle Star property unattended.

"Where do you think whoever owns that crate is?" Boyce warily asked as they reached the abandoned, crippled wagon.

Ki studied the dense woods looming on both sides of the trail. During the day they formed a dense green thicket. Now that night had fallen, they were impenetrable. "It is not our concern," he said. "We can squeeze past on the left—" He stopped in mid-sentence as his sensitive hearing heard a twig snap. "Someone is coming," he whispered to Boyce. "From the left . . ." He paused again as the soft sound of muffled footsteps reached him. "At least two . . ."

"Could be outlaws," Boyce muttered. "Blocking a trail, or railroad tracks, is the oldest trick in the book if you want to waylay somebody."

Ki nodded. He reached for a *shuriken* throwing blade inside his vest. Out of the corner of his eye he saw Boyce unholster his Colt.

"Howdy, boys."

Ki saw two men step out of the woods and onto the trail, in front of the wagon.

The last daylight had gone. The moon was barely a slit of bone, breaking through a thick hide of clouds. The crickets had started up, heralding the evening with their shrill chirping.

Ki looked at the two men out of the corner of his eyes, trying to make the most of his night vision. He really couldn't make out much beyond that the two were dressed in the simple garb of cattlemen: tight-fitting trousers, dark, solid-colored flannel shirts, and flat-topped Stetsons. They wore their gunbelts high.

"Glad you came by when you did," one of the men said.

He looked up at Ki as he spoke, and now the samurai saw that the man wore an eyepatch. "Our wheel, there, come off, and when we unhitched our team, somethin'—a coyote maybe—spooked our horses. They run off."

"We could use some help," chimed in the other man. He'd come closer, so that Ki could see that he had a long-nosed, weak-chinned face. "We've been here three hours. We gonna catch hell when we get back to the ranch."

"Which ranch?" Ki asked sharply.

"Figure Eight," the man with the eyepatch answered smoothly. "We just signed on." As he stared at Ki, the faint moonlight caught his single eye, making it gleam like a slimy stone.

These men are not cowhands, Ki thought, his warrior's instincts tingling. Not in a million years . . . "The Figure Eight, you say? I did not know know that Luke Reilly had signed on any new hands."

"Well, you're also mixed up on who owns the Figure Eight," said the man with the eyepatch. "Owner's name is Johannson."

"Yes, that is true," Ki said, suddenly uncertain. Perhaps he'd misjudged these two. He glanced at Boyce and shrugged. "The owner of the Figure Eight *is* named Johannson."

But Boyce, as well, appeared unconvinced. He still had his Colt in his right hand, his wrist resting casually across his saddle horn, but Ki could hear the tension in the rail security man's voice as he said, "I hope you good ole boys won't take this wrongly, but we're a mite spooked, seeing as how Wolf Martyn's band is said to be in the vicinity."

"Don't we know it," the man with the eyepatch said. "That's why Gus and I were hiding out in the woods. We been shitt'n bricks since we broke down here that the Wolf and his pack was gonna catch us."

"Well, then," Boyce nodded, "you two can plainly see that we aren't part of the Wolf pack, so why don't you ease our minds by taking your pistols out of your holsters—nice and slow like," the railroad man hastily cautioned, "and toss them in the wagon bed. Then my friend and I will see about helping you get that wheel back on your crate."

"Trouble is," said Eyepatch, as if he hadn't heard Boyce, "it'll take three men at least to lift the wagon, and one to slide on the wheel."

"*After* you put your guns in the wagon," Boyce repeated, a steely note of insistence appearing in his tone of voice.

Ki palmed his *shuriken*, ready for anything as the two hands looked at each other. Then the man with the eyepatch shrugged. "Sure," he said. "We'll do that." Ki watched as the two slowly drew their revolvers and then put them in the wagon bed. "Satisfied?" Eyepatch asked.

Boyce glanced at Ki, who nodded.

"I reckon so." Boyce's Colt disappeared back beneath his gray frock coat.

Ki, tucking his *shuriken* blade back into his vest, dismounted. "I will lift the wagon."

"What! By yourself?" Eyepatch blurted. "I told you it'd need three men *at least* to do the job. Your friend will have to lend a hand—"

"No," Ki quickly objected.

"You sure, Ki?" Boyce asked, sounding uncertain.

"I am sure about lifting the wagon," the samurai said meaningfully, staring at Boyce, trying to silently communicate that he still wasn't completely convinced that these two were who they said they were.

"I understand," Boyce said, casually brushing aside his frock coat, to briefly reveal his holstered gun.

Ki nodded, satisfied that Boyce would remain on his horse, where he could keep an eye on things. Anyway, his *te* martial arts training had enabled him to execute feats of raw strength and endurance far beyond his apparent ability. Someone else helping him to hoist the wagon would just be in the way.

Ki found his way around the wagon in the darkness, positioning himself to one side of the axle that was missing its wheel. Behind him, he could hear Eyepatch and his buddy lifting the wheel and rolling it into position, readying themselves to slip it on. The samurai got into his fighting stance and took deep breaths to focus his mind, imagining that he was going to flip the wagon over. He grabbed the greasy axle and lifted with his legs, exhaling sharply as he did so. The wagon, its wooden bed creaking, rose up steadily.

"Holy shit," Eyepatch breathed.

"Now," Ki muttered. He gritted his teeth against the strain and let his hands slide along the slick axle, giving the men room to slide the wheel onto it.

"Just a second, there," Eyepatch muttered, moving in close beside Ki.

"Hurry with that wheel," Ki began. Suddenly the samurai felt a knife pressing against his ribs.

"Act like nothing's happening," Eyepatch whispered in Ki's ear. "Do just as I say."

Ki looked down at the six-inch blade Eyepatch was holding against his vest, just about where his heart would be. He saw Eyepatch nod to his buddy, who began to move toward where Boyce was mounted up. Boyce could see nothing of what was happening, Ki realized.

"You there," Eyepatch called to Boyce. "I got a knife on your friend here."

"Is that so, Ki?" Boyce asked sharply.

"It is so," Ki hissed, the effort of supporting the wagon becoming unbearable. If a chance to disarm Eyepatch did not soon materialize, he would be too tired to fight!

"That's right, you just keep on holding up that wagon, son," Eyepatch said jovially. "You drop it, I'll pop your pump. It wouldn't be no trouble at all on my part. Now, then . . . In case you two ain't guessed by now," Eyepatch chuckled, "this here's a hold-up, *any way* you look at it. We'll be taking your money, your guns, and your horses." He started to pat down Ki's pockets. "All right, then, you," he addressed Boyce. "Now it's *your* turn to give up *your* gun."

"Let me have it," said the other robber, the one with the weak chin, as he sauntered over to Boyce's horse and reached up for the railroad man's Colt.

"My pleasure," Boyce said, handing over his revolver. But before Weak Chin could get a firm grip on it, Boyce slid his boot from his stirrup and kicked the man in the chest.

"Sombitch!" Eyepatch cursed, startled, as his buddy went flat on his ass and Boyce's gun went flying. Ki felt the pressure of the man's blade momentarily lessen against his ribs. It was the opportunity he'd been waiting for. He let go of the wagon. It fell with shrieking springs and the anguished groan of cracking wood. But before it could touch the ground, Ki had spun around and knocked Eyepatch's blade out of his grasp with a short, but brutally powerful wrist block.

71

Weak Chin, meanwhile, was back up on his feet. Ki knew that Boyce had been disarmed, but he expected to hear the railroad man dismounting and using his fists to put Weak Chin back down in the dirt where he belonged.

But the loud sound of the wagon falling had put the jitters into Boyce's horse! The chestnut gelding was bucking and rearing, keeping Boyce too busy struggling to deal with Weak Chin. For now, Ki realized, it was going to be two against one.

Eyepatch had found himself a long, thick fallen tree branch and was swinging it at Ki. "Gonna knock your head clean off your shoulders, son," the robber vowed determinedly.

Ki's upper rising block snapped about a foot off the branch, leaving a jagged, pointed end. Meanwhile, Weak Chin had moved in behind Ki, trying to lock him in a bear hug. The samurai countered with a rear elbow strike to the man's solar plexus that staggered him back.

The outlaw, gagging from the effects of Ki's elbow strike, gave up on the attack, and turned to hoist himself into the wagon bed. "Cut the bastard!" he called to Eyepatch as he rummaged in the darkness, trying to locate the pistols the two had earlier tossed in there.

"Can't! Lost my knife!" Eyepatch complained, lunging forward, trying to impale Ki with the branch's sharp stump.

"Here, have one of mine," Ki said, reaching inside his vest for a *shuriken*. The faint moonlight glittered against the blade's shiny steel as it left the samurai's fingers, and Eyepatch spat blood as the blade flew to his throat. He was falling to the ground as Ki heard the first shot.

Ki spun around in a crouch, fully expecting to confront Weak Chin, now armed and doubly dangerous. Instead, he witnessed four more shots fired by Boyce, who'd dismounted. Boyce was shooting into the vertical side of the wagon bed, behind which Weak Chin must have been hiding. The railroad man fanned the rounds off so quickly that the orange fire licking out from the barrel of his revolver seemed one continuous flame. Weak Chin cried out as Boyce's rounds chewed four evenly spaced, splintery holes through the side of the buckboard. Then, all was quiet, except for the thudding hooves of Boyce's horse.

"Goddamned town nags aren't worth spit," Boyce muttered, watching as his horse ran down the trail the way they'd come. "This is why whenever I can, I always try to rent me an Army mount. Those horses will go through hell and high water and be yawning while they do it. Just look at your mount," he added in disgust. "It didn't budge, not even when the shooting started."

"Circle Star horses are carefully trained," Ki said. "But no matter. Your horse will not be hard to find." He watched as Boyce shucked the spent brass from his revolver, reloaded it, and then tucked the gun into a shoulder rig. "So you had a *second* gun . . ."

Boyce nodded. "I got to figuring on how I lost my Colt during that bank robbery, and then how easily you took it away from me during our little tussle this afternoon, and I decided that maybe carrying a spare would be in order. This here piece is a match for the other one, so going from one to the other takes no getting used to."

Ki checked Eyepatch and saw that he was dead. The samurai retrieved his blade, wiping it clean on the corpse's shirtfront, and then bent to retrieve Boyce's fallen Colt. "Maybe if you tied a string to this one," he wryly suggested, handing the gun back.

"Cute." Boyce brushed the dirt from the Colt and then slid it home into his cross-draw belt holster. "Very cute."

"Not as cute as what these two tried to pull on us," Ki said.

"Amen to that," Boyce began, but was interrupted by the sound of a drawn-out moan coming from the back of the buckboard. "And maybe it ain't over yet," he muttered, his Colt reappearing in his hand.

But it *was* over, Ki saw, as he and Boyce warily approached the wagon and peeked in. The outlaw was lying on his side, with his knees drawn up, looking like a sick child. He held a revolver loosely clasped in his right hand. At the sound of Ki and Boyce's approach, he raised the handgun to wave it in their general direction.

Ki was about to warn Boyce to be careful, that while it was clear Weak Chin was dying, a man didn't need much life left in him to let the hammer down on a revolver. But Ki saw that he needn't have worried—Boyce was keeping his Colt steady on the curled-up form.

"Throw it away, fellow," Boyce gently ordered.

Weak Chin did throw it away—or rather, let it fall from his grasp. Ki reached in and took away the gun, and found and

73

removed the other one. To do so, he had to check around and beneath Weak Chin, and that revealed to the samurai the full extent of the man's wound. Boyce's .44 slug had caught him square in the chest. The man was lungshot—as good as dead.

"How am I, boys?" Weak Chin demanded. "Am I going to make it?"

"Afraid not, fellow," Boyce said evenly.

"Didn't think so." Weak Chin turned his head to spit out a mouthful of blood. "Leastways you boys ain't liars . . . Ain't liars, and ain't ordinary cowpokes, not from the way you took me and Roy."

"What's your name?" Boyce asked.

"Dick Jones. See they carve it right on my stone . . ."

"I will." Boyce nodded. "You got my word on that, fellow. You and Roy been working this wagon wheel ruse a long time, Dick?"

"Yep, and it's always worked fine. Until now that is. Wolf taught it to us, himself—"

"Wolf!" Ki interrupted. "You ride with Wolf Martyn?"

"I did," Dick said dryly. "Can't rightly say I'll be riding with *anybody* anymore."

He began to cough. Ki, listening to the rattle coming from Dick's chest, knew the man was just seconds away from dying.

"Tell us, before it's too late," Boyce urged. "Where can we find Wolf Martyn?"

"First you tell me who you both are," Dick insisted. "I got a right to know who kilt me."

"My name's Dan Boyce. I work security for the Texas and Pacific."

"Boyce, eh?" The man chuckled. "You're the cinder dick that broke up that bank robbery some of the Wolf pack was trying to pull." He looked at Ki. "And who the hell are you? Old Roy there was the best there was with a knife, but you took his blade away from him like he was a li'l old lady."

"My name is Ki." The samurai hesitated. "I . . . *ride* . . . for the Circle Star."

"The Circle Star!" Dick exclaimed. "Damn, why that's the Starbuck spread! Lord above, it was a sorry day for the Wolf Pack when we rode into this part of Texas! First you and your drovers chew up some of Wolf's boys for trying to steal Circle Star mounts. Then Wolf loses his three best men to this

74

man Boyce and Jessie Starbuck during a bank robbery a couple of weeks ago!"

"How many men does Wolf have left?" Boyce urgently demanded. "Where's he holed up?"

But the dying man seemed not to hear the questions. "Ole Wolf will teach that Jessie Starbuck filly a lesson, though," he said weakly. "Ole Wolf, he's a smart one. He's got a man on the inside at the Starbuck spread—"

"What?" Ki exclaimed. "Are you telling us the truth? Answer!"

"Never mind, Ki," Boyce said quietly as he felt for the man's pulse. "This fellow, here, he won't be doing any more answering—except, maybe to his Maker . . ."

They turned away from the buckboard that had become the outlaw's hearse. "Do you think he was telling the truth about Wolf Martyn having a man on the inside at the Circle Star?" Ki worriedly asked.

Boyce shrugged. "In my experience, dying men don't lie."

"This has been my experience, as well," Ki glumly replied. "And so if Dick was telling the truth, it can only mean one thing . . ."

"Just one," Boyce agreed. "That it looks like I was right, and you, Jessie, and Marshal Farley were wrong about young Tod Lane."

"I will go in search of your horse," Ki said.

"Ki," Boyce began, putting his hand on the samurai's shoulder. "I take no pleasure in being right."

"Understood, my friend." Ki mounted up. "I will return quickly. At the ranch they will be holding dinner."

Boyce sighed. "All of a sudden, I don't have much appetite."

★

Chapter 6

"Oh, I just can't believe Tod Lane would betray us that way," Jessie exclaimed from her place at the head of the dinner table.

"There's no other explanation, Jessie," Dan Boyce replied, toying with his brandy snifter.

"Do not forget, Jessie," Ki spoke up from his chair across from Boyce. "We were told by a *dying man* that Wolf Martyn has a contact here at the Circle Star."

"And dying men don't lie," Boyce added. "I've got to say that I suspected Tod all along."

"And your suspicion had something to do with the scheme you wanted me to play along with?" Jessie asked.

Boyce nodded. "As of this afternoon, my original idea was for you to keep Tod on, so that we could keep an eye on him in the hope that he might lead us to Wolf Martyn. But that was before Ki and I ran into those two during our ride here from town. From what that dying man told us, it's clear that Wolf Martyn feels he has a score to settle with you."

"Dan, you are saying that Martyn no longer wishes Jessie's horses, or her bank's money," Ki interjected. "The outlaw wants Jessie."

"Exactly," Boyce replied. "Taking that into account, to

have his spy hanging his hat in the Circle Star bunkhouse is just too dangerous."

Jessie shook her head. "I still don't believe Tod would betray me."

"Why not?" Boyce demanded, sounding frustrated.

"For one thing, it would mean betraying his uncle," Jessie said. "Or, you can just call it woman's intuition. I reckon what I'm getting at is that I trust Tod, and I really don't want to hear any more about firing him!"

Boyce shrugged and looked away. Jessie, seeing how uncomfortable she'd made him, sighed, thinking that the evening had started out so auspiciously . . . It had been after dark when Boyce and Ki appeared through the last of the many stands of shade trees, to ride along the path that led up to the Starbuck house. A hired hand came to summon Jessie, so that she was on the veranda to welcome her guest when he and Ki reached the house.

"Aren't you a vision!" Boyce breathed when he first caught sight of Jessie.

"Thank you, sir," Jessie demurely replied. She had her golden hair pinned up, and was wearing a low-cut, blue silk gown that she knew afforded an enthralling glimpse of her alabaster cleavage.

"Sorry we are so late," Ki apologized as he and Boyce dismounted, "We ran into some trouble . . ."

He looked as if he wanted to say more, Jessie thought, but just then Tod Lane appeared to take their horses. Jessie noticed that both Boyce and Ki were giving the wrangler funny looks, but she decided that it was just her imagination as she gave her guest a tour of the premises.

The house was built of stone. The main middle section stood three stories tall, with one-story wings jutting out from either side. Inside, the second-floor bedrooms opened out to a hallway, one side of which was a railed balcony that overlooked a huge combination dining area and living room. Darkly-stained roof rafters accented the soaring ceilings of the interior, which had polished, hardwood floors, bright scatter rugs, and a massive, gray slate fireplace, where a hearty blaze was burning. Comfortable leather furniture was arranged about the living room portion, while a mahogany dining room set commanded a generous space of its own, near the double doors that led to the kitchen.

Jessie suggested that Boyce freshen up in one of the guest rooms until dinner, when they all were summoned to the table for a delicious meal. Then Ki and Boyce began their story about why they were so late. Jessie listened, with growing apprehension, until by the time the dishes were cleared away, and coffee and brandy were served, she was more than ready for a good, stiff drink.

Now she studied a dour-looking Dan Boyce, and then turned her attention to Ki. "Do you really suspect Tod Lane?" she asked, thinking that she respected Ki's ability to judge people as much as her own.

The samurai took his time answering. "The facts do not go in Tod's favor," he admitted. "For example, we know that he is an ex-convict, that he once rode with Wolf Martyn, and that a confederate of Wolf's swore on his last breath that Wolf had a contact on the ranch."

"So, you're saying you *do* think Tod is a traitor?" Jessie demanded.

"Who else could it be?" Ki asked, sounding evasive.

"That's *not* what I asked," Jessie insisted. "*Do* you or do you *not* think he's betrayed us?"

Ki sighed. "No, I do not."

Jessie, smiling, heard Boyce mutter, "I don't believe you two. I think you're both confusing what you'd *like* to believe with the *reality* of the situation."

"I could say the same for you, Dan," Jessie countered. "You're a lawman; you know that all you have is circumstantial evidence."

"I think that you're just concerned about how your friend Marshal Farley is going to take the news that his nephew's still on the wrong side of the law," Boyce argued.

"Sure I'm worried about Joe Farley," Jessie said. "But it's more than just that. I think we need to give Tod Lane the benefit of the doubt. After all, if we were in his shoes, we'd sure want it for ourselves."

"Well put, Jessie," Ki said, sounding proud. "Dan, I think you have your answer for now as to what we intend to do about Tod."

Jessie nodded. "We'll keep on eye on him, but still keep him on, just as you originally wanted us to do, Dan."

Boyce, shaking his head, looked at Jessie. Abruptly his grim expression lightened. "Feminine intuition, eh?"

"Don't knock it if you haven't tried it," Jessie said and smiled.

"I don't suppose there's anything I could say that would make you change your mind about letting Tod stay around."

"No, Dan . . . I'm sorry."

"Hey, don't get me wrong, lady. I admire you for sticking by one of your employees," Boyce assured her. "But to be honest, I'd have to say that your decision does worry me. You've got your intuition, and I've got mine, and mine tells me that Tod Lane is hiding something. I'm worried about your safety, Jessie."

"Oh, come now." Jessie laughed. "I've got Ki here to protect me, and won't you stick close by?"

"Yes, ma'am," Boyce said softly. "Just as close as you'll let me . . ."

He reached across the table to place his fingers over her hand.

"Anyway, I want you to know that I hope I'm wrong and you're right about the kid," Boyce continued.

"Really?" Jessie asked.

"I'd surely hate to see a pretty thing like you disappointed in *anything*," Boyce murmured, giving her fingers a little squeeze.

She was *so* enjoying the arousing spark she experienced at Boyce's touch, and felt scorched by the look in his wide set hazel eyes. She wondered, If we were alone, would he try to kiss me?

She certainly hoped so. It had been a couple of weeks since the attempted bank robbery, but she still found herself daydreaming about how it had felt to be swept up in Boyce's strong arms. And today she'd been very impressed by the way he'd handled himself up against Ki. The more she'd seen of this man, the more she'd liked. And now his fiery touch had brought her around to what she reckoned she'd known from the moment she first set eyes on him—that she wasn't going to be satisfied until she'd seen, and *felt,* every bit of him!

"If you will excuse me," Ki said, standing up. "I will say good night."

Boyce and Jessie untangled their fingers as they looked up at Ki. Jessie felt as if she were awakening from a trance.

"Hey, I'm sorry, friend," Boyce began, sounding as if he'd

suddenly become aware of how Ki had been excluded from the conversation.

"No apology is necessary," Ki said and smiled. "I am still troubled by the fact that we have twice encountered Wolf Martyn's men on Circle Star land."

"Uh, yeah, me, too, Ki," Boyce mumbled.

Jessie, listening, could still feel the heat between herself and Dan. She was coming to the conclusion that Mr. Boyce was in as much of a mood to do some kissing as she was in the mood to be kissed . . .

"I am going to patrol the grounds," Ki continued.

"Good idea," Boyce said hurriedly.

"I do not suppose you wish to accompany me."

"No, maybe I ought to stay here and keep an eye on Jessie . . ."

"Yes, I suppose you had better," Ki said. "Anyway, I believe the expression is, 'two's company, and three's a crowd.' "

Jessie watched as Ki solemnly extended his hand across the table to Boyce, who just as solemnly shook it.

"We fought well together today, my friend," Ki said.

"We surely did," Boyce agreed, smiling. "We fought well against each other, and we fought well when we were both on the same side. And I've got to say, I liked it better when we were both on the same side."

As Boyce trailed off, Jessie thought he sounded tense, as if he were waiting for Ki to say something.

"So did I, my friend," Ki replied. "And so we shall remain." A faint, cryptic smile played across his dark features. "After all, two is company."

"What was that all about?" Jessie asked once Ki had left the room.

"Just something he and I were getting straight between ourselves," Boyce murmured. "He's a strange bird . . ."

"Care to join me by the fire?" Jessie asked, not willing to talk about her relationship to Ki.

"I'd care to join you just about anywhere," Boyce said as Jessie took him by the hand to lead him to the fireplace. At Jessie's behest he tossed another log into the fire, spurring on the crackling orange flames, until they cast tall shadows against the smoke-blackened walls of the great slate hearth. "Mind if I have myself a smoke?" he asked as they settled close beside each other on a leather sofa facing the fire.

"No, on the condition you'll share it with me," Jessie told him.

"You smoke?" Boyce blurted, obviously startled.

"I do when I'm with a man who doesn't consider it a hanging offense."

"My word," Boyce said and chuckled. He dug a short-stemmed black briar pipe and a worn leather tobacco pouch out of his coat pocket and tamped full the bowl. Then he took out a match, set it sputtering and flaring with the tip of his thumbnail, and got his pipe going. The sweet scent of cherry tobacco wafted over them as Boyce exhaled a series of perfect smoke rings. "You are one surprising woman."

"Oh, you haven't seen anything, *yet*." Jessie, catlike, was watching him, with both desire and promise in her intent emerald gaze. "You know, I never properly thanked you for saving my life during that bank robbery," she whispered, leaning against him, in order to begin nibbling light kisses along the strong line of his jaw. "You were *very fast* with your gun . . ."

Jessie's evening gown left her shoulders exposed. Now she trembled like a fawn as Boyce put his arm around her, to draw her even closer.

He set his pipe down in the ashtray on the low table in front of the couch, in order to gently caress her. He felt dizzied by her closeness, the tantalizing aura of perfume rising from her lovely breasts. The bodice of Jessie's gown was so wonderfully sheer that he could feel her nipples harden through the silk. His fingers went to her graceful, swanlike neck. He touched her pulse.

"Your heart's beating fast," Boyce murmured. "Almost as fast as mine."

"Fast on the draw, fast heart . . ." Jessie began.

Boyce was nuzzling her hair. "Lord, you smell grand," he said and sighed happily.

"And today you were fast with your fists," Jessie mused, just slightly pulling away in order to remove her hairpins. "Tell, me, Mr. Cinder Dick, is there any time when you *aren't* fast?"

"Oh, yes," Boyce told her as he drank in her beauty. Jessie had shaken her head to let down her hair, and now her tousled mass of blond curls glinted with a coppery sheen in the lambent firelight. "There's one specific occasion when I'm just as slow and thick as molasses . . ."

"Oh, really?" She giggled.

"You can call me Mr. Slow Poke." He winked. "Not that I'm one to blow my own horn . . ."

"Hmmm." Jessie picked up Boyce's still-smouldering pipe and took a very sensual, very suggestive puff, exhaling her own perfect smoke ring. "Then I guess I'll have to blow it for you . . ."

Boyce plucked his pipe from her grasp, blindly dropping it in the ashtray as Jessie's head tilted upward, her lips parting for a lingering kiss. He thought her mouth was like a cool drink of water to a man lost in the desert as their tongues intertwined to do a mating dance in time to the tune their bodies were just now beginning to grind out. When they finally broke their passionate embrace, Jessie's eyes in the firelight were huge, twin, green pools of surprise and delight.

"My stars," she breathed, a lovely shade of pink coloring her cheeks. "Dan Boyce! Where did you ever learn to kiss like *that*?"

"I figure anything worth doing is worth concentrating on," Boyce replied, sounding modest. He rose to his feet, pulling Jessie up with him, and then pulled her tight against him, to bury his face in her golden tresses. His hands moved over her body, lifting up her gown's skirt to trace the curve of her hip, then to fondle and stroke the proud, round swell of her bottom beneath her silky undergarments. His fingers found their way to the rear slit in her pantaloons, and gently burrowed their way inside, to teasingly trace the dividing cleft of her trembling cheeks, before ever-so-lightly brushing between her legs.

Jessie softly moaned as his fingers touched her most secret place. She folded into him, cooing like a bird . . .

Just then the double doors leading out to the kitchen swung open, spilling bright lantern light into the room. It was the housekeeper, coming in to clear away the last of the dinner things from the table, making Jessie and Boyce instinctively pull away from each other. They giggled like schoolchildren caught in some naughty act.

"I think, perhaps, we ought to continue this in my bedroom," Jessie passionately implored.

"I *always* finish what I start, Jessie," Boyce said meaningfully. He swept her up as easily as he'd done that day during the aborted bank robbery, and carried her to the staircase.

"My room is at the end of the hall," Jessie said breathlessly as Boyce seemingly flew up the stairs with her in his arms. Oh, how his masculine strength made her feel so childlike and innocent! As he strode with her down the second-floor hallway, she undid his tie and unbuttoned his shirt, her fingernails tickling the back of his neck as her hands slid beneath his collar to stroke the thick muscles of his shoulders and biceps.

Boyce felt his erection grow hard as marble as Jessie's fingers did a dance down his spine to caress his ribs. Her lips nibbled kisses across his chest as he brought her into the candlelit bedroom, quietly nudging the door shut with his heel as he crossed the threshold. The room was luxuriously furnished, as suited a woman of Jessie's station in life, but just then, Boyce, truth to tell, wasn't in a mood to notice much about the furniture—except for that big canopied bed, made up with satin sheets and a red velvet coverlet, that dominated the center of the room.

Boyce set Jessie down beside the bed. She turned her back to allow him to undo the catches on her gown, and then stepped out of the garment. She wiggled out of her lacy underthings, dropping them to the polished wooden floor, where they formed a shimmering satin puddle. Then she turned to present herself to him, placing her hands beneath her lush, bountiful breasts, and lifting them for his approval. The candlelight lent a sheen to her tawny skin, highlighting her magnificent curves.

Boyce stared, mesmerized. "Come here, you," he growled, holding out his hands.

Jessie, wriggling like a puppy beneath his exploring hands, gave herself up to myriad sensations flooding her being. There were the intermixed, sweet scents of cherry pipe tobacco and brandy on his breath, and the rough tweed of Boyce's clothes rubbing against her soft bare skin. Her hands burrowed beneath his frock coat to palm the sinewy muscles flexing beneath his sweat-damp flannel shirt. There was the stimulating rub of his close-shaven but bristled jawline as he kissed her. And then came the tickle of his tongue as he dipped his head to lick, and gently chew, her taut nipples.

84

And, always, there was his persistent, throbbing hardness, barely reined in by the stressed wool of his trousers. His erection pulsed against Jessie's soft belly like a bucking bronco, kicking to be free of its stall.

Boyce backed away from her. He kicked off his boots and began to undress, letting his clothing fall to the floor. Finally he peeled down his tight trousers, allowing his erection to jut free.

Jessie's eyes widened, and then a lascivious smile tugged at the corners of her mouth. "Remember what you said," she warned playfully, licking her lips. "As slow as *molasses* . . ."

Boyce, laughing, went to her. He buried his face in the warm valley of her sumptuous cleavage, inhaling her scent as he nuzzled her magnificent globes.

Jessie moaned with pleasure, her nipples swelling beneath his nibbling kisses. She embraced him, her palms cupping his tight, corded buttocks and cradling his scrotum. Then, all the while cooing sweet love talk in his ear, she reached down to curl her fingers around his throbbing manhood. From his groans, she knew that she was sending waves of pleasure cascading through him.

And then it was Jessie's turn to moan as they fell back on the bed, and once again her nipples tightened and rose to meet his darting tongue. Strongly, insistently, Boyce kept her on her back as he planted a line of kisses down her belly, until he'd reached the first tendrils of her golden softness. Then his tongue flicked and darted between her thighs, lapping at the sweet honey beading the warm, downy fur of her center.

Jessie tangled her fingers in Boyce's thick, curly hair as he sent waves of paralyzing pleasure riffling up and down her spine. She tried to hold back, but she was no match for Boyce's skillful mouth. She arched her back, kicking and crying, as Boyce's tongue whipped her into a long, shivering orgasm.

When she was at last able to form words, she pleaded, "Come inside me."

Silently, Boyce tried to do as he was told, but at the last instant, Jessie twisted around so that she ended up on top, straddling him. Sighing happily, she rose up, her dewy thatch brushing and tickling his sensitive tip. Boyce, groaning, drew her close for a kiss, and as their tongues dueled, his steely member twitched between Jessie's buttery thighs.

"Oh, Dan," she trilled. "I can't wait another moment!"

She thrust her rump high, her swollen, honeyed sex hovering above him for an instant, and then settled down upon him, enveloping his manhood in blissful warmth. His marble-hard shaft seemed to split her in two as he slid in her to the hilt. They began to move in an easy rhythm, like a pair of matched steeds loping along the prairie, gasping and sighing as their bodies slid and sucked and rocked together.

Low growls came from Boyce's parted lips as Jessie's inner muscles squeezed at him, snugly hugging his entire embedded length. The cool, smooth satin sheets bunched beneath his bucking, gyrating hips as each of his thrusts carried him deeper and deeper into her.

He tried to hold back; he desperately wanted to make good on his vow to prolong their pleasure, but there was no chance of that now. His climax was relentlessly, inexorably overcoming him. He couldn't do a thing about it, and he knew it . . .

Jessie knew it too. She laughed in delight, locking her strong thighs around Boyce's trembling hips, egging him on, the way a skilled rider will get every bit out of his lathered mount, overpowering him in her luscious embrace. He cried out as he spurted into her, bucking uncontrollably.

At that moment, Jessie's own pleasured purr again rose into a joyous sob. She shuddered uncontrollably as her second orgasm approached, her sassy rump frenziedly slapping wetly against the top of Boyce's ropey thighs. And then she came, collapsing upon Boyce's chest, her perspiration-beaded breasts pressed moistly against him, her sweet hips twitching as she mewled incoherently with the waves of shivery pleasure that enveloped her.

They lay quietly, listening as their rapid breathing gradually slowed, until Jessie broke the quiet.

"Hey, you," she languidly drawled, still lying on Boyce's chest, lifting her head just enough to lick his chin. "What happened to 'Mr. Slow Poke Molasses'?"

"Lord above." Boyce ruefully sighed. "You *would* be the first woman to make a liar out of me . . . I'll give you that slow poke next time." He grinned. "By the way, what happened to 'blowing my horn'?"

Like a flash, Jessie scooted around, so that her lovely, pear-shaped bottom was resting on his chest. The sight of it made

Boyce's manhood rise up as straight and hard as a creosote-soaked fence post.

"I'll keep my promise, *this* time," she said and winked over her shoulder. And then she dipped her head, turning her attention to the matter at hand. And didn't say anything. Not for a long, long time . . .

The trees surrounding the house and the ranch's outbuildings were black silhouettes against the starry moonlit sky. The cool night air refreshed the samurai as he made his rounds. Not paying attention to exactly where he was going, but feeling the need to be away from the house, he wandered toward a stand of hickory trees. The thick, leafy canopy overhead filtered out the stars and moonlight. It was quite dark in this little forest. Dark and peaceful.

Ki sat down at the foot of a broad-based tree. He crossed his legs in the lotus position, rested his palms on his thighs, and sat up straight, staring with half-closed eyes into the darkness.

I am a samurai, a professional warrior, Ki mused, taking deep, rhythmic breaths. In Japan a samurai is considered incomplete until he finds a great lord to serve. Alex Starbuck is that lord, and now that he is dead, I serve his kami, his ghost, by protecting Jessie . . .

His itchy nose intruded on Ki's contemplations. He ignored the persistent itch and gradually it went away.

In Japan an incomplete samurai is called a *ronin,* a "wave man"—a man blown here and there, like the waves of an ocean, Ki reminded himself. Slowly he found his inner peace.

Ki's thoughts suddenly turned to pretty Annie Slade, the Winchester-wielding filly who'd rescued the samurai and old Hank Tyson from Wolf Martyn's horse thieves. Ki fondly recollected his and Annie's passionate lovemaking after the battle . . .

Where are you now, Annie? he mused. Are you still on Wolf's trail? Where is your camp? And are you as lonely as I am tonight?

He stood up, brushing the dirt from his jeans, and began to head back to the house, thinking to go up to his room and read for a while. He was just stepping out from the hickory grove when his keen ears picked up the faint sound of doors squeaking open on rusty hinges.

Ki froze, confident that he was well hidden by the night. With an absolute minimum of movement he drew a *shuriken* throwing blade from his vest and then glided as stealthily as a predator in the direction of the sound, which he thought had come from the stables. He hunkered down behind a watering trough, watching and waiting. Sure enough, after a moment he saw Tod Lane exiting from the stables, leading a saddled-up mount.

The young wrangler paused to shut the stable doors, then swung himself up into the saddle and trotted off. An instant later, Ki hurried into the stables, feeling sick to his stomach.

Could Jessie and I be so wrong about Tod? the samurai asked himself. Was the boy on his way to meet Wolf Martyn? There was only one way to find out, and that was to follow Tod.

The interior of the stables reeked of horseflesh. Ki found a lantern just inside the entrance and struck a match to light it. The horses were all in their stalls. Ki grabbed his saddle from the long wooden rack and went to the third stall on the right, where a black gelding he favored was waiting.

Two's company, the samurai sardonically repeated to himself as he saddled up the gelding, but this time a feral grin crossed his features. If Tod Lane were indeed on his way to meet Wolf Martyn, then Ki would be at hand to kill two birds with one stone—

Or, perhaps, one *shuriken* would be more apt, the samurai corrected himself, seeing as there was no time to go back to the house to fetch his bow.

Ki led the saddled gelding out of the stables, extinguished the lantern, and closed the doors. Then he mounted up and rode off in pursuit of Tod Lane—

Hoping for the best. Prepared for the worst.

★

Chapter 7

Time to hunt, Ki thought as he followed Tod Lane through the dark night. Time, perhaps, to kill . . .

He slowed his mount to ascertain that he was still on Tod's trail. It wasn't difficult. There was a sliver of moon to see by, and Tod, unaware that he was being followed, was making no effort to camouflage his direction. Closing in on Tod—and Wolf Martyn—would be child's play.

Ki continued on, toward a sandstone rise, and then abruptly reined in the gelding. He smelled something. It was wood burning. But that didn't make sense, the samurai thought. Surely Tod wouldn't be foolish enough to build a highly noticeable camp fire if he were going to be rendezvousing with a wanted man?

Ki nudged the gelding into a walk up the rise, letting the horse pick its own way along the treacherous, crumbly footing in the dark. He paused at the top of the rise. Sure enough, down below, through some trees, he saw a small fire glimmering, its skein of pungent smoke winding and twisting into the night sky. A new smell reached Ki, wafted along by the night breeze: It was the aroma of coffee brewing!

Tod Lane was either very stupid, Ki decided, or he was up to something other than an outlaw rendezvous. He rode on down the rise and then dismounted, in order to close in on the young wrangler on foot. Ki was well acquainted with the terrain surrounding the Circle Star spread and thought that Tod had chosen well for his meeting place in terms of comfort, if not privacy. Soil, washed down from the surrounding cliffs of sandstone, had given rise to dense stands of hardwoods—pecan, walnut, and oak. There was plenty of brush to fuel a fire, and a nearby brook of pure, sweet water to fill a canteen—or a coffeepot.

At last, Ki, moving soundlessly through the woods, was close enough to spy on Tod, but what the samurai saw only further confused him. Tod's horse was unsaddled, its forelegs hobbled with braided leather. The mount was idly grazing on the tender shoots of grass springing up beneath a leafy hickory tree. Tod had spread out a tarp and a bedroll and was sprawled before his fire, using his saddle for a backrest. Beside him was a tin mug of coffee. The pot itself was nestled in the burning embers on the edge of the fire.

This isn't a rendezvous at all, the samurai realized. It's a campsite! The young wrangler was clearly intending to spend the night here.

Ki, crouched in the shadows, watched Tod for a while. There was nothing about his posture to indicate that he was expecting anybody. Just to see what would happen, Ki reached out and snapped a twig. Tod, seemingly lost in thought as he stared into the fire, seemed not to have heard it.

Enough of this, Ki decided. "Tod," he called out before standing up and revealing himself. He didn't want to frighten the young man, who he presumed was unarmed. Ki had never seen Tod wear a gun and didn't think the young wrangler owned one.

"Who's there?" Tod demanded. "Oh, it's you, Ki," he said as the samurai approached the fire. "I know what you're thinking."

"You do?" Ki gracefully settled into a cross-legged lotus position beside Tod.

"Yeah, sure!" Tod said quickly, sounding agitated as he ran his fingers through his long blond hair. "You think I stole that horse over there. But I didn't! I was going to bring it back tomorrow morning, I swear!"

"Calm down," Ki said to soothe the young wrangler. "I never thought you stole a horse. But I am curious as to why you are here. Are you meeting someone?"

"No!" Tod said loudly, sounding even more upset. His blue eyes glittered in the firelight.

He protests too loudly, Ki surmised. I have touched a sore spot. But there was time enough to get into that. "Then why are you here?"

"I-I needed to get away from the others," Tod began. "To go somewhere quiet and peaceful to think. The other hands have been treating me like horseshit since this afternoon, when that cinder dick rousted me in town. A couple of them even threatened to do me in once I fell asleep. That made me think I'd sleep healthier under the stars."

"I see," Ki said and frowned. "I will speak to them."

"Dammit, Ki, that won't do no good." Tod scowled. "You can't *order* those men to like me." He wistfully shook his head. "Now it's all spoiled for me hereabouts. It's bad enough being an ex-con as far as the other hands are concerned, but to have ridden with Wolf Martyn when it was Wolf's men who wounded Hank Tyson and gunned down that kid who had the assistant wrangler's job before me—"

"You mean Joady Cooper," Ki softly interrupted.

"Yeah." Tod nodded. "Hell, Ki . . . I was five years in prison. Now that I've paid my debt to society, I'm sick of being treated like dirt. It just ain't right. I got five years. I didn't get *life!*" He shrugged. "Anyway, I decided to come out here to camp and do some hard thinking, and talking it out with you has kind of helped me ponder it through. There's no point in my hanging around. I'll hand in my resignation to Miss Jessie first thing tomorrow morning."

"She will not accept it," Ki said.

"Huh?" Tod looked surprised.

"She will not let you run off with your tail between your legs," Ki said. "And neither will I." He paused. "That coffee smells good . . ."

Tod poured fresh, piping hot coffee into the tin mug. "I don't have another cup, but you're welcome to share this one."

"Thank you." Ki accepted the mug and took a sip of the strong, hot brew. "Tod," he began. "You must realize that for

91

you to run off now would only confirm everyone's worst suspicions about you."

"What do I care about that?" Tod moped. He reached into the breast pocket of his denim jacket for a hunk of chewing tobacco and bit off a piece. "Everybody already thinks the worst of me, anyway."

"That is not true," Ki firmly insisted. "I, for one, do not think the worst of you. And neither does Jessie, nor your uncle, Marshal Farley."

"But the other hired hands—"

"Do not matter in the least," Ki said and paused. "The only opinion that matters is your own. And you cannot expect folks to think well of you when you hold yourself in such low esteem."

Tod's eyes went wide, and his fists clenched. "Well, if that don't beat all. You got a lot of bark on you to talk to me that way! There you are, sitting all high and mighty as Miss Starbuck's right-hand fellow, lecturing me about pulling myself up by my own bootstraps! I bet you ain't never been down and dirty. Kicked around like a stray dog—"

"I was not always so high and mighty, if that is how you see me," Ki quietly interrupted. He took another sip of coffee and then handed back the mug. "As a matter of fact, I once *fought* with stray dogs for scraps of food in the gutter."

"Go on," Tod said. He sounded unconvinced, but his eyes were wide over the rim of the coffee mug.

"I will tell you a story," Ki said. "My father was a New England sea captain. My mother a Japanese, of noble heritage. They met and married in Japan. When I was very, very young both my parents died and I was left alone."

Ki betrayed no hint of emotion as he spoke. "By then, my mother had already been shunned by Japanese society for marrying a 'round-eyed barbarian,' and I was treated as an outcast of society, a half-breed. At that time in Japan, orphans were taken in at monasteries, but none would have me, because of my Caucasian lineage. So I lived in the streets, wore rags, and, near starvation, did as I have said: I fought with the mongrel dogs—my *fellow* mongrels—for scraps of food in the gutter . . ."

Watching Ki's profile in the flickering firelight, Tod

caught a glimpse of the samurai's feral smile and shivered. "So what happened to you?" Tod asked. "I mean . . . How did you survive?"

"I almost did not, but then I was taken in by a great master warrior, a samurai named Hirata," Ki replied. "He trained me in the martial arts, and tempered my spirit . . ."

Ki reached out for the coffee mug and took a swallow. "More about that I may tell you some other time. For now, you should understand that when you speak of your misfortune, I can be sympathetic, but when you *give in* to misfortune, I can have no patience."

"I hear you, Ki," Tod said quietly. "And I feel kind of foolish about what I said before . . . about you being all high and mighty. I'm real sorry . . ."

"It is forgotten," Ki said, and then abruptly quieted.

"What? What is it?" Tod asked. "Oh, now I hear it, too—"

Ki waved the boy silent, his attention captured by the faint whickerings. Tod's hobbled mount had pricked up its ears as well and was now whinnying softly.

It made sense, for horses had a way of calling to each other, Ki knew. Especially at night, when darkness reinforced a steed's instinctive tendency to run with the herd and in that way gain some safety from the world of predators that craved horseflesh.

The samurai, listening intently, picked up the sound of footsteps approaching through the woods. "Someone is coming!" he hissed at Tod while palming a *shuriken*. "Tell me now and tell me quickly," he sternly demanded. "*Did* you lie to me, before? *Are* you expecting someone? Wolf Marytn, perhaps?"

"Christ! No!" Tod exclaimed. "I swear, on my mother's life!"

"Yo, hello there, you two!"

The old boss wrangler, Hank Tyson, stepped into the clearing, leading his own horse and Ki's. He was wearing a long, tan canvas duster that more or less matched his visored leather cap. "This here a private powwow?" Hank asked. "Or can I join you for a cup of that sweet-smelling Joe?"

"Come and sit down by the fire," Ki said, relaxing, and putting away his *shuriken*.

"Don't mind if I do," the boss wrangler said and sighed, brushing aside his duster to rub at his side beneath his brown flannel shirt. "I reckon I ain't quite all healed up from that bullet I took, 'cause riding any distance at all surely gives me in to the miseries."

"Ki," Tod began. "What you just said, accusing me of being here to meet with Wolf Martyn—"

"I spoke rashly," the samurai said. "And now it is my turn to apologize."

"But—"

Ki held up his hand to silence Tod. "What are you doing out here, Hank?" he asked.

"I found it hard to get to sleep after listening to that ribbing young Tod here took from the other boys, so when he slipped out of the bunkhouse, I was awake, and like you, I thought I'd follow the kid."

"You could have ridden with me, then," Ki told the old wrangler.

"Hell, no," Hank snorted. "Like I said, I ain't one hundred percent yet. I didn't want to slow you up. I figured I'd ride by myself, and get to where I was going in my own sweet time." He stifled a yawn. "How about some of that coffee, son?" he asked Tod.

"We just got this one cup, but you're welcome to share it with us." Tod handed over the mug.

"Thanks. You boys don't mind if I add a little something to give it some kick, do you?" Hank took a battered metal flask from his duster's side bellows pocket. "I've always found that bourbon and coffee hits the spot around a camp fire."

"We were discussing Tod's future at the Circle Star," Ki said. "It seems he was thinking of quitting his job."

"Boy ain't quitting," Hank declared, taking a swig from his flask before pouring a generous dollop into the tin cup. "He ain't quitting 'cause I won't allow it. He's the best damned wrangler I ever worked with."

"Then you don't blame me, Hank?" Tod asked cautiously. "For getting shot by one of the Wolf Pack, I mean?"

"Course not, you danged fool!" Hank grumbled. "You didn't have nuthin to do with that."

"You see?" Ki nudged Tod in the ribs.

The young wrangler smiled, shyly. "I reckon I didn't know how many good friends I had all along."

"And now that you do," Ki replied, "We had best start back to the ranch."

"Before we go," Tod said and sighed, "and seeing as how we're all friends, I've got something to confess . . ."

Ki stiffened, thinking sadly, I suspected there was something he was hiding. How he hoped Tod would not disappoint him, after all.

"Well, go on, boy, spit it out," Hank urged. "Whatever it is, it can't be all *that* bad."

"Oh, no?" Tod took a big swallow of bourbon-laced coffee. "Maybe *that* will give me the courage I need to get this off my chest," he muttered, wiping his mouth with the back of his sleeve. "Ki sort of brung it up already, by asking me if I was here to meet Wolf Martyn. You see, last week, when Ki and Miss Jessie were in town, a couple of Wolf Martyn's boys came around, to try and recruit me back into the pack."

"Git out!" Hank sputtered angrily. "You say'n a pair of them brazen outlaws rode in—and *out*—of the Circle Star and you didn't raise a ruckus?"

"I didn't dare, Hank!" Tod said, sounding upset. "They were professional shootists! If you or any of the other hands who were around had braced them two, they would have planted you in the ground."

"I agree," Ki said. "Jessie does not expect her cowboys to go up against gunslicks. Tod did the right thing."

"Well, I suppose," Hank grumbled, sounding somewhat mollified. "Well? What did they want?" he asked Tod.

"Horses," the young wrangler said. "They told me that Wolf was planning a train robbery sometime soon, and that the gang was going to need fresh horses to make its getaway after the dirty deed was done."

"Circle Star horses," Ki added softly.

Tod nodded. "They said that seeing as how I was a wrangler, I was in the perfect position to bring them fresh Circle Star horses after the robbery."

"And what did you tell them, boy?" Hank demanded.

"Why, I said no, of course!" Tod insisted, sounding affronted.

"Too bad," Hank muttered. "But maybe it's not too late to make contact with Wolf and tell him that you changed your mind."

"What? Changed my mind?" Tod asked, astounded. "What do you mean by that? Why would I change my mind?"

"To lure the Wolf Pack into a trap," Ki said. "You see, Tod, if you had agreed to help Wolf Martyn's band by bringing horses to a prearranged spot . . ."

"I could have led the law there, instead . . . ," Tod slowly mused, as what Ki and Hank were driving at finally dawned on him. "Damn, I'm sorry, Ki, but I was so upset about Wolf Martyn's boys seeking me out in the first place that a clever ruse like that never struck me."

"I understand," Ki said. "In a way, I am glad." He smiled. "It proves your lack of guile. And as far as the ruse is concerned, it may not be too late."

"That's what I was getting at, boy," Hank said. "If you could make contact with those owlhoots and and tell them you've changed your mind, we might yet be able to set the leg-hold trap that finally brings down the Wolf."

"I'm willing to do it," Tod said and nodded. "But how would I get in touch with them? They didn't tell me where their hideout was, or nothing."

"Perhaps Dan Boyce might have some ideas on that point," Ki said, standing up.

"Where we going to find *him* at this hour of the night?" Tod asked.

The samurai smiled wryly. "I have reason to believe he is spending the night at the ranch. Come, we must break camp and get back to the Circle Star."

Jessie's eyes sprang open. She wondered what had awakened her. During the previous few hours she and Dan had enjoyed a wondrous and exhausting spell of lovemaking, so she should have been sleeping like a newborn babe.

She held her breath, straining her ears as she stared into dimly lit corners of her bedroom.

Everything *seemed* normal. The darkness outside her windows told her that it was still a long way from dawn. The house was deathly still. She could hear its timbers creaking and the night's cool breezes whistling faintly in the eaves. Beside her in her canopied bed, Dan Boyce was sleeping soundly.

She reached across Dan to squint at his pocket watch where he'd left it on the nightstand. By the faint glow cast by the last smidgen of burned-down candle she could see that it was 3 A.M.

Jessie, yawning, decided that it was her imagination, or

maybe she had reacted to some fleeting dream. She was turning over, plumping up her featherdown pillows, when she froze—

That *sound* . . . It wasn't the timbers at all that were creaking, but the hallway's floorboards. Now she knew why she had awakened. It was her sixth sense, warning her of danger. Somebody was standing just outside her closed bedroom door!

"Dan," Jessie whispered. When there was no response, she nudged him hard in the ribs. "Dan!" she hissed, her mouth pressed against his ear. "Wake up!"

"Huh? Whuh?" Boyce mumbled, coming awake. "Jessie? . . . Aw, honey, I'd love to," he began, feeling Jessie's lips against his ear. "The spirit is willing, darl'n, but the flesh is weak." He patted her bare rump, warm and moist under the covers.

"That's not what I'm after." Jessie giggled, reaching down to give him a little squeeze. "Leastways, not at the *moment*." She paused, becoming serious. "Dan, I think there's somebody standing just outside the door."

Boyce sat up, now fully awake. "I don't hear anything." He frowned. "Are you sure you're not just imagining it? I mean, all that wine at dinner, and then the brandy, after—"

"Dan Boyce, I don't imagine things!" Jessie hotly whispered. "I tell you I just know that there's someone out there!"

"Not female intuition again," he groaned, and then shrugged. "Ki, maybe?"

"Loitering outside our door?" Jessie sarcastically asked.

"No, I guess it wouldn't be Ki," Boyce murmured. "I'll go see." He hesitated, scratching and yawning. "You wouldn't happen to have a gun handy, would you? Mine are in my room," he added sheepishly.

Jessie nodded. "Right there in the nightstand you'll find my Colt."

Boyce was just reaching for the drawer when the bedroom door burst open and several silhouettes appeared from out of the dark hall to crowd the doorway.

Jessie let out an involuntary shriek as Boyce, evidently deciding that there was no time to fumble with the strange drawer, dove out of the bed to tackle the first figure into the room—a man dressed in leather and denim, with his hat pulled low and a dark bandanna across the lower half of his face. The intruder was holding a gun, but he hesitated using it, evidently taken aback by the fact that the man attacking him was naked as a jaybird.

That hesitation was all Boyce needed. He drove his fist into the man's belly, just above his belt buckle. As the man grunted and doubled over, the wind knocked out of him, Boyce connected with a right cross, catching the man on the tip of his jaw, just below his ear. The intruder fell to his knees, and then slumped.

Boyce dropped to his own knees and reached for the man's fallen gun. His fingers were just wrapping around the revolver when the next intruder into the room, also masked, rushed at the railroad man and kicked out savagely, the tip of his boot thudding against Boyce's head. Boyce fell over on his side and lay still.

Jessie, meanwhile, heedless of her nudity, had kicked off the covers and thrown herself across the bed. She yanked open the nightstand drawer and extracted her Colt.

"Go ahead and shoot, Miss Starbuck."

Jessie froze. The outlaw who Boyce had knocked down had retrieved his gun and was now pointing it at Boyce's unconscious form.

"Maybe I will," Jessie said, slowly bringing her gun around to bear on the outlaw trio. "I think what we have here is a Mexican standoff."

"Do you, Miss Starbuck?" The lead outlaw shook his head. "I sure don't. Think it through, ma'am," he continued, strangely, almost politely, given the circumstances. "You try and shoot one of us—"

"I hit what I aim at," Jessie warned.

"And then one of us wings you," the outlaw continued on, as if he hadn't heard her. "Of course, first thing, I'll shoot this fella, here," he indicated Boyce, "who I reckon you must be kind of attached to."

The outlaw smiled confidently, evidently reading the expression on Jessie's face as she thought about Dan being executed. "And all that shooting will wake your hands. Being stalwart old boys, they'll feel the need to try and stop us, so we'll have to shoot some of them as well. That's a lot of folks getting hurt, and when it's all over and done, you'll still be coming along with us. The question you got to answer is,

Do you want to do it that way, or quietly, with nobody getting hurt?"

"Who are you?" Jessie demanded, still clutching her pistol, although she was coming around to thinking that she wasn't going to be able to shoot her way out of this. "What do you want?"

"We belong to Wolf Martyn, ma'am," the outlaw said, "And what we want is you." He paused, as he thumbed back the hammer of his revolver, to let the ominous, metallic click fill the quiet bedroom. "Ma'am? You're still holding your gun. I'm getting a mite impatient . . ."

He trailed off, leaving his threat hanging in the air. Jessie realized that these three did hold all the cards. Sighing, she tossed her gun toward the foot of the bed.

"Wise decision, Miss Starbuck," the lead outlaw said, lowering his own gun.

"What do you say we have some fun with her before we go?" the outlaw who'd kicked Boyce said lewdly, feasting his eyes on Jessie's nakedness.

Jessie looked him in the eye. "Just try it, mister, and see what you get."

"Nobody touches her," the lead outlaw gruffly reprimanded.

"But she looks so purty lying there," the man complained.

"Wolf said bring her back untouched," the lead outlaw countered. "You want to explain to Wolf why you disobeyed his order?"

The outlaw shut up. "Good." The leader nodded and then turned back to Jessie. "Now, get dressed, Miss Starbuck, unless you want your pretty, bare bottom spanked by the saddle. You got some hard riding to do."

★

Chapter 8

"I reckon you got caught with your pants down, all right."
Hank Tyson stood in the doorway of Jessie's bedroom and
glared at Dan Boyce.

"Very funny," Boyce muttered, grimacing as he pressed
a damp cloth to the side of his head. He looked at Ki. "As
long as we're on the subject, would you mind *handing* me
my pants?"

"I'll do it," Tod Lane said, hurrying to gather up Boyce's
garments from where they were draped on the mirrored
French vanity and its matching chair upholstered in red
velvet.

Ki stonily watched the boy hop to it. Then the samurai
stared into the mirror, where he saw Boyce sitting on the edge
of Jessie's bed. Boyce sat with his bruised head in his hands,
a blanket around his shoulders. It was about an hour before
dawn. When it is always the darkest, Ki thought wryly. And
then: Jessie, how shall we ever rescue you out from Wolf
Martyn's clutches?

Ki, Hank Tyson, and Tod Lane had made it back to the Circle Star in time to see the French doors to Jessie's bedroom
being thrown open, and then Dan Boyce, bare-assed naked,
appeared on the balcony. Ki had felt his heart all but stop as

Boyce began yelling that Jessie had been kidnapped. Within moments Boyce's shouts had awakened the hands sleeping in the bunkhouse, throwing the ranch into turmoil.

Ki, Hank, and Tod had all crowded into the bedroom to hear Boyce recount what had happened.

"I remember tussling with one of them, and knocking the jasper down," Boyce muttered as Tod set his clothes down beside him on the bed. "I was reaching for his gun when the lights went out."

"Shouldn't we be sending for my Uncle Joe?" Tod Lane asked the railroad man.

Boyce seemed ignore the young wrangler, so Ki spoke up. "Marshal Farley has no jurisdiction outside of Sarah Township limits," he explained. "We will of course inform your uncle as to what has happened, and he will wire the appropriate Federal authorities."

"Course, it'll be days at the earliest before any federal law can arrive," Hank snorted.

"And while I could send for additional railroad security men, it'd take even longer for my office to round them up and get them here," Boyce added.

"We must handle this on our own," Ki agreed.

"Are you sure you don't need a doctor?" Tod asked Boyce, who was gingerly dabbing with the damp cloth at the bruise that ran along the front of his ear.

Again Ki saw Boyce seem to ignore the young wrangler. "I blame myself for letting Jessie be abducted," the railroad man said and sighed. "Hank is right. I was caught with my pants down."

"Perhaps you would have been better advised to have brought your guns with you into Jessie's bedroom," Ki said. "But under the circumstances, I think that you handled yourself admirably."

"If I'd had my own guns within easy reach, it would have made all the difference," Boyce sadly admitted. "It was my fumbling with that danged night table that gave them the time they needed."

"And if *I* had been here to protect Jessie, *that* would have made all the difference as well," Ki said, walking over to the bed to glance again at the ransom note that had been left on Jessie's pillow by the departing outlaws. "But rather than the two of us wasting our time in self-recriminations, we should be putting our heads together trying to devise a way to rescue Jessie."

"You know, Ki, that's a good point," Boyce growled as he began to get dressed, all the while glaring at Tod Lane. "You *would* have been here to protect Jessie, if Tod hadn't lured you away . . ."

"What? What are you saying, Mr. Boyce?" Tod had backed into the room's farthest corner and was now imploringly holding out his hands to Hank and Ki as he frantically asked, "You two don't think I had anything to do with Miss Jessie being kidnapped, do you? Why, I'd rather *die* than let any harm come to that lady."

"That's very touching, son," Boyce said skeptically. "But let's look at the facts—you're an ex-convict who once rode with Wolf Martyn. You expect us to believe that you just *happened* to go out for a late-night ride, decoying Ki, on the same night that Martyn's men chose to invade Jessie's home and kidnap her?"

"I-I swear I didn't know n-nuth'n about this," Tod blubbered, sounding close to tears.

"I hear you, but I don't believe you!" Boyce declared, buttoning up his trousers and then advancing on the frightened young wrangler. "I want you to tell us the truth," the railroad man spat. "Don't make me beat it out of you—"

"Hold on, Dan." Ki stepped into Boyce's path, blocking him. "I know you are upset, and that your head hurts, but you should not let yourself go off half-cocked."

Boyce frowned at Ki. "You saying you *buy* his story?"

"I do," Ki said quietly. "Now it is your turn to look at the facts. Yes, Tod rode off tonight, but he had no way of knowing that *I* would be outside to see him go. And no way of knowing that I would follow him."

"Well . . . ," Boyce said, taken aback. "I guess that's true."

"And there's another thing," Hank Tyson spoke up. "I was there in the bunkhouse when the other hands lit into Tod about how he wasn't going to be safe falling asleep in their vicinity. In other words, he didn't just up and decide to go camp'n tonight. He was driven out of the bunkhouse by some of Miss Jessie's oldest, most trusted hands."

Boyce, sighing, let his shoulders slump. He stepped around Ki to approach Tod, who was watching warily from his place in the corner.

"Son," Boyce began, "I guess that kick in the head did rattle my brain. This is the second time I've jumped to rash conclusions about you. I don't recall making an apology for the way I treated you yesterday afternoon, so let me apologize now." Boyce stuck out his hand.

Tod, smiling, shook it. "The best way you can apologize to me, Mr. Boyce, is to let me help rescue Miss Jessie."

Boyce, nodding absently, turned to Ki. "That ransom note says that Wolf Martyn wants a dozen horses in exchange for her freedom, right?"

The samurai scowled. "It is such a laughably small request in exchange for a human life that I am almost insulted."

"What Wolf Martyn lacks in human intelligence he makes up for in animal shrewdness," Boyce said. "Those horses he wants might be just the *first* ransom he demands."

"I don't follow you," Hank said.

"I'm willing to bet that Wolf doesn't bring Jessie to the exchange site," Boyce explained. "I think he's starting small with his demands just to see if we're willing to play along. When he sees that we are, he'll raise the stakes."

"Damn, that *is* shrewd," Hank agreed.

"He knows that as long as he has Jessie, he's got the winning card," Boyce finished. "So why *not* keep bidding up the pot?"

"I am afraid that you are right," Ki said. "I just hope for Martyn's sake that he has the intelligence not to . . . ," he paused, almost choking on the word, " . . . *molest* Jessie. If he or any of his men have touched her, they will find themselves embracing their deaths like long-lost loves by the time I am finished with them."

"Amen to that, fellow," Boyce fervently vowed.

"Wolf will be able to control himself and his men in the beginning," Tod said. "I reckon he's got respect for you, Ki, and Mr. Boyce, here, on account of the two of you have already planted so many of his men into the ground. I remember that about him. He really does run his gang like a wolf pack, you see. He rules by force. With them outlaws, fear equals respect." Tod shook his head. "The problem will come if the abduction stretches on. Once we start dancing to Wolf's tune, he'll start to lose respect for us."

"Stop being afraid of us, you mean," Ki interrupted.

"Just right," Tod said and nodded. "And if or when that happens, he'll figure he doesn't need to treat Miss Jessie right, or even . . ." He abruptly trailed off, suddenly looking sick to his stomach.

Ki understood. The samurai hadn't needed Tod to complete his thought to know where it was going. "You were going to say that once Wolf stops being afraid of us, he will realize there is no need to keep Jessie alive."

"Yes." Tod nodded.

Ki looked around Jessie's bedroom. Being here in this chamber, surrounded by Jessie's most intimate possessions, only intensified the heartrending sense of loss the samurai felt over her forced absence.

It was Boyce who broke the oppressive silence. "We've got to do something," he said, frustrated. "But *what*?"

"We got to somehow gain the upper hand," Hank Tyson chimed in. "It's like when you're try'n to bust an ornery bronco. You don't just react; you take the offensive and surprise the hell out of the critter!"

"I think I know the way to do that," Tod Lane said quietly. He looked very self-conscious as all eyes in the room turned toward him. "That note says Wolf wants a dozen horses, right? Well, that's what Wolf's men wanted when they contacted me here at the ranch last week."

"What?" Boyce exclaimed. "Wolf's men were in *contact* with you?"

"I will fill you in later," Ki said, waving Boyce quiet. "Go on, Tod."

"Remember what you and Hank said earlier about how it was too bad I couldn't think fast enough at the time to agree to what Wolf wanted, and in that way get the opportunity to lead you to him? Well, I'm thinking fast now. Say you let me take those horses to the meeting spot Wolf put in the note. If he's got Miss Jessie with him, and he's willing to stick to his half of the bargain and let her go in exchange for the horses, all well and good. If he ain't, then what I'll do is volunteer to rejoin his gang."

"What good would that do?" Hank asked.

"Don't you see, Hank?" Tod replied. "If Wolf ain't willing to give up Miss Jessie right off, it'll mean he means to play us out like a fish on a line. In that case it would be worth a lot to Wolf to know what we're thinking." Tod winked. "I'll

105

tell Wolf that I'm fixed real pretty here at the Circle Star, that Ki and Mr. Boyce keep me privy to all their plans. I'll offer to *spy* on what goes on here *for* Wolf . . ."

"But what you'll *really* be doing is spying on Wolf for us," Boyce said. When Tod nodded, grinning, Boyce's own smile lit up. "And once you find out where he's keeping Jessie, and report back to us, we can stage a rescue. I like it, son . . . I *like* it . . ."

"And I do *not*," Ki declared. "Tod, the role you're describing is the most dangerous in espionage," the samurai warned. "There is much that can go wrong, and if it does, your life will be worth nothing."

"It's my life to risk," Tod declared. "Sure it's a gamble, but I got a lot to win. Number one, I can pay back Miss Jessie for giving me a chance at a new life after I come out of prison. Most folks would have turned their backs on a jailbird. Number two, I can prove my innocence, once and for all, to Mr. Boyce, here—"

"No need for that, son," Boyce said.

"Pardon me, Mr. Boyce, but I think there's plenty of need," Tod countered. "Just now, after everything, as soon as you heard that I'd been contacted by Wolf's men, you started to suspect me all over again."

"Well . . . I-I . . ." Boyce stuttered.

"Don't deny it, sir," Tod said firmly. " 'Cause I saw it in your eyes. I reckon the only way I'm going to prove I don't belong to Wolf is to actively help bring him down. And it's not just you, Mr. Boyce. I've got to prove something to all the Circle Star hands, which brings me to reason number three." The young wrangler turned to Hank. "I reckon that if I'm involved in Miss Jessie's rescue, it'll put me back in the fellows' good graces."

"Reckon so," Hank softly agreed.

"There you have it, Ki." Tod smiled. "I want go back to the bunkhouse as a hero rather than a villain."

"There is one situation you seem not to have considered," Ki said.

"Which is?" Tod asked.

"Wolf Martyn could shoot you."

Tod shook his head. "Like I said, Wolf ain't book-learned, but he ain't dumb," he said confidently. "He won't kill a man who could be useful to him."

"He could shoot you on sight, once the horses are within his grasp," Ki persisted. "Shoot you before you can even offer him your services."

Tod looked less confident. "Well, I can't say that possibility doesn't trouble me. But there's no way I can't take this opportunity to repay Miss Jessie and turn my life around."

"And there's no way I ain't go'n with you," Hank Tyson announced.

Tod, frowning, shook his head. "No, sir, Hank! No disrespect intended, but you'd just be in the way! How'll I be able to volunteer to be a spy for Wolf if you're around?"

"I'll make myself scarce, to give you the opportunity," Hank promised. "Anyway, there ain't nothing to talk about, 'cause I *got* to come. Elsewise, how you gonna herd a dozen rambunctious horses over rough terrain all by yourself?"

"He is right, Tod," Ki said.

"Damn," Todd sighed. "I hadn't thought about that." He shrugged. "All right, I reckon Hank comes."

"We ain't got much time to get ready," Hank said, looking satisfied. "That note read that Wolf expects us at the parley by ten this morning." He glanced at Ki. "You got any problem with me pick'n the horses?"

Ki shook his head. "Choose neither the worst nor the best."

"No point in piss'n Wolf off," Hank agreed, starting for the door.

"And no point in giving him the means to outrun a posse if it comes down to that," Tod added, following Hank out.

Once the two wranglers were gone, Ki told Boyce, "I will trail behind them without their knowledge to see what happens at the rendezvous. If Jessie is freed at this exchange, I want to be in a position to take care of Wolf Martyn, once and for all."

"I'll come with you," Boyce said.

Ki peered at him. "Are you feeling fit enough?" he asked doubtfully.

"Well, I guess I'm still a little wobbly on my feet from that kick I took, but I'll keep up."

"No, my friend," Ki said softly. "I am familiar with the surrounding territory, and so I know very well the site Wolf has chosen. I can only approach it by horseback, and then I will need to continue on foot, rock climbing, in order to put myself at the vantage point I have in mind."

"Rock climbing, huh?" Boyce shook his head, wincing in pain as he did so. "Hell, I guess I'm in no condition to go rock climbing." He sighed reluctantly.

"You regain your strength here," Ki said. "If all goes well, Jessie shall be back with us by this afternoon."

"And if all doesn't go well?" Boyce asked.

Ki bared his teeth. "Then, sooner or later, Wolf Martyn will pay, with his life!"

Hours later, the sun was a pale, round disk occasionally peeking through an overcast sky. Ki sat perched on a granite ledge, waiting for the exchange to take place.

We are going to get wet, he thought as a breeze picked up, bringing with it the scent of rain. Oh well, the rain would make him even less visible to the expected participants.

About twenty feet below him and no more than ten yards away was a stretch of grassy pasture, commanded by a single massive oak tree. That tree was the site Wolf Martyn had specified for the exchange.

The area was empty now, but Ki, glancing up at the midmorning sun, guessed that it was still a few minutes before ten o'clock. As the samurai waited, he thought about how glad he was that he'd convinced Dan Boyce to remain behind. Getting to this spot, and getting himself settled before the others could arrive, had turned out to be a rigorous if uneventful journey . . .

It had been just dawn, with lustrous bands of crimson, yellow, and blue suffusing the Texas sky, when Ki left the ranch, about a half hour after Tod and Hank had set off with their herd of Circle Star horses. There was no dust cloud for Ki to follow, for the ground was still wet with last night's dew, but then Ki didn't need to trail Tod and Hank. After all, the samurai already knew where they were going. The trick was to get there first, without alerting any of the sentries Wolf Martyn had likely posted to guard against just such an ambush.

Ki had left his horse about two miles back, moving on foot into the higher windswept landscape of peaks and ridges where little grew but scrub. His concentration was total as he painstakingly flitted from rock to rock, regularly pausing to survey the area for outlaw sentries. He knew that stealth, not combat prowess, would save the day, for he could not actively confront any of Wolf's men. The sounds of battle reaching Wolf Martyn would jeopardize Jessie's sa[...] ing the exchange, if Wolf meant to hold up his end [...] bargain, or compromise Tod's risky ploy if the outlaw l[...] did not.

And, anyway, eventually Wolf would notice if men were missing. What would become of Jessie and Tod if Wolf began to ponder who had been in the vicinity to kill his sentries while the young wrangler was offering his services?

Accordingly, Ki had used all of his stalking skills to avoid dislodging a single pebble as he'd picked his way slowly and carefully along the rock outcroppings. But so far his care had been for nothing. He was certain that he was alone in these rocks. For some unknown reason, Wolf Martyn had chosen not to deploy some of his pack to watch his back during the rendezvous.

This troubled Ki. Yes, it was conceivable that Martyn might think that holding Jessie was all the insurance against ambush that he needed . . . But still . . . It was not like a crafty outlaw to neglect stationing a couple of men with rifles on the high ground, just to make sure that things went his way . . .

I might as well chalk up the mystery as a lucky break and leave it at that, Ki supposed, turning his attention to his weapons.

With him he had his bow and his leather quiver packed with an assortment of arrows. He checked the glittering array of *shuriken* blades and stars lining the inside pockets of his vest. In addition to these, he had the pair he carried in sheaths strapped to his forearms.

Hopefully, I will have to use none of these things, Ki thought, recalling Boyce's last words just before the samurai left. Dan Boyce had warned that kidnapping-hostage situations were tricky affairs, and that ultimately, Jessie's well-being would depend on Ki's restraint.

I will do my best not to lash out, Ki now vowed as his keen hearing picked up the sound of many horses approaching from the southeast. That would be Tod and Hank, driving their herd.

I must remember that in these circumstances a blow against Wolf Martyn will ultimately become a blow against Jessie, Ki told himself as he watched a line of black shapes moving across the grassy prairie from the north. Ki stared at the

..apidly approaching riders, counted six, and saw that Jessie was not among them.

It is going to be as Boyce said, Ki bitterly realized. Wolf means to keep Jessie and constantly raise his demands.

The samurai withdrew into the shadows cast by the rocks as Tod appeared around a narrow bend in the trail. The young wrangler rode his chestnut mount through the cut in the rocks leading into the pasture, and then the dozen Circle Star horses followed, channeled like cattle down a chute. The horses fanned out to nibble on the sweet grass as Hank, wearing a bandanna across his nose and mouth, brought up the rear. The old wrangler evidently had been riding sweep the entire way. He looked like a stone statue come to life, for he and his lathered mount were caked with dust.

Ki watched as Tod adjusted the Peacemaker riding on his right hip. The unfamiliar weight of the gun must have chafed during the ride.

The samurai smiled as he recollected how Hank had seen to it that word spread through the Circle Star bunkhouse about what Tod had volunteered to do for Jessie. Before the young wrangler could set off, a number of hands had approached to offer their apologies for doubting him—and to lend him the pistol and holster rig.

It looked as if Tod had been right, Ki now thought as the pair of wranglers waited under the dappled shade of the oak tree. Tod *had* won back all of his friends at the Circle Star by going through with this dangerous ploy. Now, Ki could only hope that Tod would survive to *enjoy* those friendships.

The half dozen outlaws were just reaching the oak tree. Hank removed his bandanna in order to spit, and then asked Tod, "Which one's Wolf?"

"The one wearing the derby," Tod replied.

Ki couldn't help staring at the man Tod had identified as Wolf Martyn. The infamous outlaw leader looked more like a down-and-out drummer than a badman. He had a hatchet-shaped face, made even more gaunt by a three-day growth of beard. Along with the derby, Wolf wore a dusty, black three-piece suit, with a soiled but heavily starched white collar, and a black ribbon tie.

And while Wolf's garb came as a surprise to Ki, what most startled the samurai was that the man was so little.

Wolf was riding a bay pony, which fit him just fine, since the outlaw leader couldn't have been much more than five feet tall, or weighed more than one hundred and twenty pounds, even with the brace of pistols he wore butt-forward in a crisscross holster rig around his waist.

Wolf Martyn's five men were dressed more ordinarily, in that mix of leather and denim, chambray and flannel, that could signify anything from honest, hardworking cowpokes to hardened gunslicks. Ki noticed, however, that all of Wolf's men had at least one six-gun strapped on, and a rifle sheathed in a saddle boot.

"I see you brought my horses," Martyn said. He had a high-pitched voice laden with the clipped nasal inflections of New England.

"We brought them, just like you wanted," Hank said. "But I don't see Jessie Starbuck."

"You, I don't know, old man," Wolf said, pointing a grimy finger at Hank. The finger moved like the barrel of a pistol to Tod. "You, I do—You're the youngster who showed so much promise riding with the pack some years ago."

"Yessir, Tod Lane's the name, sir."

"Ah, Tod Lane." Wolf removed his derby to scratch his head. He was wispy bald on top, with what remained of his dark, greasy hair plastered across his scalp in a futile attempt to hide his baldness.

"Tod, I believe some of my boys have been trying to bring you back into the pack." Wolf smiled. "But you've been playing hard to get . . ."

"Where's Jessie Starbuck?" Hank broke in.

"She's at my hideout with the rest of my men," Wolf said. "No harm will come to her, provided I get back safely, of course."

"We brought the damned horses," Hank said angrily. "Why ain't you kept your part of the bargain? A man puts his word on paper, he ought to keep it."

"You saying I'm a liar, old man?" the outlaw demanded.

Ki stiffened. Wolf looked to be trembling with anger. He is a little man with a chip on his shoulder, Ki realized. One who has likely been bullied in his life, and is now quick to take offense . . . A little man in a derby, with a stone-cold killer's heart.

111

"I asked you a question, old man. Are you calling me a liar?"

"If the shoe fits," Hank said.

"Hank," Tod warned softly.

"Hush up, boy," Hank snapped. "I'm talking to that little man with the big guns, over yonder."

Tod moaned. One of Wolf's men let loose a highly audible gasp.

Ki, without realizing he'd done it, had nocked an arrow and aimed his bow. He expected the worst, but was not sure what he could do about it. If Wolf attempted to shoot Hank, Ki would have to do his best to protect the old wrangler, but then what would become of Jessie?

The pasture suddenly seemed very quiet. There was just the breeze rustling the oak tree's leaves, and the nickerings of the grazing horses.

"Hank," Tod began loudly. "Why don't you go round up those mounts that have wandered off down the far end of the pasture." He paused. "If that's okay with you, Mr. Martyn?"

"Ya . . . ," Wolf said slowly. "Ya, that's all right with me . . ."

Hank was opening his mouth to say something, but Tod sharply cut him off: "*Do it,* Hank!"

Hank, frowning, wheeled his mount and set off for the far end of the pasture.

"You just saved that old coot's life," Wolf said crisply.

Saved a lot of lives, Ki thought, lowering his bow.

"Yessir." Tod nodded. "But that's not why I sent him off, sir. You see, I got something to talk to you about."

"You do?" Wolf sounded amused. "And what might that be, sonny?"

"The way your boys just up and barged into the Circle Star and took Miss Jessie opened my eyes, Wolf," Tod said quickly. "It showed me that I've been a fool bust'n my ass for ten dollars a month wages when an outlaw can just up and take what he wants, the way you took Miss Jessie."

"So you want to rejoin the pack, after all, is that it?" Wolf asked, sounding bored.

"Yessir!"

"Well, I could always do with a wrangler—"

"Sir, I was think'n I could do more than run your remuda," Tod said. "You see, they *trust* me at the Circle Star, so I could go on back there and spy for you."

"Spy for me, you say?" Wolf cocked his head, studying Tod.

"Yessir, and then meet you now and then at your hideout."

"My hideout," Wolf echoed, smiling now.

"To report on what they got planned, and—" Tod broke off, glancing anxiously over his shoulder. Hank was on his way back to the oak tree. "Wolf, don't say nothing to Hank about this," Tod urged. "That way I can spy with none of them being the wiser . . ." He trailed off as Hank brought his horse to a stop beside Tod's.

"Old man," Wolf began. "Your young friend just offered to be my spy at the Circle Star for me, now what do you think of that?"

Hank opened his mouth and then closed it. "I-I don't know what to think . . . I . . ."

Wolf threw back his head and laughed as the two wranglers exchanged confused and anxious glances. Ki too was perplexed. Things were not going as planned.

"Don't get me wrong, old man," Wolf said. "I think it's a fine idea, except for one little hitch, and that's since I just *told* you what his plan is, it looks like you've got to be *eliminated* for it to work."

Wolf gestured over his shoulder to his men, and a pair of outlaws kneed their mounts forward, to take up positions bracketing Tod and Hank.

"You've got a gun, Tod," Wolf coaxed. "Use it."

"I-I don't understand," Tod stammered.

"You don't?" Wolf shook his head. "And I thought you were such a bright lad. Let me spell it out for you: I want you to shoot your friend."

"You son of a bitch," Hank cursed as the outlaws surrounding them drew their guns and the man closest to him reached over to pluck his Colt from his holster. "*You no good son of a bitch!*"

"Yes, I am," Wolf agreed. "And you're a dead man. Have you finally realized that?"

Hank stared, dumbfounded.

"Ya," Wolf said jovially. "I think you have."

"I can't shoot him, Wolf." Tod was pleading. "I can't—"

"You're going to have to prove yourself if you want to rejoin the pack," Wolf said, waiting.

113

"I can't," Tod whined. He kept swiveling his head, peering first at Wolf and then at Hank.

"I'll count to ten," Wolf declared.

Ki, looking down from the rocks, brought up his bow.

"Do it," the outlaw leader declared. "Do it, or my men will kill you both."

"B-but Wolf . . ." Tod looked at Hank, who was sitting ramrod straight in the saddle, glaring at Wolf Martyn.

"One, two, three," Wolf began to count.

Boyce has counseled restraint, but I cannot stand by and do nothing, Ki thought.

" . . . four, five . . ."

Ki shifted his elbows on the rock he was crouched behind, ignoring the gnat buzzing his ear and the rivulet of sweat running down the line of his jaw to bead upon the lacquered wood of his bow. The razor head of his arrow was centered on Wolf Martyn's chest.

If I can kill Wolf, it might throw his men into confusion, Ki told himself. In the space of a few seconds I can hit one or two more of them, drawing the surrounding men's fire. Perhaps it will allow Tod and Hank to get away.

" . . . six, seven . . ."

Creating enough of a distraction to allow Tod and Hank to get out of immediate danger was all that Ki could hope for. Hank was disarmed and Tod's gun was still holstered.

Too bad it is not the other way around, Ki mused. Hank could shoot when the chips were down, but while Tod was brave, the samurai doubted he would be much good in a close-quarters gunfight.

" . . . eight . . ."

Jessie, I will do my best to find you before the men holding you realize their leader is not coming back to them, Ki vowed, feeling sick to his stomach. He was very aware of the increased danger Jessie would be in the moment Wolf died. Once the the men holding her realized they were leaderless, they would panic. Would they kill Jessie to keep their identities secret?

Ki reminded himself that he would have to keep one of the outlaws down below alive. Then, when the others are dead, I will make that one tell me the whereabouts of the hideout, he thought. And there was no question in the samurai's mind that when he was finished, the outlaw *would* talk.

" . . . nine . . ."

Ki held his breath, prepared to let his arrow fly. But Wolf Martyn had abruptly stopped counting.

"You failed the test, youngster," Wolf told Tod.

"You going to kill us?" Tod gulped.

"Nah, you ain't worth killing," Wolf said idly.

It was all just Wolf's idea of a joke, Ki realized. Relieved, he lowered his bow.

"You ain't worth killing, youngster," Wolf repeated to Tod. Then he grinned at Hank. "But *you* are."

Fast as a rattler striking, Wolf drew a pistol and fired once, hitting Hank in the chest. Blood geysered from Hank's shirtfront, but the old wrangler never made a sound. He just fell back, knocked out of the saddle by Wolf Martyn's round the way a tin can gets knocked off a fence post. His body limply hit the ground, facedown.

"*You bastard!*" Tod screamed at Wolf, clawing at the Peacemaker on his hip. "*I'll kill you, you murdering bastard!*"

He'd just managed to clear leather when the outlaw beside him clubbed Tod behind the ear with the barrel of his gun. The young wrangler slumped in his saddle, his borrowed revolver slipping from his grasp to the ground.

"What clowns," Wolf smirked. He glanced over his shoulder. "You four round up those horses and start back to the hideout."

Ki had again brought up his bow, but still he held back from slaying Wolf. Restraint, he urged himself, struggling to rein in his fury. Hank has been shot, but you cannot retrieve that bullet. So now concern yourself with Tod and Jessie.

"What do you want to do with the kid, Wolf?" one of the outlaws asked.

Answer wisely, you bastard, Ki thought fiercely, staring down the shaft of his arrow at Wolf. Inevitably I shall be the means of your death, but for now, answer well and carry your miserable existence through one more day.

"We'll take young Tod with us," Wolf replied. "Who knows? He might make a useful bargaining chip with Jessie Starbuck's people, later on."

"I'll kill ya . . . ," Tod groggily murmured, only semiconscious.

115

"Better tie his hands, though," Wolf told his men. "Kid's so riled up about that old coot I put down, he might try something stupid." He chuckled. "Other than trying to make me think he was going to be my *spy* . . . and drawing on me, of course."

Ki, not trusting his willpower, put aside his bow. Every muscle in his body was clenched against his overwhelming desire to skewer Wolf Martyn.

He watched the outlaw leader dismount, to approach Hank's still body. Wolf took a folded piece of paper from the inside breast pocket of his frock coat and bent to tuck it into Hank's empty holster. As Wolf straightened up, the sky grew suddenly darker, and a cold rain began to slant down.

"Grab the old man's horse, and let's ride," Wolf said, turning up the collar of his coat. He swung himself up into the saddle, wheeled around his pony, and set off.

And I cannot follow, Ki thought in frustration, watching the outlaws ride off across the prairie, with the Circle Star horses and Tod Lane in their possession. Ki felt himself burning inside with pent-up fury, even as the rain soaked through his clothes and plastered his long black hair to his skull.

I cannot hope to follow men on horseback across open country on foot, he thought. But my horse is miles back. By the time I fetch it and return, the rain coming down will have washed away the outlaws' trail.

And Wolf Martyn still held Jessie, which meant that the outlaw now had even more cards than when this fiasco of a plan started. Ki brooded as he grabbed his bow and hurried down the incline to check on Hank.

The rain had intensified into a windswept downpour, making the oak tree's branches creak and moan. Ki knelt beside Hank, gently turned the fallen wrangler onto his back, and wiped the mud from his face. He wanted to do what he could for his friend, which was very little.

Hank had been shot in the heart. He had likely died before he hit the ground.

"I will avenge your death," Ki murmured, gazing down at the body. The samurai hoped that the wrangler's *kami,* his spirit, was hovering nearby to hear his oath, and take it with him to heaven.

Meanwhile, Hank's sightless eyes filled and overflowed with rain, as if his corpse were crying. Ki gently lowered the lids.

He took Wolf Martyn's note from Hank's holster and gingerly unfolded the sodden sheet of paper. The pelting rain had turned the ink to blue streams running down the page, but the block printing was still legible.

Ki read the note's contents through twice and then let the wind snatch away the wet scraps. He then sat with his back against the oak tree, with his head slumped and his bow resting across his knees, pondering Wolf's words to Hank.

"... *You're a dead man* ... *Have you finally realized that?*"

"Have you, Wolf Martyn?" Ki fiercely murmured, as the rain washed away his own tears of mourning. "*Have you?*"

★

Chapter 9

"Oh, my head . . ." Tod Lane's eyes fluttered open.

"Easy, Tod," Jessie murmured. She'd been waiting for the young wrangler to awaken ever since Wolf Martyn and his men had tossed Tod's limp body into the shack where they'd been keeping her prisoner.

"Miss Jessie, is that you?" Tod weakly mumbled.

"Yes, it's me." Jessie stared down at him with concern. He was lying stretched out on the hard-packed dirt floor. Jessie was cradling his head in her lap and pressing a cool, damp cloth to his forehead.

"Rest easy," she said soothingly as Tod tried to rise. She adjusted the blanket she'd covered him with when he was first brought in. "Don't try to get up just yet."

"Yes, ma'am, I guess I'll take that advice." Tod winced, letting his head settle back into Jessie's lap. "It feels like I got a cavalry troop riding hell-bent for leather inside my skull." He sighed, looking rueful. "And I'd give anything if that cavalry troop was real, seeing as how I reckon we're now both in Wolf Martyn's clutches."

"I'm sorry to say that's right," Jessie said. She dipped the cloth into a pan of water, then wrung it out and gently pressed it behind Tod's ear. "You've got a bad bruise." She traced it lightly. "There's no bleeding, but you've been unconscious since they brought you here."

"How long have I been out?" Tod asked.

"I'd say several hours," Jessie replied, shaking her head. "But it's been hard for me to keep track of time because I've been locked up in here."

She glanced around the one-room shack. It was barren of furniture except for a backless bench along one wall and a couple of stools. A pile of blankets like the one covering Tod had been her bed the night before. There was a pair of windows left partly open for ventilation, but they were covered over with sturdy wire mesh, to prevent any chance of escape. The shack's walls were studded with wooden pegs from which hung a motley collection of tack gear— bridles, halters, reins, harness equipment, and so on. The tack's brightwork was all tarnished and rusting, the leather green with mildew.

"I've been measuring time by when my jailers bring me my bread and water," Jessie wryly remarked.

Tod again tried sitting up, this time managing the feat. "I guess now I know how Mr. Boyce was feeling." He grimaced, taking the cloth from Jessie and then gingerly holding it against his ear.

"How was Dan when you last saw him?" Jessie asked, with a look of concern. "Wolf Martyn's men hardly gave me time to get dressed," she continued, indicating her denims, "before they dragged me away. Dan was still stretched out on the floor."

"Oh, Mr. Boyce is okay," Tod reassured her. "He had a little headache last I saw him, but that's all."

"That's a relief," Jessie said. "But tell me, how did you come to be caught by Wolf?"

"That's kind of a long story, ma'am," the young wrangler frowned, "a long story that concerns both Hank Tyson and me. One that has a very sad ending."

"I see . . ." Jessie paused. Something—the look in Tod's eyes?—warned that she had best steel herself for what was coming. "Maybe you'd better tell me all about it."

Tod did.

Jessie sat cross-legged on the dirt floor, listening quietly as Tod filled her in on how Ki and Dan and Tod and Hank had concocted their plan to get the best of Wolf Martyn. She struggled against her tears as Tod told of how the plan went awry, ending with his anguished description of the way Wolf Martyn had cold-bloodedly gunned down Hank.

"That bullet took old Hank smack dab in the chest," Tod managed to say, fighting back a sob. "I saw the way he fell . . . the way he hit the ground and lay so still . . ."

"You're saying you think Wolf killed him?" Jessie asked.

"Yes, ma'am, I surely think that's so," Tod moaned. "And I blame myself for letting it happen! I shouldn't have let him come!"

"It sounds to me like the decision wasn't up to you, Tod," Jessie softly said. "From what you told me, you tried hard to convince Hank to stay behind, but both Ki and Dan overrode you."

"Yes, ma'am, that's so, I reckon." Tod slowly nodded, momentarily looking relieved, but then he frowned. "But I had a gun! Maybe if I'd been faster, I could have beat Wolf to the draw, and saved Hank—"

"Now you're talking nonsense," Jessie said, gently admonishing him. "You had about as much chance of beating Wolf to the draw as you would have had trying to snatch that bullet out of the air before it hit poor Hank." She shook her head. "Face it, Tod, there was nothing you could have done."

"You're sure about that, Miss Jessie?" Tod asked plaintively.

"I'm sure," she said to comfort the young wrangler, and then her voice hardened. "Just as I'm sure that Wolf Martyn will pay for all of his crimes, including Hank's shooting."

She paused, swallowing hard, thinking to herself, Or Hank's murder, if Tod's right about the severity of the old man's wound . . .

Tod shook his head. "I reckon old Hank would have come through it all right if he hadn't gotten so riled at Wolf for not bringing you to the exchange site."

"There was never any chance of Wolf bringing me," Jessie said fiercely. "A few hours ago, when Wolf had you carried in here, he bragged to me about his plans. He's figuring on robbing the train, day after tomorrow."

"The one carrying the government payroll to the Army station at Bent Hollow?" Tod asked, his eyes widening.

"The very one," Jessie replied. "Wolf knows the train is going to be loaded down with troops to protect that payroll,

121

with even more soldiers standing guard at every station along the way."

"Then how's he going to do it?"

"When he first came to these parts, his plan was to hit the train head-on," Jessie explained. "He rode into Texas with over twenty men, figuring it would be easy pickings to steal some horses to supply his pack with fresh mounts for their getaway once they robbed the train, and to knock over Sarah's bank for a little dividend while waiting for that government payroll to come around."

"But he figured wrong, didn't he, Miss Jessie?" For the first time, Tod managed a slight grin.

Jessie nodded, smiling proudly. "Ki, Dan Boyce, and I, *have* whittled down his numbers. Now the wolf pack's down to around half a dozen men."

"That's what I don't understand," Tod began. "Taking on a train bristling with troops was gonna be hard enough for twenty men. How does Wolf expect to do it with just six?"

"He doesn't expect to do it, any longer," Jessie replied. "He now expects *Ki and Dan Boyce* to see to it that the payroll is handed over to him, nice and easy like."

Tod Lane was staring at her, looking dumbfounded.

"You see, I know lots of influential people," Jessie elaborated, "including the governor, the Lone Star State's senators, and the president of the Texas and Pacific Railroad."

"I guess it's gonna be like what Mr. Boyce said," Tod slowly mused. "Wolf's upping the ante."

"It's Wolf's notion that once those bigwigs get word that I'm his hostage, they and the government will turn over that payroll in exchange for my freedom," Jessie said.

"And will they?" Tod asked.

She shrugged. "It's my intention not to let things get to that point. I intend to escape."

"But how?" Tod demanded. "How are you planning to get out of here?" He paused. "By the way, just where, exactly, are we? We could be anywhere!"

"Oh, now, it's not as bad as all that," Jessie said and chuckled. "I know the terrain surrounding the Circle Star. This happens to be the old stagecoach depot ten miles southeast of Anvil Rock."

Tod looked confused.

"Don't fret," Jessie said to reassure him. "Remember, I grew up in these parts. I know my way around like I know the back of my hand. Wolf Martyn has got us locked up in what used to be the tack room. Just behind this shed is the stables. I guess Wolf is using the station house across the yard from this shack as the barracks for himself and his men."

"Well!" Tod sounded impressed. "You *do* know this place, Miss Jessie."

"This depot was abandoned when I was a little girl, when the railroad came through. There's a pretty little pond over yonder where my father and I used to come for picnics." She rolled her eyes. "I could just kick myself for not thinking of this site earlier as a likely place for Wolf Martyn to make his hideout."

"Maybe Ki will think of it?" Tod asked hopefully.

"Maybe . . ." Jessie was doubtful. "But this place was abandoned before Ki came to the Circle Star. If *I* didn't think of it . . ." She trailed off.

"But if we can get out of here, you can find your way back to the Circle Star?" Tod persisted, sounding worried.

"Blindfolded," Jessie promised.

"And you have got a plan for getting us out of here?" Tod pressed, his worry now replaced by skepticism.

"Yep," Jessie replied. "The seed got planted after Wolf let on to me how few men he's got left, but it blossomed when you told me how Wolf rode to the rendezvous with five men. You see, Wolf said he'd be meeting with Ki and Dan Boyce tomorrow to get word on how they intend to meet his demands. I expect he'll be riding with the same five-man escort."

"I get it!" Tod said excitedly. "That means there'll only be one man left behind to guard us!"

"Right." Jessie nodded. "He'll be armed, but if we can take him by surprise . . ." She paused meaningfully.

"There's certainly plenty of horses for us to make our getaway," Tod mused.

"So you're with me?" Jessie asked. "It could be dangerous," she added in warning.

"You know I'm with you, come hell or high water, ma'am," Tod said stoutly. "But there's one thing I still don't get."

"What's that?" Jessie asked.

"Come tomorrow, once Wolf and the rest of his pack ride

123

off, we'll still be locked in here, and our guard will be out there. How are we ever going to take him by surprise?"

"Why, Tod, didn't you know?" Jessie winked. "Women are just full of surprises!"

"I just hope we can get out of here in time to keep Ki and Mr. Boyce from doing Wolf Martyn's bidding," Tod fretted.

"Don't you worry," Jessie said. "Martyn may *think* he's got the upper hand, but this is one time the wolf has caught the tiger by the tail!"

"How are you feeling?" Ki asked Dan Boyce.

"All right," Boyce replied, fingering the fading bruise that ran along his temple. "I'm just about over that kick in the head I took." His expression hardened. "Over it, that is, until I think about how Wolf Martyn cut down old Hank in this very spot, and then my skull starts to throb all over again."

Ki nodded. It was almost noon on a sunny day. He and Boyce were on horseback. They were waiting for Wolf Martyn, as instructed in Wolf's second ransom note. They were waiting beneath the same oak tree where two days ago the outlaw had cut down Hank Tyson.

Now Ki found himself involuntarily scanning the bright green pasture beneath his chestnut gelding's hooves, as if Hank's blood might still stain the blades of grass. But the heavy rain two days ago had washed away all traces of Martyn's heinous crime.

"You know," Ki began, "when all this is finished, I think I will gladly never again set foot on this stretch of ground."

"I hear you," Boyce replied, shuddering. "You had a tough row to hoe, fellow, having to stand by while Wolf plugged Hank, then making your way along those rocks over yonder to fetch your horse so that you could bring Hank's body back to the Circle Star."

Ki silently stared up at the sunlight filtering through the oak's leafy boughs. It *had* been a long and morbid trek back to the ranch, leading his horse with Hank's corpse draped across the saddle. Yesterday morning, with the Circle Star hands looking on, Hank Tyson had been buried in a quiet grove on the outskirts of the Starbuck holdings.

Jessie said that you would always have a place at the Circle Star, Hank, Ki now silently told his friend's *kami,* in case the spirit was still lurking in the vicinity. And Jessie, if she could have been at your funeral, would have been glad that I saw to it that her word was kept . . .

"We got riders coming in from the north," Boyce announced.

As he had done two days ago, Ki watched the line of black shapes moving across the grassy prairie. Today, however, his bow was tucked into its saddle boot, and, in addition to the *shuriken* throwing blades stashed in his vest, he had a pair in the leather sheaths strapped to his forearms beneath the floppy sleeves of his shirt. Boyce, as well, was heavily armed, Ki knew. The railroad security man had a Winchester in his saddle boot, and both of his Colts: one strapped around his waist, the other holstered under his left armpit.

"Here we go," Boyce said. "Good luck, Ki."

"Same to you," Ki murmured. He found himself reaching out to rest his hand on his bow as the riders came closer.

Boyce evidently caught the movement out of the corner of his eye. "Steady now," he cautioned. "Remember our plan. Whatever happens, stick to the strategy we worked out."

Ki scowled. "If I could restrain myself two days ago, when that vermin shot Hank, I can certainly restrain myself today, knowing that Jessie's and Tod Lane's lives are in the balance."

"Good man," Boyce muttered underneath his breath as Wolf Martyn and his five-man escort reached the oak tree. "We're gonna skin this bastard. We just have to bide our time."

"Well, howdy-do," Wolf Martyn called out, reining in his bay. "I see you two jaspers are nice and punctual." Martyn laughed scornfully. "I like it! I like men who can follow orders!"

Hold your temper, Ki told himself. Hold your tongue. Once again the samurai was struck by just how little the outlaw leader was. Martyn was wearing the same filthy dark suit as when the samurai had last seen him, and he still needed a shave.

"Well, now, Mr. Dan Boyce," Wolf said and smirked. "Mr. hotshot cinder dick for the Texas and Pacific." Wolf doffed his derby to deliver a mocking salute. "You caused me a lot of trouble these past couple weeks, but I see you've gotten right tame now that I got you by the short hairs."

"*Who* you've got is Jessica Starbuck and Tod Lane," Ki said evenly. "Are we here to negotiate, or do you just want to gloat?"

"Well, well, you surely do talk pretty, for a Chinaman," Wolf spat, staring at Ki. Wolf had gray eyes, as hard as granite, and Ki saw a lifetime's worth of bottled-up loneliness, resentment, and pain in the scrawny little outlaw's stare.

Perhaps it was not your fault that you became a monster, Ki pondered, staring back at Martyn. But while it is not the dog's fault if it becomes rabid, it still must be put down to protect others.

"It seems that you cost me a lot of men, Slant-eyes," Wolf continued. Suddenly one of his pistols appeared in his right hand. "Persuade me why I shouldn't cut you down right here and now."

"Because then you won't get what you want," Boyce quicky interjected. "Ki, here, is Jessie Starbuck's right-hand man."

"So?" Wolf muttered, pointing his gun at Ki. "I got you, Boyce, to do my bidding. What do I need this Chinaman for?"

Ki, not trusting himself to speak, tried to center himself, vainly attempting to throttle his rising fury. It would be so easy to put a *shuriken* throwing blade right between Wolf's eyes! But there were five hard men backing up the little outlaw, with the rest of the pack guarding Jessie and Tod . . .

"Yeah, you got *me,* Wolf," Boyce was saying, obviously trying hard to sound ingratiating. "But Ki knows his way around these parts. He knows the local law. If you want that payroll, you need *him* to help *me* get it for you."

"All right." Martyn scowled, holstering his gun. "I'll let the slant-eyes live."

Oh, thank you so much, Ki thought sarcastically.

"Let's get down to business," Wolf decreed. "How and when are you going to deliver that payroll to me?"

"Before we talk about that," Boyce countered. "I presume that both Jessie Starbuck and Tod Lane are alive and well?"

"Yeah, yeah, they're fine," Wolf said impatiently.

"How do we know that?" Ki asked quietly.

Wolf glared at him. "Well, now, Chinaman, you'll just have to take my word for it, won't you?"

"That is not good enough, Wolf," Ki replied.

"Keep talking Chinaman," Wolf threatened. "You'll eat lead—"

This time Ki indulged himself. "Have you noticed it, Dan," the samurai said and chuckled, meanwhile casually folding his arms across his chest, "the littler the man, the louder the lingo?"

"That tears it!" Wolf snarled, going for his guns. His men, taking their cue from their leader, reached for their own weapons. The pasture was abruptly filled with harsh breathing and the serpent hiss of blue steel sliding against waxed leather.

But this time Ki was ready. He slid his arms apart so that the inner sides of his forearms and the palms of his hands rubbed together. The smooth motion forced the two *shuriken* throwing blades out of their hidden sheaths. Ki's hands rose up and the four-inch blades glinted in the sunlight as he twirled them in his fingers.

As Ki had hoped, the sudden appearance of his *shuriken* gave Wolf and his men pause.

"Careful, boss," one of Wolf's band whispered to the outlaw leader. "I heard tell about that Chinaman with his knives. He's as dangerous as any gunslick with them blades of his!"

Ki glanced at Boyce. The railroad security man had produced his Colts, and both barrels were trained on Wolf.

Wolf's hard gray eyes took in the show of force arrayed against him. "It's still six against two," he said.

"Oh, we know we're certain to die," Boyce said cheerfully. "But *you'd* better know that you're gonna be the first to go, Wolf."

"My two blades and at least two of Boyce's rounds have your name on them, Wolf," Ki added. "There will be no deal. No payroll. Just death."

Wolf licked his lips. "Jessie Starbuck will die if anything happens to me," he warned.

"Maybe she will, and maybe she won't," Boyce said and shrugged. "In any case, it won't make no never mind to us three, will it, Wolf? Because you and I and Ki, here, will all be dead."

"You and your men had better put their guns away," Ki said. "Before something rash happens."

Wolf seemed to think it over. "Do as he says, boys," the outlaw leader said dully, holstering his own Colts. The other outlaws tucked away their pistols.

127

"I like a man who follows orders," Ki said tauntingly.

Wolf's gaze was murderous. "You and me, Chinaman. We've got a score to settle one of these days."

"I look forward to that, Wolf," the samurai said evenly, matching Wolf's stare.

"Ki and I will just keep our own weapons handy to make sure this palaver stays peaceful," Boyce announced.

Wolf shrugged. "Just remember that I'm holding Jessie Starbuck, and if I bleed, she bleeds!" he said harshly. "Now talk to me about that fucking payroll! When's the railroad going to hand it over?"

"The railroad *won't* hand it over—" Boyce began.

"Then Jessie Starbuck dies!" Wolf shrieked.

"Simmer down and listen, you little shit!" Ki shouted. "The railroad will not hand it over, so Boyce and I are going to *steal* it for you!"

"W-what?" Wolf blurted, incredulous.

"You heard us," Boyce said. "The railroad has a policy of not giving in to hostage demands." He scowled. "I hope you don't think you're the *first* jasper to come up with this kidnapping scheme, Wolf? Because you ain't. Other desperadoes have nabbed themselves Texas and Pacific employees and tried to shake down the railroad for ransom, but the bigwigs in charge don't play that way. If an employee gets killed being a hostage, the railroad pays their next of kin a pension and spares no expense in hunting down them that done the dirty deed. But no ransom, period."

"But this isn't no two-bit railroad employee we're talking about," Wolf Martyn sputtered. "This is Jessica Starbuck! She hobnobs with senators!" He slapped his saddle horn in frustration. "I *know* she does!"

"That is true," Ki said. "And if we had more time, perhaps we could bring all that political influence to bear on the railroad management to bend their no ransom policy—"

"But we *don't* have that kind of time," Boyce interrupted. "That government payroll comes through tomorrow afternoon, and when it's gone, it's gone. All the influence in the world ain't gonna get that money out of the paymaster's safe once it's inside the walls of the army fort at Bent Hollow."

"So you two intend to steal it?" Wolf skeptically demanded. "How? How are *you* two gonna pull that off?"

"That's our business," Boyce said evenly. "Yours is to make sure Jessie Starbuck and Tod Lane are delivered safe and sound to us in exchange for the money."

"We're pulling the robbery at two o'clock," Ki added, addressing Wolf. "That's when the payroll train is due into the Goat Creek way station." He paused. "You know where that is?" the samurai demanded.

"I do." Wolf nodded.

"Then be there, with Jessie and Tod, at two-thirty," Ki ordered. "We'll make the exchange, and it will be good-bye and good riddance!"

"You just better have that payroll ready to be handed over," Wolf hissed, wheeling around his horse. "Or it will be good-bye and good riddance to Jessie Starbuck! Let's go, boys!"

"Well, what do you think?" Ki asked as they watched the outlaws ride off. "Do you think he fell for it?"

Boyce holstered his guns. "Hard to say," he drawled thoughtfully, rubbing his chin. "He's a sly one, but you sure enough had him fit to be tied when you made all those remarks about how puny he is. With that temper of his raging, maybe he wasn't thinking too clearly . . ."

Ki grimly shrugged. It was Hank Tyson's insult about Wolf's size that got him killed, so the samurai had figured that insulting Wolf in the same fashion would rile him, thereby muddling up the outlaw's thinking so that he wouldn't too closely question their explanation about why the payroll couldn't just be handed over to him.

"So," Ki said, "do you think he swallowed our story about how the railroad has a policy of not paying ransom?"

"I think so . . ." Boyce said, and frowned. "At least, I *hope* so . . ."

"I still think we should contact the railroad and get them to cooperate with us," Ki added and sighed.

"I tell you, it wouldn't work," Boyce replied. "Sure, they'd hand over the money, but they'd insist on getting the Army involved, having bluecoats stake out the exchange site." He looked at Ki. "Now, the Army may be hell's bells when it comes to quelling Indians, but this here hostage exchange business is tricky—it ain't no standard military operation—and Wolf Martyn's pack is an experienced and cagey lot. Do *you* want to put Jessie's life in the Army's hands?"

Ki shuddered at the thought. "So, I guess we will be robbing the train tomorrow after all." He hesitated. "But Dan, you realize that we cannot hurt any innocents in the process, and that we cannot actually hand over that money to Wolf Martyn?"

"I realize that, Ki," Boyce said quietly. "Just as I realize that Wolf Martyn likely has no intention of giving us back Jessie and Tod Lane alive." He winked at Ki. "But together, if we're lucky, we just might have those two, the payroll, *and* *Wolf Martyn* safely in hand, come tomorrow sundown."

★

Chapter 10

"What time do you think it is?" Jessie asked.

"Reckon it's about fifteen minutes later than the last time you asked," Tod Lane replied. "Begging your pardon, ma'am, but you been pacing back and forth like a she wolf trying to coax her cubs out of her den."

Jessie glanced at the young wrangler. He was sitting on a folded blanket, leaning against the wall, but despite his relaxed posture, she could feel his tension.

"Speaking of wolves, I don't think we can wait any longer," Jessie said. "We heard Wolf Martyn and his men saddling up and riding out what must have been hours ago."

"We can't be sure Wolf has gone to meet up with Ki and Mr. Boyce," Tod said fretfully.

"We can't be sure of anything in our situation," Jessie pointed out. "For all we know, Wolf is on his way back from his rendezvous with Ki and Dan. We've got to make our move sometime. I say we make it now."

Tod looked unconvinced. "What's wrong?" Jessie coaxed gently.

"Reckon I'm scared, ma'am," he said. "Reckon being locked up in here has kind of reminded me of my years in prison, which has put me back into a convict's way of thinking," he added, sounding sheepish. "There's two kinds of men in prison, Miss Jessie. Them that wants to rule the roost, and them that just wants to do their time and get through it." He shrugged. "Reckon I was the second kind."

Jessie knelt beside Tod and took his hand. "I want you to know that I think you're a good and brave man," she told him.

"Really?" He was watching her from out of the corners of his eyes.

"Really." Jessie nodded, smiling. "Why, the only reason you're locked up in here with me is because you bravely volunteered to rescue me, right?"

"Yes, ma'am!" Tod turned his head to face her. "That's right!" he resolutely declared.

Jessie reached out to brush aside the comma of blond hair above Tod's eyes, and chastely kissed his forehead.

"G-golly, Miss Jessie!" Tod's blue eyes went wide. He blushed cherry red.

"That's for being my hero," Jessie murmured. "Now, then, hero. Are you with me?"

Tod lightly squeezed Jessie's fingers before letting go. "I'm with you till hell freezes over!" he passionately declared. "Let's do it!"

"Let's do it," Jessie repeated, getting to her feet. "And you know what to do, right?"

Tod nodded. "But I sure don't feel like much of a hero by playing dead," he muttered as he stretched out in the middle of the packed earth floor. "I sure wish you'd let me be the one to tackle that guard."

"That's brave of you to offer," Jessie said, moving toward the shack's locked door, "but this is the only way. Don't you see, Tod? If we exchanged roles, the guard would suspect something. This way, he'll hopefully figure that there's no way I can hurt him."

"That's just it, Miss Jessie," Tod replied. "How are you going to knock him out?" He sat up and glanced around the tack shack. "There ain't nothing in here to use as a weapon."

"Oh, don't be too sure," Jessie murmured, taking a mildewed bridle from its peg on the wall and stuffing it into the back pocket of her jeans.

"What are you going to do with that?" Tod asked, sounding bewildered. "Try and choke him?" he added dubiously.

"It's obvious you haven't read your Old Testament in a while," Jessie said playfully.

"Huh?"

"Never mind," she chuckled. "You'll see. Now lie down and look sick!" she ordered.

Tod, looking skeptical, did as he was told. Jessie went back to the door and began to pound on it with her fists. "Help! Help!" she shouted. "Guard! We need help!"

Presently she heard someone fumbling with the lock on the shack's door. The door opened, and a man with a bristly walrus mustache stuck his head in. He had mounds of scar tissue above his eyes, and a nose that had been squashed flat in some ancient brawl. "What's going on?" he demanded.

"He just fainted dead away," Jessie whimpered, pointing down at Tod's still form. "I think his head is hurt bad."

Laughing, the guard sauntered into the shack. Jessie's stomach lurched. Wolf may have only left one man to guard us, but this one is more than big enough for the job, she thought.

He was six-feet-four, and looked to be about 240 pounds, and Jessie wagered to herself that every bit of that was muscle, not fat. The guard was wearing a collarless union shirt, baggy canvas trousers, a worn-out Stetson, and scuffed tan boots. The six-shooter riding on his hip looked as little as a toy as he rested his huge hand on the gun butt and stared down at Tod.

"He needs a doctor," Jessie said.

The guard shrugged. "Ain't no doctor here, lady." Still gazing down at Tod, he nudged the young wrangler with his toe.

Here goes nothing, Jessie thought, pulling the bridle from her back pocket. She gripped it by the reins and began to swing the metal bit end around and around. The reins pulled taut with centrifugal force as the weighty bit orbited her head.

"I can't do nothing for him," the guard began. He paused to glance over his shoulder, his attention caught by the whistle of the bit slicing through the air . . .

Jessie whipped the bit against the side of the guard's head. His Stetson went flying, revealing the fact that he was totally bald as he toppled like a felled tree, and lay still.

Tod sprang to his feet, laughing. "Old Testament, eh? I get it, Miss Jessie! David and Goliath!"

Jessie, grinning with relief, let the bridle slip from her fingers. "Get his gun," she ordered Tod, and as the young wrangler plucked away the guard's revolver, she held out her hand. "Maybe it would be better if I held on to that," she softly suggested, hoping that she wasn't ruffling Tod's feathers. Men could be so touchy in matters such as these. "No offense . . ."

"None taken," Tod grinned, handing over the six-shooter. "I'm the first to admit that I ain't much with a gun, and *everybody* knows you can shoot the wings off a fly at twenty paces."

"Thanks, Tod," Jessie murmured, quickly checking over the gun. It was a blued double-action Colt .44 with walnut grips, a heavy trigger pull, and the hammer resting on an empty chamber. Just five rounds, Jessie noted broodingly.

She glanced at the guard. His gunbelt was smooth. Maybe he kept his extra rounds in his pockets.

"Ohhhh . . ." The guard began to stir.

Five rounds will have to do! Jessie decided. "Come on, Tod!" she exclaimed, starting for the door.

The young wrangler hesitated. "Don't you figure to shoot him, Miss Jessie?"

Jessie, pausing in the doorway, frowned at the prostrate, groaning man. "I'm sorry, Tod, but I can't cold-bloodedly execute someone."

Tod ducked his head, looking embarrassed as he followed Jessie out. "Of course you're right, ma'am. I don't think I could do it either, especially seeing as how I've never shot nobody, no way, at all!"

"Well, I have, Tod," Jessie said quietly. "And I don't look for opportunities to repeat the experience unless it's absolutely necessary."

Outside the shack Jessie paused long enough to check its door. An unlocked padlock hung from the opened hasp. She locked the semiconscious guard inside, telling Tod, "I know that giant can tear this place down with his bare hands from the inside, but at least we'll hear him coming."

With gun in hand, Jessie looked around and listened hard. As she'd hoped, the old stage depot compound was deserted. Across the yard the rambling, one-story stone house that was the depot itself was still. "This way," she told Tod, leading him around the shack, toward the stables.

"You let me get our horses ready," Tod said, taking the lead as they raced past the blacksmith lean-to that fronted the stables. "Reckon I'm as fast cinching a saddle as you are with a six-gun, Miss Jessie."

Jessie glimpsed darting movement from within the blacksmith lean-to's shadowy interior and whirled in a crouch to confront it, her gun at the ready. But it was just a scrawny calico cat, evidently startled by their sudden appearance. Jessie's eyes flitted over the lean-to's raised stone hearth overflowing with ashes, its rotted leather bellows, rusting tools, and the huge black anvil, on top of which rested a sledgehammer. All was quiet within.

Inside the stables it was dark and cool, the air pungent with the scent of oiled leather and healthy horseflesh. As Tod had surmised, there were plenty of mounts in the stalls to choose from.

And every one of them wears the Circle Star brand, Jessie wryly mused. When she got back home she would send a couple of hands along with the posse to retrieve her property.

Several wooden racks near the doors held an assortment of saddles and tack, but this was well-cared-for gear, not like the rotting stuff that lined the walls of the shack that had been their prison. As Tod grabbed what they needed and hauled it over to the stalls, Jessie stood lookout by the stables' tall, chinked double-doors. She strained her ears and wondered what in tarnation they would do if Wolf Martyn and his escort were to suddenly gallop into the yard.

"Tod, hurry it up, would you?" Jessie said admonishingly, nervously gripping the Colt.

"Going fast as I can, ma'am," Tod mildly replied. He already had one horse, a chestnut gelding, ready to ride, and was flinging a saddle on a tan mare.

Jessie heard the sound of wood splintering, coming from the direction of the shack where they'd locked in the guard.

Tod must have heard it, too. "Reckon I could go a little faster, after all . . ."

"I wonder if five rounds will stop that giant," Jessie muttered to herself. She again heard wood giving way, and then the shriek of metal screws being torn loose from their wood anchorings.

Then abrupt silence.

"Tod," Jessie hissed. "I think he's broken out."

"There! All done!" Tod cut her off, leading the two saddled horses by their reins to the front of the stables. "Let's ride!"

Thank the Lord! Jessie thought as she jammed the Colt into her waistband and pushed wide the stable doors. Once they were mounted up and riding, what could the unarmed guard do but shake his fist and fume?

"Take the mare," Tod said, mounting the gelding.

Jessie swung herself into the saddle and kneed her mount forward, with Tod bringing up the rear. "We made it!" Jessie called out joyously as she rode out into the bright sunlight, past the blacksmith lean-to.

A few hours from now we'll be safe and sound at the Circle Star, she thought as she glanced over her shoulder at Tod and saw the guard lunge from out of the lean-to's shadows, directly into the path of Tod's horse!

There's nothing the unarmed guard can do once we're mounted up and riding hard, Jessie had thought, but she'd been wrong.

"Look out!" she cried out to Tod, knowing even as she spoke that her warning would come too late. She wheeled her horse and found herself struggling to control the confused and frightened mare as it reared. Unable to take her hand from the reins to go for her gun, she could only watch in amazement as the guard grabbed hold of Tod's gelding by its head and twisted the horse off its feet, the way a cowpoke wrestles a calf onto its side prior to hog-tying it.

The screaming gelding, its eyes rolling in fear, went crashing to the ground. Only Tod's quick reflexes saved him from being crushed beneath the horse's thrashing bulk. As soon as the horse had begun to topple sideways, Tod had kicked his boots free of the stirrups and launched himself out of the saddle.

The young wrangler landed hard on his side, and lay still, the wind knocked out of him. At least he's managed to fall with the horse between himself and the guard, Jessie thought. But then Tod's mount regained its feet and trotted off, leaving Tod exposed.

She was just settling her own horse and tugging the Colt from her waistband when the huge guard crossed the expanse of earth separating himself from Tod in a few steps and scooped up the fallen wrangler as if Tod weighed nothing at all.

"You let him go!" Jessie ordered the guard, thumbing back the Colt's hammer. "You let him go, or I'll shoot you with your own gun!"

"I don't think you will, lady," the guard said with a smirk. He was still hatless. Jessie could see the angry scarlet welt the bridle bit had branded into the big man's bald dome.

"I don't think you'll shoot," the guard continued. "Not when it means causing this here squirt's death."

He was standing with Tod in front of him. He had his left arm around Tod's throat, the palm of his right hand pressed up against the wrangler's ear.

"You're a mighty big target, and Tod, there, is a mighty small shield," Jessie called threateningly. The giant's shoulders and head were fully exposed.

"Oh, I know you can shoot me all right," the guard continued, "but you can't *kill* me before I snap this here pipsqueak's neck like it was a twig!" As if for emphasis, he tightened his grip around Tod's throat.

Damn, thought Jessie disgustedly. The giant was absolutely right. This had turned into exactly the same situation she'd faced in her bedroom, the night she was kidnapped.

"Don't you listen to him, Miss Jessie!" Tod implored her, his voice sounding strained as the giant further constricted his grip on Tod's throat. "You never mind about me. You shoot this bastard and ride out of here before Wolf comes back!"

Jessie gazed at the young wrangler. He looked blue. She guessed he was near to passing out if the guard didn't let him get some wind into his lungs.

"How about it 'Miss Jessie'?" The big guard continued to smirk. "You want this little shit's death on your conscience?"

"You win," Jessie said dully, lowering the Colt's hammer. She tossed the gun into the dust a few feet in front of where the guard was standing with his huge, meaty hands still wrapped around poor Tod's neck.

"Good." The guard nodded. "Now get off that horse."

"Darn, Miss Jessie," Tod murmured sorrowfully as Jessie dismounted. "You should have done what I told you—"

"Oh, how could I have, Tod?" Jessie asked with a sigh. She watched her mount trot away a few steps, and with it went her hope for freedom.

"They're just gonna kill us, anyway," Tod replied bitterly. "Least my way, you would have lived."

"That's right, we are going to kill you both, anyway," the big guard said jovially. "I won't get the pleasure of doing you, Jessie Starbuck, 'cause Wolf will want that honor." He tightened his grip on Tod. "But I got to pay you back for busting my head, so I guess I'll just kill this little shit, *right now*—"

"No!" Jessie cried out, hurling herself toward the gun lying at the giant's feet. She knew she had no chance of reaching it before he did, but as she'd hoped, he had to let go of Tod to prevent her from getting the weapon. The young wrangler dashed away as the big guard lumbered forward to kick away the pistol. As Jessie dropped to her knees to reach out for the gun, the shooting iron skittered past her, to disappear under some debris in the blacksmith lean-to.

As Jessie got to her feet, the guard tried to grab her. She hastily backpedaled out of reach.

"At least you don't have the gun, either!" Jessie spat at the hulking guard as the two warily circled each other.

"Do you think I need a weapon for the likes of you two?" The guard laughed, looking down at her. He shucked off his collarless shirt. His belly was washboard ridged. His broad pectorals moved with a life of their own.

My word, Jessie worried. I wonder if even Ki could take this brute bare-handed?

Just then Tod darted in beneath the giant's outstretched arms to deliver a pair of right and left jabs to the big man's already ruined nose. The guard took the punches without so much as allowing his bald head to rock back, and then swiped out at Tod with the back of his hand, the way an upright grizzly will swipe at its adversary. Tod, throwing up his arms, managed to block the blow, but the giant's strength was such that the young wrangler still ended up sprawled in the dust.

Jessie took advantage of the guard's distraction to execute a *te* roundhouse kick to the guard's ribs. It was a fine kick, the technique delivered just as Ki had taught her, but it felt as if she'd kicked the anvil over yonder, and with just about as much gain. The guard absorbed her kick without flinching. All she seemed to have accomplished was to make the giant even madder, if that was possible.

"Wolf or no Wolf, I'm gonna break your back," the big man snarled, coming at her.

Jessie, nearly frozen with fear, watched this freight train of fury barreling down on her and wondered if her end were at hand.

But Tod tackled the guard from behind, locking his arms around the man's legs, forcing him to fall to his knees. Tod's bravery on her behalf snapped Jessie out of her funk. She ran into the blacksmith's lean-to, scooped up a double handful of cold ashes from the hearth, and tossed them into the giant's face.

"My eyes!" the guard cried out, coughing and rubbing at his stinging eyes. "I can't see! You bitch!"

"Nice move, Miss Jessie!" Tod cheered. He moved in close, pummeling the giant with punches.

Now where the hell did that gun go to? Jessie wondered, frantically searching through the piles of debris within the lean-to. She looked back to see the guard still on his knees, as Tod delivered two solid uppercuts to the man's chin. This time Tod's efforts earned him a grunt of pain from his opponent. But the big guard's vision was evidently clearing. He managed to grab hold of the young wrangler's shirtfront and deliver a punch to Tod's solar plexus.

Tod, moaning, fell to lie curled on his side. He'd done his best, Jessie knew, but from the way he was gasping, she was certain he was out of the fight for the near future.

"Now it's your turn, bitch," the guard growled, getting to his feet as he wiped the last of the ashes from his eyes.

He rushed into the lean-to after Jessie, who scurried to put the anvil between herself and her adversary. As he leaned across the anvil to grab hold of her, she barely managed to twist beneath his outstretched fingers and into the relative safety of the yard. Shouting in frustration, the guard grabbed the sledgehammer lying atop the anvil and lumbered out after her.

"I thought you said you didn't need a weapon for the likes of us," Jessie said tauntingly, desperate to buy time for Tod to recover and occupy this brute so that she could resume her search for the pistol lost within the lean-to.

"You use a rolled-up newspaper to swat a fly," the guard grumbled. "Same notion here." He shouldered the sledge-hammer. "I figure once I smash your kneecaps, you won't be so limber."

The guard attacked, sweeping low with the hammer, trying to catch Jessie's legs. Jessie jumped back, and the hammer walloped the ground. There was a splintering sound as the steel hammerhead met the rock-hard packed ground. The small wedges holding the hammerhead in place gave way, and the hammerhead thudded to the ground, leaving nothing but the stick in the surprised guard's hands.

"Hell with this," he snorted in disgust, halfheartedly hurling the handle at Jessie. "I'll tear you apart with my bare hands."

Jessie easily dodged the thrown stick and picked it up.

"You gonna hit me with that toothpick?" The guard laughed.

Jessie was smiling as well. What she now had was a polished hardwood stick which was approximately a yard long and a uniform inch and a half wide. Traditional *jo* sticks were fifty inches long and fashioned of white oak, but in a pinch this hammer handle would do just fine.

Ki had taught Jessie basic *te* weaponry skills, including the allied techniques of fighting with the *bo* staff and *jo* stick. She was certainly no expert in the martial arts, or a match for someone with a samurai's mastery of esoteric weaponry and *te* open-hand combat techniques—her ineffectual roundhouse kick had nicely proved that! Yet she was reasonably confident that with the aid of the hardwood stick she could teach this lumbering giant a thing or two—and she aimed to!

The guard was closing in. This time Jessie stood her ground because it suited her tactics, not because she was rooted in place by fear.

And as she'd hoped, the guard misunderstood that. "Ah, I see you're ready to give in," the big man said and grinned.

"I'm ready to give you a beating, you mean son of a bitch," Jessie replied, hoping to make the guard careless by increasing his rage.

"*You'll* take the beating, you bitch!" the guard roared wildly. He shuffled forward, aiming a right punch at Jessie.

She used the first hold that Ki had taught her, the *gyaku-nigiri,* or reverse hold. She placed her hands about shoulder width apart, palms facing down, centered along the length of the horizontal stick. As the guard's fist hurtled toward her face, Jessie slammed the hammer

140

handle against the guard's knuckles, cracking his finger bones.

The guard howled, but before he could back away, Jessie quickly thrust upward, and the middle section of the handle smashed into his throat. He collapsed backward, falling hard on his rump in the dust, his broken right hand trailing limply as he clutched at his throat with his left.

I should finish him off, right now, Jessie told herself. But she couldn't do it. It just wasn't in her to administer a cold coup de grace to another human being, no matter how despicable.

"Had enough?" she asked hopefully.

"I'll show you enough," the guard snarled, his breath rattling harshly through his swelling throat. "I'll fix you good," he continued, lumbering to his feet.

Like something out of a nightmare, the big man loomed over Jessie, reaching out for her with his one good hand.

Jessie saw her opening and danced in. She rapped the stick against the side of the guard's knee. The man yelped and tried to back away. Jessie stepped in and thrust the stick into the guard's lower belly, doubling him over. Then she twirled the stick like a baton, just the way that Ki had shown her, brought it around behind her and then up over her head in a powerful arc that ended with the business end of the hammer-handle slamming against the back of the guard's bald skull.

The guard nose-dived to the ground, and stayed there, out cold.

"Where the heck did you learn to do *that*?" Jessie heard Tod gasp in wonderment. She turned to see the pale wrangler getting to his feet.

"Ki taught me," Jessie brightly remarked, tossing aside the stick. "How are you feeling?"

"I'll make it," Tod said and coughed, wincing. "Leastways, I don't *think* that big lug broke anything when he punched me."

"Good," Jessie nodded. "Then, if you're feeling up to it, please fetch the horses."

"Oh, I'm up to it, all right." Tod grinned. "I reckon I'd climb out of my *grave* if it meant getting out of here!" he called over his shoulder.

"That's the spirit." Jessie laughed. "I want to find that handgun, and then we'll be on our way home!"

• • •

An hour later, Jessie and Tod were slowing their mounts to let the horses pick their way along the narrow trail that led through a dense grove of pecan trees. It was late afternoon. The sky was darkening, casting the trees in purple shadows.

"How much farther back to the Circle Star, Miss Jessie?" Tod asked.

"About two hours," Jessie replied. "Once we're through this grove, we'll be traveling wide-open country, and we can make better time."

"I sure hope we don't run into Wolf Martyn coming back from his parley with Ki and Mr. Boyce," Tod said with worry in his voice.

"Not much of chance of that," Jessie reassured the young wrangler. "I know a roundabout way to get home. It'll take us a little extra time, but it'll pretty much guarantee we won't be seeing Wolf."

"The next time I see that jasper, I want him behind bars," Tod muttered.

"Don't worry, he will be," Jessie promised. "If Wolf has any sense at all, he'll hightail it out of Texas before Ki and Dan Boyce show up at that hideout of his!"

They were coming to the end of the pecan grove. "Our troubles are just about over," Jessie had begun to say, when she saw the flicker of movement on her right, in the shadows. "Tod! It's a trap!" she shouted. She pulled hard on her mount's reins, twisting the horse sideways and forcing it to rear up, but with Tod's gelding crowding the narrow trail behind her, there was no way to go back the way she'd come.

Jessie heard the reedy, whistling sound as the lariat came drifting down and the loop cinched tightly around her, pinning her arms to her sides. She stared, helpless, as the rider dressed in denims and a tan canvas range jacket kneed his horse out of the woods to trot backward, jerking upon the rope as he rode. Jessie was jolted out of the saddle. She hit the ground hard, the revolver she'd taken from the guard falling from her waistband upon impact.

Can't hold onto that shooting iron for nothing, Jessie sorrowfully thought as she was dragged, jouncing and jolting along behind the rider, for around twenty feet before the rider stopped.

Jessie lay gasping in the dust, the breath knocked out of her. She tried to move her arms, but the lariat loop was being kept tight. She was helpless, she realized, as she stared at her captor. Whoever he was, he was clearly an outlaw, one of Wolf Martyn's band. The rider wore his wide-brimmed hat tugged low, and a red bandanna covered the lower half of his face.

As Jessie stared, she saw the rider swing what looked to be a sawed-off lever-action rifle out from beneath his baggy, tan canvas jacket. "You stop right there!" he called out in a reedy voice.

Jessie looked over her shoulder. Tod had dismounted and was crouched low, reaching out for Jessie's fallen six-shooter.

"You ain't taking us!" Tod fiercely shouted, glaring at the rider. "Not again!"

"Tod, don't!" Jessie blurted.

"I got to try, Miss Jessie!" The young wrangler made his move.

But the shooter on horseback was far too quick for Tod. He levered off rounds from his stubby rifle almost faster than the eye could follow.

Jessie cringed at the weapon's rapid-fire staccato whine. She rolled to one side, off the trail, as her mare and Tod's mount, spooked by the gunfire, galloped off the way they'd come. Jessie looked back over her shoulder, expecting to see Tod Lane turned into a bloody corpse.

But the shooter's rounds were geysering dust spouts all around the fallen six-gun, setting up a barrier of lead that kept Tod from snatching the weapon. Then the rider zeroed in on the handgun itself, his rounds plinking against the Colt as if it were a tin can, moving it across the narrow trail until the pistol fell out of sight into a hollow.

Tod, shaking his head, peered into the hole at the six-shooter. "It won't do, Miss Jessie," he muttered. "That fella shot it up so bad that the barrel's bent."

"You're lucky I didn't do the same to you!" the rider said, feeding fresh cartridges into his rifle.

"All right, you've caught us," Jessie told the man. "Can I at least get up?"

"Why not?" the rider said and chuckled, kneeing his horse forward a few steps to put some slack in the rope.

Jessie, shrugging off the lariat loop and getting to her feet, thought to herself, There's certainly something odd about this fellow. His voice is so high-pitched . . . She peered, trying to see something of the rider's features, but with that hat of his pulled down so low, the rider seemed nothing but a pair of big eyes, the color of old pennies. This one's either very young, Jessie thought, or else . . .

The rider, holding his little rifle at port, swung one long leg over his saddle horn, slid down out of the saddle, and then sauntered over to where Jessie was slapping the dust off her denims.

Jessie stared at the figure—at the way he moved, the swivel of his hips through his baggy denims. She abruptly exclaimed, "Why, you're a woman!"

The rider froze for an instant, then defiantly whipped off the red bandanna and the sombrero-like hat, releasing a mass of auburn curls.

"So I'm a woman. What of it?" she spat. "I've got the two of *you* dead to rights, nice and proper!"

"Lord above." Tod rolled his eyes. "Here I am with *two* fillies, both of them pretty as a picture, and the *devil* when it comes to handling shooting irons!"

Tod was right on both counts about this newcomer, Jessie thought. This young woman was certainly pretty. She looked to be just this side of twenty. She had those big, dark eyes, a smattering of freckles across her upturned nose, and that unruly tousle of dark curls. And now that Jessie was looking closely, she could make out the girl's bountiful breasts and curvaceous, sassy rump, now and again straining her baggy clothing. And whoever this mysterious woman was, she *could* shoot like the devil with her little rifle!

"What's your name?" Jessie asked.

"What's yours?" the young woman demanded, holding up her weapon. "Seeing as I'm the one holding Li'l Pete, I'll be asking the questions!"

"Li'l Pete?" Tod burst out laughing.

"What's so funny?" the girl demanded, glowering.

"I ain't never heard of no one naming their gun, is all . . . Not since Davy Crockett, leastways . . ."

The girl pointed her rifle in the general direction of Tod's boot tips. "Maybe if Li'l Pete sets you dancing, you won't think he's so funny," she threatened.

"Here, now," Jessie interrupted, wanting to put a stop to this before it got out of hand. "I'm sure Tod meant no insult. The both of us have been through a hard time. We've been held prisoner by Wolf Martyn and his gang—"

"You were his prisoners, you say?" the girl interrupted. "How do I know you aren't part of his gang?"

"What?" Tod exclaimed. "Are you loco? This here's Jessica Starbuck! She ain't no outlaw!"

"So, you are Jessica Starbuck," the girl said with a sigh.

"That's right," Jessie nodded. "And you are?"

"Annie Slade."

Jessie was relieved to see Annie tuck her deadly rifle away into some sort of shoulder sling beneath her range coat. She had no doubt that this spitfire and her Li'l Pete were quite capable of setting Tod to some very high-stepping dancing, indeed!

"I apologize for roping you," Annie said. "But what with it getting dark and all, I didn't realize you were a woman until I heard you call out to your friend here."

"Tod Lane, ma'am," Tod said, doffing his hat. "And while I'd be honored if Miss Jessie here called me a friend, I reckon it's more proper to say I'm her employee . . ."

Jessie, laughing, said, "Well, Tod happens to be *both*. He's the boss wrangler at the Circle Star."

"Boss wrangler?" Tod repeated, sounding surprised at his sudden promotion.

Jessie nodded. "Certainly, and I'm lucky to have you to fill the slot," she continued. "With Hank either seriously wounded, or dead, I'm going to need someone to take over his duties." She glanced at Annie. "Tod, here, is the best there is when it comes to handling horses."

Annie, looking him over, nodded. "Anyway, like I was saying, I didn't know *who* I'd caught in my ambush . . . Just that I'd snared myself a couple of pigeons. Then I heard your voice, and knew you were a woman, but by then I was committed, so I figured I might as well play the hand and sort out what was what later."

Annie glanced at Tod. "*You* ought to be mighty thankful for your choice of words back then."

"How so?" Tod asked.

"You calling her 'Miss Jessie' got me thinking she was Jessica Starbuck. That's why I gave you the benefit of the doubt, and shot up that six-gun you were going for, instead of you."

Tod shrugged. "Ain't the first time I fast-talked myself out of trouble with a pretty girl," he said and winked.

It was getting dark, but in the dying light Jessie could still make out Annie's big brown eyes growing wide as she stared at Tod. "Well, aren't you the one, Mr. Lane!" the girl murmured.

"Call me, Tod, please . . ." For the second time the young wrangler doffed his hat, and this time he actually bowed!

Jessie couldn't help smiling to herself. It certainly seemed as if Tod was smitten by the young woman. But there would be time enough for the wrangler to do his wooing once they were all safe and sound back at the Circle Star. "Tod, would you see to our horses?" Jessie asked.

"Yes, ma'am."

As Tod started down the trail, Jessie turned to Annie. "You mentioned something about laying an ambush?"

"For Wolf Martyn," Annie explained. "I've been tracking him for a long time. For example, I know his hideout is about an hour due north of here. I was hoping to catch Wolf in my ambush during his comings and goings," she paused, "but I caught you instead."

"But why would you be after Wolf?" Jessie asked.

Annie sighed. "It's a long story."

"One you'll have plenty of time to tell," a gruff, male voice said. It was Wolf Martyn, stepping out of the shadows, a gun in either hand.

Jessie spun around, going into a crouch, her right hand instinctively pawing at her right hip for the gun that wasn't there. She sighed and straightened up, glancing at Annie Slade, relieved to see that she had had the good sense not to pull her rifle.

Three of Martyn's men stepped out from behind the trees, with guns drawn. Jessie, hearing footsteps, looked behind her to see Tod being herded at gunpoint by the Wolf Pack's remaining two members.

"How'd you get away from Big Joe?" Wolf asked idly. "Keep them covered!" he ordered his men as he holstered his own pistols.

"Big Joe ain't so big anymore!" Tod taunted. "Miss Starbuck here cut him down to size!"

"Well, I wouldn't have thought that *you* could have done it," the bantam-sized outlaw replied, effectively shutting Tod up. He turned to Jessie. "We were on our way back to the hideout along a trail about a half mile west of here, when we heard shots, and thought we'd mosey over to investigate." He looked Jessie over. "But where's the gun? I don't see it."

"Over here, Boss," one of the outlaws called, holding up Annie's midget rifle. "Strange-looking piece it is, too . . ."

"Well, well, what do we have here?" Wolf said. His lips curled into a quizzical smile. "I *never* forget a pretty face . . . And you *do* look familiar to me . . . Have we met?"

"Someday I'll tell you," Annie snarled. "Right before I send you to hell!"

"You need a lesson in manners, young lady!" Wolf Martyn's open hand lashed out, slapping Annie's face. Her head rocked, and an angry red splotch appeared on her cheek where Martyn had struck her, but she remained silent.

"Damn you!" Tod cried. Enraged, he reached out as if to throttle Wolf, but the outlaws surrounding him blocked his path before he could reach their leader.

"Enough of this," Wolf snarled. "Take them back to the hideout and this time lock them in good and proper!"

"What about the girl?" one of the outlaws asked.

"Take her, as well," Wolf replied. "We'll kill 'em all in front of Dan Boyce and that Chinaman—after they pull that train robbery and hand us over the Army payroll!"

★

Chapter 11

"I sure hope you know what you are doing," Ki said. He was holding the reins of both his own horse and Dan Boyce's, watching as Boyce climbed up the telegraph pole.

"Don't worry, this is going to go just fine," Boyce assured him.

But Ki had his doubts. The samurai was feeling awfully exposed. They were out in the open, on a thickly grassed prairie dusted with wildflowers, the bluebonnets just now giving way to asters, daisies, and goldenrod. About a quarter mile away, paralleling the line of telegraph poles, the steel rails of the Texas & Pacific track cut through the grass like a silver ribbon glinting in the sun.

The track ran north to south in this part of Texas. To the north was Gray Marsh Station. About ten miles due south of their position was the Goat Creek Way Station. There, the track split, with one branch following Goat Creek in a southwesterly direction to Sarah Township. The other branch wended its way through rough country to the Army fort at Bent Hollow.

"You just keep a sharp lookout and we'll do fine," Boyce called down from the top of the pole.

149

Ki looked around. There is no way to keep a lookout, he thought. Surrounding the prairie were wooded hills providing plenty of cover from which an Army patrol could easily be watching them.

The samurai craned his neck, shielding his eyes from the sun as he watched Boyce dig a folding knife from the pocket of his frock coat and set to work splicing his portable telegraph key into the strung wire.

"Hurry up," Ki demanded.

"Some things you just can't rush, fellow," Boyce muttered. He severed the wires that ran to Goat Creek and spliced in his portable key. "There. If I did this right, and I calculate I did, from here on, everybody up the line will be figuring they're sending to Goat Creek, when really they'll be sending just to us."

"So now we can intercept all messages?" Ki asked.

"Right. With Goat Creek getting nothing at all." Boyce fell silent as his portable key abruptly sprang to life, chattering away like a squirrel. Ki was feeling impatient, but he kept his mouth shut, letting the railroad security man concentrate on the rapid-fire clicking.

"The government payroll train has pulled out of Gray Marsh . . . ," Boyce began translating for Ki. " . . . Everything is under control . . . Train expected into Goat Creek ahead of schedule, at one-thirty . . ."

Ki glanced at the sun's position in the clear, blue sky. That would be about three hours from now, he estimated.

" . . . Goat Creek Station is to relay the message to Bent Hollow Fort . . . ," Boyce continued. "Goat Creek is to notify a squad of Troopers waiting at the fort. When the Troopers get the signal, they'll ride out to get the payroll and escort it on the last leg of the journey, to Bent Hollow . . ."

The key fell silent. Boyce tapped out a short confirmation that the message had been received. "There, that's it," he said. "Gray Marsh thinks Goat Creek has gotten the message. Good thing I'm a railroad man and know all the rail stations' telegraph procedures and call signs."

Ki shook his head. "You say just one squad is waiting for the signal to ride out to Goat Creek? That is only eight men. That does not sound right."

"I know what I heard," Boyce said and shrugged. "And it makes sense if you think about it. We're talking about an understrength, peacetime army. Bent Hollow has already stretched itself thin by stationing squads at potential trouble spots between Goat Creek and White Marsh."

"And the other day you did mention that there will be a contingent of cinder dicks on board the train," Ki mused.

"Right. The government has contracted with the railroad to have those dicks team up with the Army to escort the payroll to the fort." He paused. "I figure, all told, including the soldiers stationed at Goat Creek, those on board the train, and the cinder dicks, we're going to have to best near eighteen heavily armed men."

"Without seriously hurting any of them," Ki added wearily. "Well, let's get on with it. We do not have much time. At two-thirty Wolf Martyn will be meeting us at Goat Creek Station with Jessie and Tod." The samurai paused. "And then the fun will really begin."

"Just a second," Boyce said. He fiddled with the connections to his portable telegraph key, hooking things up so that Gray Marsh was cut out but he could send to Goat Creek. He paused to take a scrap of paper out of his pocket and peer at it.

"Well?" Ki demanded.

"I just want to check that I've got my code right for our message," Boyce explained, studying his paper. "One little mistake and the operator at Goat Creek will smell a rat, and then where will we be?" He nodded to himself, pocketed the scrap, and began sending code. "First the call sign . . ."

Ki knew what message Boyce was sending to Goat Creek. It was all part of the plan. Boyce was telling Goat Creek that the payroll train was having engine trouble and would be delayed at Gray Marsh until four-thirty this afternoon. He was also ordering Goat Creek to relay the information of the delay to Bent Hollow, so that the squad escort could stand down for the time being.

"All done," Boyce said. "Just got to wait for Goat Creek's confirmation that they received the message—" The key began clicking. "That's it!" Boyce exclaimed. "It appears they don't suspect a thing."

Ki sighed in relief. "Now, if all goes according to plan, the men at Goat Creek will be at ease when we move against them. And the escort squad will not arrive until hours after everything is all over."

"Sure," Boyce agreed. "Goat Creek now thinks they got the whole day to hang around waiting for the train."

Boyce disconnected his equipment from the line. "As we agreed, I'm leaving the wire cut between here and Gray Marsh. It'd take the army a whole day to find the break, once they realize it exists, assuming they even have the men to spare to look for it, which they don't."

"And this way Gray Marsh Station can't contradict our phony message to Goat Creek." Ki nodded. "As long as Goat Creek doesn't try to send a message up the line, or vice versa, the break should remain undiscovered for the time being."

Boyce climbed down the pole and then brushed himself off. "All right, fellow. I've done my part. Now it's your turn."

They mounted up and rode off in the direction of Goat Creek Way Station.

A couple of hours later Ki and Boyce were approaching the mesquite-studded butte where they were to meet up with Mikey and Jimmy Flame. Goat Creek Way Station was just a quarter mile away.

"You're sure you can trust those two men of yours?" Boyce demanded as they came to a halt amidst the rock formations that formed the foot of the butte.

"I am sure," Ki replied. "Both men have been at the Circle Star for many years."

"I don't know." Boyce shook his head. "Seems awful quiet around here. Being good and true cowhands is one thing," he pointed out. "Being good and true train robbers is another."

"Well, none of us has much experience robbing trains," Ki replied.

"That's a fact," Boyce agreed and chuckled.

"The important thing is that over the years Mikey and Jimmy Flame have proved to me that they will do what they say they will. And both men are devoted to Jessie."

"Well, I still think your men have chickened out," Boyce said, looking around. "Bet you two bits we're gonna have to pull this off all by ourselves after all—"

"Well, you jest lost that bet, Mr. Boyce!" Jimmy Flame cackled, popping up from behind a boulder. The bright sun turned his carrot-colored hair and bushy mustache to fire.

"I reckon the two of us have been late a'fore try'n to catch a train," Mikey added as he followed Jimmy out from behind the rock. The grizzled old hand scratched his whiskery chin. "But we don't plan to be late rob'n one!"

Ki looked both men over. As he'd requested, they were dressed in their most nondescript, tattered work outfits, and both had plain brown bandannas around their necks, to use to cover their faces during the robbery. His eyes fell to the revolvers on their hips. "Are your guns unloaded?"

"Yes, sir," Jimmy replied. "Ain't got a round between us, jest like you told us, Ki. We also brought old clothes for Mr. Boyce."

Mikey looked worried. "I jest hope you two will be able to keep things under control, like you said you could," the old hand said broodingly. "I don't feel too comfortable go'n into this situation like a toothless dog about to bait the bear!"

"Do not worry," Ki said. "You and Mikey will only be required to keep the soldiers covered once they have been disarmed. By then, the fight will be out of them."

I hope, Ki added to himself. Getting the better of almost twenty trained, armed men without seriously hurting any of them was a tall order, even for a samurai!

To hide his nervousness, Ki occupied himself checking his weaponry. He had his bow and arrow quiver, of course, strapped to his saddle, and he had a glittering array of *shuriken* blades lining the inside pockets of his vest, in addition to the pair he carried in the sheaths strapped to his forearms. But the blades would not be enough against the soldiers at Goat Creek. Ki would have to rely on other weapons, too—for instance, his *nunchaku*.

Next to his bow, the *nunchaku* was Ki's favorite weapon. This was because its effectiveness was derived in large part from the fact that it appeared to be only a harmless farm implement, a tool of the common people. The Okinawans had originally used the forerunner of the *nunchaku* as a grain flail. It was only after Ki's own people, the Nipponese, had confiscated all of the Okinawans' real weapons that these proud people developed *te,* and *kobudo,* the art of using tools as weapons.

A *nunchaku* consisted of two short sticks attached together at one end by a few inches of braided horsehair. Ki owned many different sorts of *nunchaku*. The one he carried today was cut from dense hickory, each stick a little over a foot long and octagonal in cross-section. Ki kept the weapon tucked into his waistband like a dagger. With it, he could effectively perform virtually every *te* block and strike, and with the extra power brought to the techniques by the hard wood of the *nunchaku*'s handles and the centrifugal force generated when he whipped those handles around on the end of their horsehair braid, flail-like blows from the weapon could shatter a man's bones.

And there were other, more subtle techniques that could be applied with the *nunchaku,* provided the adept had the skill and the time.

Yes, Ki thought. Today is going to be challenging indeed! To surprise . . . To disorient . . . To intimidate—these are my tactics for the coming battle.

To that end, in addition to his bow, *shuriken* blades, and *nunchaku,* Ki had with him an assortment of *nage teppo.* These were egg-sized grenades developed in centuries past by the *ninja* of the samurai's homeland. Each *nage teppo* was dyed a different color. The red ones created a smokescreen. The white ones erupted into flame. The yellow ones exploded in a flash of light that was harmless but temporarily blinding. The green ones exploded with the destructive power of a stick of dynamite. In Ki's quiver were arrows onto the tips of which the *nage teppo* could be fitted for long-range delivery of the grenades.

Boyce was changing his clothes, exchanging his suit for tattered canvas pants and a worn-out chambray shirt to make him appear like a run-of-the-mill outlaw. "I'd sure feel better if you'd agreed to wear a disguise," the railroad man grumbled.

"I do not intend to allow anyone to see me," Ki replied. "Besides," he shrugged, "my weapons and methods of combat are such that my actions would immediately identify me in this part of Texas, no matter what disguise I wore."

"Reckon there *ain't* all that many samurai wandering around to confuse you with," Boyce agreed.

"Jimmy," Ki reminded the carrot-topped ranch hand, "be sure all of your hair and that fiery mustache of yours is covered up. You will not want the authorities coming around at some later date looking for a redheaded train robber."

"Yes, sir." Jimmy nodded vigorously. "I already thought of that." He pulled a small, flat tin out of his jeans. "This here's boot black. I'm gonna rub it on my mustache and any hair that shows from under my hat. By the time I'm done, ain't nobody gonna think Jimmy Flame was anywhere in the vicinity!"

Boyce, who had finished changing his clothes, checked his pistols. "I presume, then, that I'm the only one carrying loaded guns?"

Ki nodded. "There will be no accidental shootings. It is the only honorable way to proceed with this endeavor. Our honor as warriors on the right side of the law decrees that we must make as certain as possible that no innocent participants get seriously hurt."

The railroad man nodded. "Then let's get going. It's time."

"Our horses are tethered just on the other side of these rocks," Mikey said.

Jimmy, who was putting the finishing touches on his now coal-black mustache, glanced at Ki. "You scared?"

"Fear is a state of mind," Ki remarked amiably. "Let us say that I am invigorated by the prospects of what we are about to attempt."

"Yeah, I'm scared too," Mikey sighed.

Ki laughed appreciatively. "Come on, my friends, Jessie and Tod are counting on us. We have a train to rob."

"You know, this is all your fault," Tod Lane scolded Annie Slade. "If it wasn't for you, Miss Jessie and I would be back at the Circle Star by now!"

"Oh, really?" Annie Slade shot back, her big brown eyes blazing with indignation. "How do you think I feel? I've been on Wolf Martyn's heels for months, and I was doing just fine—until I met up with you!"

"If you two could just stop your bickering for a few minutes, we could start to formulate a plan," Jessie tried to interrupt, but it was hopeless.

She attempted to ignore them by examining their surroundings for a countless time. There was just this one large room, with a fire burning in the slate hearth and a lantern glowing on the oval table in the room's center. Jessie, Tod, and Annie Slade were all huddled on a throw rug near the fire to keep warm against the stone house's chill. The rest of the room consisted of unadorned whitewashed walls and

155

a few sticks of rudely knocked-together furniture not worth sitting on. A rear doorway led to the kitchen, but that door was locked. Shutters that were nailed closed covered the windows, and the locked front door was no doubt also being guarded by Wolf's men.

No, Jessie thought. There's no getting out of here until Wolf lets us out.

And since Wolf Martyn had escorted them back to the stagecoach depot and locked them up in the main house, Tod and Annie had been at it like cats and dogs.

"Honestly," Jessie now chided the both of them, "if I didn't know better, I'd say the two of you were sweet on each other."

"Me, sweet on the likes of him?" Annie blurted. "That's a laugh!"

But Jessie noted that Tod was blushing furiously. I do believe I've inadvertently struck on the truth, at least as far as Tod is concerned, she thought, amused.

"Just what's so funny about it?" Tod asked evenly. "And if there was any laughing to be done, I reckon I'd ought to be the one doing it."

"You?" Annie sputtered.

"Yes, me," Tod replied evenly. "I got myself a respectable job as boss wrangler of the Circle Star. But what about you? Imagine! The likes of you running around the woods taking potshots at people with that midget rifle of yours. And the way you look—"

"What's *wrong* with the way I look?" Annie demanded.

Tod shrugged. "I reckon you're a mite skinny, but then again, with your face scrubbed and something frilly-like to wear, you might be a comely filly."

"*Face* scrubbed?" Annie squeaked, trembling with indignation. "Something *frilly*? *Might* be comely?"

"And are you saying you don't find *my* looks pleasing?" Tod pressed, coolly.

Jessie shook her head in amazement. She'd never seen this side of Tod, and frankly, she hadn't thought the young wrangler had it in him.

"Well, I guess you're passable handsome," Annie murmured, and now it was her turn to blush.

"And I guess that when you act tame, you are just about the prettiest little thing I've ever seen," Tod murmured, "even

156

with that dirt smudged across your nose, and those baggy men's clothes you're wearing."

"Well, just you remember that even though I might be acting tame, I *ain't*."

"You know, I've met up with a wild filly or two in the corral that played the same game," Tod remarked. "What I done to break 'em was just give 'em a firm hand, and now and again a slap on the rump to settle 'em down, and in no time at all I'm sitting tall in the saddle . . ."

It was all Jessie could do to keep from laughing. Tod was running rings around the girl. He was calm, collected, masculine. Put that together with those big blue eyes and good looks of his, and Tod Lane had the makings of a lady-killer for sure!

"Well, you try sitting tall in the saddle with me, Tod Lane," Annie warned, "and you'll be one stallion turned into a gelding, understand?"

"Yes, ma'am," Tod said and laughed. "I understand that some wild fillies need more time than others to accept the fact that they've met their match—"

"What do you mean by *that*?" Annie sputtered.

Tod ignored her. "Imagine! A girl like you setting out after Wolf Martyn all by her lonesome," he said, changing the subject.

Jessie rolled her eyes. To wile away the hours locked up in here, the three had exchanged stories. It seemed that Tod had just about gone plumb loco after he'd heard about poor Annie Slade's misfortunes, brought about by Wolf Martyn.

"What I intend to do concerning Wolf Martyn is a subject you'd better just shy away from—" Annie began.

Just then the front door swung open, flooding the interior with daylight. Big Joe stood in the doorway. Jessie was gratified to see that the big man had a grimy bandage wrapped around his bald skull.

"How's your head from that drubbing I gave you?" Jessie asked with mock sweetness.

Big Joe's hand rose up to cradle his sore head. "You'll get what's coming to you soon enough," he growled. "But now you've got some riding to do. Wolf wants to take you to Goat Creek Station. Get on your feet and get moving!"

As they were filing out of the room under Big Joe's watchful eye, Tod took a moment to whisper in Jessie's ear, "Annie may be slow to realize it, but she's the girl for me!"

"Care for a look?" Boyce offered Ki his small brass spyglass.

Ki shook his head. "I have traveled through the Goat Creek Way Station enough times to know it by heart," he told Boyce.

The station was a one-story red brick building with an outdoor waiting platform, littered with baggage and freight carts, alongside the track. Inside, a small front office for the telegraph operator and ticket clerk adjoined the passengers' waiting room. The waiting room was a low-ceilinged chamber with light green walls covered with large arrival and departure chalkboards. The room was furnished with backless benches that were likely just now taken up with soldiers, Ki thought, as he listened to the boisterous laughter coming from the station.

"It sounds like they are having a good time," Jimmy Flame muttered.

"Looks like it," Boyce replied, peering through his spyglass. "Reckon they're taken a spur-of-the-moment holiday now that they think the train's been delayed a few hours."

"Mikey, stay down," Ki reminded the ranch hand. The four of them, along with their tethered horses, were just fifty yards away from the station, hidden in a grove of hickory that bordered the track.

"Can you see how many there are?" Mikey asked Boyce.

"Nope. The way the sun's reflecting off the station's windows, I can only catch a glimpse now and then. I *can* tell you their NCO's a corporal who doesn't look old enough to shave."

"Excellent," Ki replied. "A young commanding officer combined with the soldiers looking forward to an afternoon of leisure suggests that discipline inside the station will be lax."

The samurai drew a special arrow from his *ebira*, the leather quiver strapped to his hip, and fitted a red *nage teppo* grenade into its hollow tip. "You three put on your bandannas and move into position," he said. "Mikey, Jimmy, remember to let Boyce do all the talking. All you two need do is wave your guns around and look dangerous."

"Tall order for one of us," Jimmy Flame said with a smirk, as Mikey glared.

Ki chuckled. "Remember, I will keep you covered from here. If all goes well, I will head off to intercept the train."

"I still don't see how you're gonna commandeer an entire train carrying a passel of armed guards," Boyce grumbled. "*And without anybody seeing you do it!*"

"You merely do not see the light," Ki said and smiled, his almond eyes glinting merrily. "Now off with you all. Into position. It is time." The samurai watched carefully as Boyce, Mikey, and Jimmy Flame fitted their bandannas into place to hide their faces and then flitted from the trees, to take up positions around the station.

It is fortunate for us that the soldiers inside, not expecting the payroll train for hours, have posted no sentries, Ki thought as he nocked his arrow, brought up his lopsided bow, pulled the string well past his ear, and let the red-tipped arrow fly. The twang of the hemp cord resounded as the shaft streaked toward its target, twirling through the air.

The arrow crashed through the station's window, shattering the glass, and the *nage teppo* erupted in a thunderous blossom of black smoke. Tendrils of the oily, choking smoke began billowing out of the broken window. The rest of the noxious haze, Ki knew, would be forming a blinding, suffocating fog inside the station.

"Holy shit!" one of the soldiers cried out.

"What's happening!" shouted another.

"Fire! There must be a fire!" another began to shriek in fear.

Ki watched, satisfied, as the station's door slammed open. The ticket clerk and telegraph operator were the first out, followed by the soldiers in their blue uniforms with yellow stripes down the trousers' legs. The soldiers spilled out in a ragtag bunch, coughing and rubbing their eyes. The samurai counted five troopers, including the corporal. As Ki had hoped, none of the frightened, choking men had thought to grab his regulation-issue Spencer or Henry repeating rifles before quitting the building. They were all wearing sidearms, but Ki doubted that any of them could get to their single-action Colt .45s, inside their flapped holsters, before Boyce took charge of the situation.

"All right, all of you!" Boyce shouted, coming around from behind the station, both of his guns drawn. "This is a holdup! We ride with Wolf Martyn! Surrender and you won't be hurt!"

One of the troopers began clawing at his flapped holster, but he quickly put up his hands when Boyce fired a warning shot in the air. A couple of the soldiers looked rambunctious, but the fight went out of them when Mikey and Jimmy Flame came around the other side of the building with their own guns drawn.

The soldiers, seeing they were surrounded by masked desperadoes, all put up their hands. Then the young corporal in charge drew himself to attention and announced in a shakey, high-pitched voice, "We surrender!"

So far, so good, Ki thought, vastly relieved. The battle for Goat Creek Way Station is over with no one hurt.

The samurai waited another moment, observing as Boyce had the troopers line up with their hands laced behind their heads. Then the railroad security man and Jimmy Flame kept the soldiers covered as Mikey relieved them of their revolvers.

"And that is that," Ki murmured. He left his bow and quiver hidden beneath some brush—he would not be needing them for what he next had to do—and made his way to his horse. He mounted up and wheeled the animal around, goading it into a flat-out run through the woods in the direction opposite the way station.

Ki rode hard along the dusty, sagebrush-choked trail that paralleled the railroad tracks. He had a particular spot picked out from which to intercept the payroll train. Five miles up the line from Goat Creek Station was a stretch of elevated land, studded with rock outcroppings. Here the train would have to slow to make the upgrade as the track snaked between the bluffs. Ki intended to position himself on a suitable overhang, wait for the train to pass beneath, and jump onto the roof of one of the cars.

And Anvil Rock is the perfect place, he thought as the huge landmark came into view around a bend in the narrow, rutted trail. Anvil Rock was a steeply walled chunk of granite thirty feet high. The rock's flat top, which had earned the outcropping its name, culminated in a lip that extended out over the track.

Ki hauled back on his mount's reins at the foot of Anvil Rock and then vaulted out of the saddle, landing lightly on the soles of his bare feet before his lathered gelding could even come to a full stop. He had arrived not a moment too soon, for his keen ears had picked up a metallic whispering. It was the twin steel rails of the track, beginning to sing. Soon, he knew, he would hear the first, faint rumblings of the approaching locomotive.

He stood still a moment, with his hands on his hips, breathing deeply to calm and center himself as he stared up at the vertical sheet of rock he was about to climb. Normally he enjoyed climbing. For Ki it was a form of moving meditation to press himself against the rock many feet above the ground while his fingers and toes searched for minute purchases . . . But normally climbing was a sort of game of chess between himself and the rock. He might freeze into a meditative state for as long as an hour while contemplating his next move against his stony adversary . . .

But now there was no time for a serene match of wills, samurai versus mountain. Now the rock was merely another adversary to be vanquished along the way on his relentless quest to rescue Jessie and Tod Lane.

Think of the ant, the fly, the bee, the samurai willed himself to remember, feeling himself becoming physically lighter as he went into the position known as the "horse stance." His legs were bowed as if he were straddling a horse, while his head, neck, and back formed a straight line, even with the heels of his feet. Think of the spider clinging to its web . . .

Then Ki sprang up, not like a bird, but like an insect taking wing. And the resemblance of his actions to those of an insect showed his good form, for the ancients had long ago devised this climbing technique. The secret was simple: If a man moved fast enough, he would have no time to fall.

Ki scuttled up the sheer rock face as if gravity did not exist. Within ten seconds he was twice as many feet off the ground.

Think of the monkey, Ki reminded himself. For a *te* adept soon learned that his bare toes could flex and bend to grip like fingers, just as he learned the art of sticking, of infinitely shifting one's center of gravity to transcend nature's physical laws. Falling simply was not a possibility . . .

Anyway, this tall rock was part of the world, and who could fall off the world?

Ki's fingers hooked themselves over the top. He bent his elbows, flexed his biceps, and lightly hauled himself up onto Anvil Rock's summit. He stayed low. Anvil Rock could be seen for miles around, and he didn't want to be spotted, on the unlikely chance that the payroll train had posted a lookout. Keeping his belly pressed against the cold granite, he slithered like a snake the length of the shelflike crest, until he was on the lip that protruded out over the track, thirty feet below.

At this height there was a steady wind blowing, creating a dirge-like sigh as it wove its way through the rocks. Ki stared down the track that laced through the bluffs, glinting in the sun like a narrow river cutting through a valley.

A thin skein of dark smoke appeared, curling against the blue sky until the wind snatched it away. Ki heard the rhythmic chug of the locomotive as it labored its way up the grade. The steam-powered grunt and exhalation came faintly at first, but built steadily in intensity.

A low, mournful steam whistle sounded as the train, belching black smoke, jerked and jolted its way around a particularly steep bend and then began to pick up speed as it approached Anvil Rock. There wasn't much to the train, just the locomotive and wood car, a baggage and mail car where the payroll was likely being kept, and a passenger car, where the cinder dicks and army escort were riding.

Ki let the coal-black locomotive pass beneath him and then quickly rose up, positioning himself with his toes hanging over the ledge's lip, like a diver about to go off a cliff. He waited until the baggage car had begun to pass beneath him and then pushed off into thin air, arching his back like a pole vaulter and then extending his arms and legs until he resembled a *shuriken* star spinning on the way to its target, cartwheeling sideways through the void. Beneath him the narrow roof of the baggage car rose up crazily, and yet the fall seemed to take forever, as in a dream, or a nightmare—

Ki touched down on the swaying planking feet first, as lightly as a cat, bending his knees to absorb the impact of his landing. An instant later he was making his way along the length of the roof, toward the locomotive. The train rocked and shuddered as it lurched along the steeply inclined, narrow-gauge track, and the curved wooden roof was slick with oil and soot, but Ki cupped his feet as he used his *te* training to maintain his balance. In no time at all he was at the wood car, and he rested a moment, hidden from view amidst the stacked cords of firewood, as he decided upon the course of action that would expose himself—and the locomotive crew—to the least amount of danger.

There were three of them manning the engine in their cramped compartment: an engineer, a brakeman, and the stoker. They were dressed in grimy overalls and chambray work shirts minus the sleeves. Their sweat had soaked the red bandannas around their throats and darkened the crowns of their leather-visored caps.

Ki needed to time his attack just right if he was to strike unseen. The engineer and the brakeman would be no problem: They both faced forward, with their backs to Ki, attentive to their dials and levers. It was the stoker who was making things difficult. One moment he would be facing in Ki's direction as he gathered up wood, and the next his back would be turned as he fed the blackened furnace.

Ki pulled his *nunchaku* from his belt, and waited for the right moment. In just a few seconds it came: The stoker had turned his back to hunch over the furnace and adjust the damper. Ki dropped down into the compartment. Inside, the cramped space stank of oil, and the floor was greasy. Ki almost lost his footing as he landed, but he managed to keep his balance, and then quickly made his move against the stoker, who evidently sensed movement behind him, and began to turn . . .

Ki held his *nunchaku* with both hands, one stick in each, with the braided end toward himself, so that the weapon resembled a set of tongs in his grasp. As the stoker straightened up, the samurai caught the man's neck between the two octagonal hardwood sticks and squeezed the sticks together, the way a scorpion will capture its prey in its pincers. The technique was an advanced form of *atemi*, the "soft sleep," the art of applying pressure to certain nerve centers in an adversary's body to kill, cripple, or, in this case, merely send the individual into unconsciousness.

The stoker emitted a soft sigh as he sank to the floor, but with the noise of the engine within the compartment's confines, Ki doubted that even a shout would have been heard by the two remaining members of the crew, who still had their backs turned to Ki. The samurai took out the brakeman by pressing the *nunchaku*'s blunt tip against a pressure point below the side of the man's jaw. Ki took a moment to break the unconscious man's fall and then dispatched the oblivious engineer in the same manner.

It was over in seconds, with Ki certain that the three men would eventually come awake none the worse for their experience, but without a clue as to what had happened to them.

And now it was time to rid the train of its passengers, Ki thought as he pulled the brake levers. The world around him erupted into sparks, and one long, banshee-like scream, as locked metal wheels filed shavings off the tracks. Its boiler head bleeding steam, the big locomotive's pistons slowed until they were barely moving. The train jolted several times, then came to a stop.

Ki checked the pressure dials on the boiler, and quickly stoked the furnace with wood. He wanted a big head of steam ready and waiting so that the train could move out smartly when the time came.

Now that the engine was idling, the din inside the compartment was vastly decreased. Ki could hear the shouts coming from the cars in the rear.

"What's going on?" somebody was yelling.

"What's wrong, engineer?" called another. "Why have we stopped?"

Taking care to stay out of sight, Ki shouted, "Help! Help! We need help up here!" He peeked out, again being careful to avoid being seen, to watch soldiers in blue and cinder dicks in civilian clothes tumbling out of the passenger car.

He counted thirteen men in all rushing toward his position with guns drawn. He'd seen no one disembarking from the mail car, and Boyce had told him that there were sixteen guards on the train, so Ki guessed that three of them had had the presence of mind to stay with the payroll. It meant little to Ki; the baggage car was windowless, so those inside couldn't see him.

Oh well, Ki now thought as he took a yellow *nage teppo* grenade from his vest pocket. I suppose Boyce, Jimmy, and Mikey can deal with the three that are left, the way we planned . . .

The soldiers and cinder dicks were almost to the engine compartment now. As Ki had assumed, the rock wall close by the far side of the train had kept all the men to one side. Ki waited until the first men were no more than ten feet away from his position and then shouted, "Everybody, watch out, he is going to try and make a break for it!"

There, Ki thought. That ought to get them looking. He squeezed his own eyes shut and tossed out the *nage teppo* . . .

He could only estimate the intensity of the white flash of light by the way the world turned fiery red through his own closed eyelids. Immediately Ki heard the mewling cries of terror.

"W-what happened?"

"W-what was it? I'm blind!"

Ki stood up—there was no longer any need to shield himself from view—and looked out at the damage. All the soldiers and cinder dicks were kneeling in the dust, their weapons fallen away and forgotten as they rubbed at their eyes and bemoaned their misfortune. Ki quickly unloaded the still-unconscious locomotive crew to the side of the track, then climbed back up into the locomotive and released the brake. As the train pulled away on the final leg of its journey to Goat Creek, Ki couldn't help feeling smug. Things had gone exceedingly well . . .

The locomotive crew would awake in about ten minutes, without the slightest notion of what had hit them. And just about that time, the temporarily blinded men would begin to regain their vision. Within twenty minutes everyone would be completely recovered . . .

Of course, they would also be stranded five miles from Goat Creek Station.

"You might as well enjoy your walk, gentlemen," Ki said with a chuckle, letting the breeze blow back his hair. "By the time you get to Goat Creek, everything will be long over . . ."

Ki couldn't resist blowing the train's whistle as the locomotive picked up speed. The end of the line, and Jessie's rescue, was in sight.

★

Chapter 12

"There comes the train now," Wolf Martyn said.

Jessie, Tod, and Annie Slade watched from horseback as the locomotive puffed its way toward Goat Creek Way Station. The three of them, surrounded by Wolf and his half dozen men, were on a grassy knoll on the far side of the tracks, looking down on the action. Silhouetted on this rise, they were in clear sight of anyone down below, but thanks to his hostages, Wolf was feeling brazen and had decided that there was no need to hide.

"After all," the bantam-sized outlaw leader had said with a laugh to Jessie, "I ain't the one robbing no train . . ."

Wolf had bragged to his hostages about how he had ordered Jessie's friends to filch the government payroll for him. Now Jessie was watching and waiting, wondering just how Ki and Dan Boyce were going to pull off the theft . . .

"Everything looks pretty normal," Tod murmured to Jessie.

Jessie shook her head. "If there's one thing that Ki has taught me, it's that appearances are deceiving."

"I see a lot of bluecoats around," Annie Slade piped up. "I wonder when Ki and your friend are planning to make their move." Annie had mentioned that she'd run into Ki out on the range some weeks ago, but had remained vague about the circumstances of that meeting.

"If I know my friends," Jessie replied, "they already have."

"Quit your talking, you three," Big Joe growled from behind them.

Jessie twisted around in her saddle to stick out her tongue at the guard. Tod and Annie laughed.

"Keep it up," Joe grumbled. "You'll get yours, and soon, too . . ."

"We'll see about that, baldy," Jessie said tauntingly. "Does your poor noggin' still hurt very much?" She grinned. "That bandage wrapped around your head looks cute."

"*You* won't be so cute when I'm done with you," Joe fumed.

"You talked big before too," Jessie told him. "And what did it get you, besides that bandage?"

"Goddammit, lady," Joe snarled.

"Easy, Joe," one of the other outlaws cautioned, riding to take position beside the angry guard.

Jessie looked the newcomer over, trying to evaluate his potential in a fight. He was a tall, rangy fellow with long dark hair. He had what looked to be a double-action Colt Lightning riding on his right hip. Jessie noticed that he also had Annie Slade's sawed-off rifle and shoulder rig sticking out of his saddle-bag.

"You remember what Wolf said . . . ," the long-haired out-law told his partner in crime.

"Don't worry none, Burt," Joe snapped. "I can follow orders!"

Jessie nodded to herself as she remembered how Big Joe, still nursing his grudge against Jessie, had volunteered to guard them. Wolf, explaining that the trio might be needed as leverage over Ki and Boyce, had cautioned Joe about prematurely doing them any harm.

"The train's pulling in now!" Wolf excitedly exclaimed. "We're going to be rich, boys!"

Don't count your money too soon, Jessie thought. She couldn't be sure, but she thought she had caught a glimpse of Ki in the locomotive.

"The train's blocking our view, Boss," one of the outlaws complained as the train came to a stop in front of the station.

168

"We're on the wrong side of the tracks," Wolf agreed. "We'll have to ride down if we want to see what goes on. Joe, you and Burt stay up here, and keep these three safe and sound. The rest come with me."

Here comes my chance, Jessie thought. Joe stayed behind them, but Burt kneed his horse forward, to take up a position alongside Jessie. Burt's Colt was within her easy reach, but did she have the nerve—and *speed*—to snatch it?

If I can get that gun, turn around, and shoot Joe before he can draw, we might have a chance . . .

She took a deep breath. It's now or never, she thought.

Ki eased up on the throttle as Goat Creek Station appeared around the bend. He began to apply the brake, stopping the train as the baggage car drew parallel with the station house, where four soldiers stood waiting. The samurai released the boiler's pressure and set the brake. He next slipped out of the cab when he was sure no one was looking and darted around the station house, where, according to plan, he found Boyce.

"Did you notice them up there?" Ki asked.

"Of course, I did," Boyce replied. He showed Ki his spyglass. "It's Jessie and Tod, all right."

"Surrounded by Wolf and his men," Ki noted.

"The two of them look healthy, and that's all that matters," Boyce said.

Just then Ki heard the rattle of the baggage car's door sliding open. He and Boyce edged around the side of the building for a better look.

There were three cinder dicks inside the car, all right. They had their guns drawn, and now shouted to the four soldiers on the platform: "It's a holdup! Outlaws got the train!"

"No shit," one of the soldiers on the platform replied dryly as Jimmy Flame and Mikey, still masked, appeared from out of the station with their guns drawn.

"You're surrounded by none other than the Wolf Pack," Jimmy warned the trio of security men who were peering out from within the dark confines of the baggage car.

"Damn, I heard Wolf Martyn had his sights set on this here payroll," one of the cinder dicks said fretfully.

"We got the rest of the soldiers tied up inside," Jimmy continued. "You three are surrounded by the toughest gang in the West!"

169

"Easy, there, Jimmy," Ki murmured to himself. "Do not overdo it . . ."

"Throw out your guns, and then the money," Mikey spoke up, "or else the Wolf Pack will fill that car full of lead."

"All right, we know when we're licked," the same cinder dick said. "You boys know we can't see out of this box to defend ourselves."

"I'm going to retrieve my bow and head on up that rise," Ki said as the security men in the baggage car tossed out their guns. "Perhaps I can free Jessie and Tod."

"Everything here is under control," Boyce said with a nod, as the three canvas bags containing the government payroll hit the platform.

Ki circled around the back of the building, then sprinted the fifty yards that separated the station from the wooded grove where they'd left their horses and he had left his bow.

The samurai was just reaching the first of the trees when he heard shots coming from where Jessie and Tod were being held—first one shot, and then three more in quick succession.

Jessie is in danger and I am stuck down here! Ki realized. But before he could finalize a plan of action he heard Boyce yelling, "Texas and Pacific Security! Wolf Martyn, you're under arrest!"

Whatever was happening was taking place out of Ki's line of sight. He needed to be on the far side of the train, the side opposite the station. He ran out of the grove, angling back to the train and then around the rear of the passenger car that he'd cleared of soldiers and security men at Anvil Rock.

I don't believe it, Ki thought as he stared, dumbfounded. Boyce was single-handedly facing down Wolf Martyn and his three men!

Boyce had removed his bandanna mask and pinned his five-pointed star to his shirtfront. "I said I'm railroad security!" Boyce repeated, drawing both his Colts. "Give up, or I'll shoot!"

Wolf's men, caught by surprise, were trying to wheel their horses around and ride back up the slope. They'd drawn their guns, and now began shooting, but since they were trying to aim and fire from horseback, they were no match for Boyce.

The cinder dick raised his guns and began to blaze away, making short work of the three outlaws, knocking them out of their saddles as if they were tin cans lined up on a fence.

Wolf Martyn had his guns out, but he quickly tossed them away as cinder dicks and soldiers, now re-armed, appeared from around the front of the train.

"All right, you win," Wolf snarled. "I give up."

Ki watched as the little outlaw was dragged off his horse. It looked like it was all over. The Wolf had been caught, at last . . .

But what of Jessie and Tod?, the samurai worried. What were those shots all about?

He peered up the slope, but Jessie and Tod were no longer visible. Grabbing the nearest horse, Ki mounted up and rode like a bat out of hell through the grove to his friends' rescue.

It's now or never, Jessie told herself.

Wolf and his three-man escort were already halfway down the slope. I've got to make my move, she thought.

But before she could, Tod Lane made his!

With an agility that would have made Ki himself proud, the young wrangler kicked his boots free of his stirrups and somersaulted backward out of his saddle. In midair Tod arched his back, twisting around so as to slam Big Joe with his shoulder, knocking the surprised guard out of his saddle.

"Ker-rist! Look out, Joe!" Burt began, but he froze as Jessie took advantage of his surprise to snatch his revolver. The Colt slid easily into her hand and out of the outlaw's waxed holster.

"Hands up, or I'll shoot," Jessie warned, pointing the Lightning at its rightful owner.

"A purty thing like you, shoot me?" Burt said and chuckled, ignoring her command to put up his hands. "I don't think so . . ."

"You're making a big mistake," Jessie warned him, thumbing back the Colt's hammer. "One that will cost you your life!"

Out of the corner of her eye she saw Tod and Big Joe rolling around on the ground as both struggled for possession of the latter's revolver. Annie Slade had dismounted and was making a beeline for Burt's saddlebag, in order to retrieve her own weapon, Jessie realized.

Just then Burt took advantage of her momentary distraction to try and grab back his gun. Jessie shot him once, in the chest. Burt gasped in surprise, then fell off his

171

horse, which had begun to rear in startled reaction to the Colt's report.

"Damn," Annie cursed in frustration, backing away from the thrashing mount and the saddlebag across its tossing rump that held her sawed-off rifle.

Jessie could understand the girl's frustration. Her midget Winchester was so close, and yet so far!

Jessie twisted around in her saddle, trying to bring her Colt to bear on Big Joe. So much was happening!

From down below, in the vicinity of the station, there was a flurry of shots and the cries of what sounded like wounded men. Meanwhile, Big Joe and Tod were still wrestling for the gun that was out of sight somewhere between their two writhing, entangled forms.

"Joe!" Jessie commanded. "Give it up! I've got you cov—"

Her final words were lost as the gun Joe and Tod were fighting over fired once, twice, three times. Both men went still.

Jessie, too, froze, with her heart in her mouth. She could only stare, wondering which man were going to rise . . .

"Tod Lane," Jessie heard Annie whisper fiercely. "Don't you *dare* be dead!"

"No, ma'am," Tod muttered, kicking free of Big Joe's limp form and getting to his feet. "I'm not dead *yet*, anyway . . ."

"Tod!" Jessie exclaimed. "Where did you learn a move like that backward somersault?"

"Oh, that?" Tod modestly shrugged, as he brushed himself off. "Any decent hand who calls himself a wrangler had best know how to get out of the saddle right quick when a bronco goes loco on him."

"And how did you best that big man in your wrestling match for the gun?" Annie chimed in.

"I reckon my smaller size was to my advantage there," Tod said and smiled. "My quick little fingers found their way past the trigger guard faster than Joe's clumsy big ones. By the time he gave up trying to get control of the trigger, and started to bend my wrists to aim the piece in my direction, I already had my first bullet in his chest . . ."

"Well," Jessie marveled at his skill, "you certainly are full of surprises!"

"And as for you, young lady," Tod said to Annie. "I'm glad to see you were worried about your lover man—"

"My lover man!" Annie sputtered, turning beet red. "You're badly mistaken, Tod Lane!" She stamped her foot. "I was just worried that—"

But Tod didn't let her finish her tirade. "You were just worried that you wouldn't get a chance for *this*," he declared, grabbing hold of Annie's arm.

"W-what do you think you're doing?" she managed to ask, an instant before Tod silenced her by pulling her close for a passionate kiss.

"My, my, Tod," Jessie said with a laugh. "You really *are* full of surprises!"

The kiss went on and on. Jessie would have intervened, but Annie seemed to be coming around to enjoying herself. Her initial struggle had subsided to a halfhearted squirming.

And Jessie guessed that there was no need to hurry things up on account of Wolf Martyn. The gunfire from down below was over now. Looking down the slope, she could see that all three of Wolf's men were lying on the ground, either dead or wounded. Wolf, himself, was standing with his hands above his head, surrounded by bluecoats and what she took to be railroad security men. The diminutive outlaw looked even smaller now that he'd been shorn of his guns and was surrounded by authority.

Annie finally broke free of Tod's romantic clinch. She seemed a little weak-kneed as she backed away from the beaming young wrangler.

"How dare you?" she said, sounding a mite uncertain.

"It was easy," Tod said and chuckled. "Want me to show you again?"

"Yes!—I mean no!—I mean . . ." Annie trailed off, groaning. "Darnit, Tod, you've got me so flustered I don't know what I mean . . ."

"And I mean to keep you that way too," Tod said softly. "Keep you all topsy-turvy, all the days that we're man and wife . . ."

"Oh, Tod . . ." Annie's fingers rose to her lips, where the taste of his kiss still lingered, and she smiled.

"Well, hasn't everything worked out just fine?" Jessie said. "You two have found each other, and Wolf Martyn has been captured."

"Wolf's been captured?" Annie asked sharply.

173

"Yes." Jessie nodded, turning to look down the slope. "He's down there—and look! Here comes Ki riding up toward us."

"Well, I'll be," Tod murmured, looking over Jessie's shoulder. "It appears you were right about Ki being nearby. I reckon Mr. Boyce must be down there as well."

"You two!" Annie cried. "Out of my way!"

Jessie threw herself sideways and Tod was all but bowled over as Annie rode past them hell-bent for leather down the slope. She had Burt's horse and rode with the reins in one hand and her sawed-off rifle in the other.

"She's going down there to have it out with Wolf Martyn, I just know it!" Jessie exclaimed.

"But he's been unarmed, taken prisoner," Tod cried. "If she shoots him now, she'll stand for murder."

"Oh, Tod . . ." Jessie said with worry.

He was right, she knew. Poor Annie Slade had found a second chance for happiness with the young wrangler, but the girl was about to throw it all away.

"Grab a horse, Miss Jessie," Tod said, mounting up on Big Joe's tan gelding. "We've got to get down there to stop her. I just got out of prison, and I don't aim to be visiting my fiancée in the hoosegow!"

Jessie tucked the Lightning into her waistband just in case, and then did as she was told. She and Tod ran into Ki on horseback when they were a quarter of the way down.

"Are you all right?" the samurai asked her, wheeling around his horse.

"Fine," she said and smiled.

"Who was that who just rode by me?" Ki continued.

"Annie Slade."

"Annie Slade?" Ki gasped. "What's *she* doing here?"

"She's about to ruin her life," Tod shouted.

"It's a long story," Jessie told the confused samurai. "Come on, Ki! I'll explain later."

The three rode the rest of the way down the slope to the station and quickly dismounted. Tod led the way. With Ki's help, Jessie was able to climb over the coupling linking the baggage and passenger cars and out onto the station platform—

Stepping into a scene from out of a nightmare . . .

Wolf Martyn, his hands cuffed in front of him, was backed up against the side of the baggage car. Annie Slade was standing beside him, with her midget rifle pressed up against the trembling outlaw's head. The soldiers and cinder dicks had all formed a loose semicircle around the two.

"Y-you can't let her k-kill me!" Martyn blubbered. "I-I surrendered! I-I'm cuffed and unarmed! I-I'm a p-prisoner!"

"Come on, now, miss," a young corporal was coaxing Annie as the others looked on helplessly, "you don't want to shoot nobody . . ."

"Stay away, all of you!" Annie commanded, her eyes fixed on the little outlaw. She pressed her rifle even more firmly against Martyn's head. "I mean it, now . . . Stay away!"

Jessie saw Dan Boyce standing off to one side and went over to join him. "She came out of nowhere," Boyce whispered to Jessie. "Before we could react, she had that little rifle screwed tight to Martyn's head."

"Dan, we can't let her do this," Jessie said.

Boyce frowned. "Do *you* know a way to talk her out of it?"

"Annie, remember me?" Ki began, taking a step toward her. "Remember what I told you about being a warrior?"

"Stay away from me, Ki!" Annie warned the samurai. "I don't want to listen to you—"

"Then maybe you'll listen to me," Tod Lane said firmly, striding through the line of onlookers, coming to within a few feet of Annie and her captive outlaw.

"T-Tod, make her get a-away!" Wolf wailed. "I-I don't want to d-die!"

"Tod, I've got to do this." Annie sniffled, near tears. "You can't understand—"

"Who says I can't?" Tod replied.

"I told you what he did to my parents," Annie cried out. "He ruined my life!"

"No, *you* ruined your life," Tod calmly corrected her. "You ruined it when you decided that you had nothing left worth living for but your *vendetta* against that sniveling little coward you've got there."

"Tod—" Annie began.

"And I *can* understand how you feel," Tod cut her off, "because thanks to Wolf Martyn, I ruined my life, as well." He paused. "Annie, I haven't had a chance to tell you, but I've been in prison."

"What?" Annie glanced at him. "You? Prison?"

"I spent five years in jail," Tod continued. "And it gets even worse. I spent those five years on account of joining up with the Wolf Pack—"

"*You?*" Annie gasped. "*You* rode with *him*?"

Tod nodded. "I was a boy. I didn't know any better. My dad was dead, and I reckon I thought I needed a man's approval. I'd heard the legends about Wolf Martyn, so I found my way to him. Even in those days I was good with horses. Wolf took me on as the gang's junior wrangler." Tod's voice grew harsh. "But my first time out with the Wolf Pack, holding onto their horses while they pulled a bank job, they left me high and dry. And I got five years . . ."

"Oh, Tod." Annie shook her head.

Jessie, watching, thought that Annie seemed to falter a bit. She let the rifle sag. Wolf, seeing his opportunity, tried to sidle away—

"Stay right where you are," Annie snapped, putting her gun back against his head.

"Oh g-god!" Wolf bawled. "*S-somebody help me!*"

"You're right to call to God, Wolf!" Annie hissed. " 'Cause you're going to *meet your Maker* in just a few moments—"

"Annie, listen!" Tod fervently said. "I *know* what prison is like. I was sent there because of him. It'd bust my heart if the woman I love ends up in the same place on account of that little bastard." He spat at Wolf's feet. "Look at him! Crying and begging . . . Near to wetting his pants, if he hasn't already. He's going to *hang* for his crimes, anyway." Tod glanced around at the soldiers and cinder dicks. "Ain't that right?"

"Count on it, son," Dan Boyce replied.

"You see, Annie?" Tod said, taking another tentative step toward the girl and holding out his hand to her. "Please now, come away. Leave the past behind. Don't let it ruin your future."

Jessie held her breath as she watched Tod gently rest his hand on Annie's shoulder. The girl seemed to sag beneath his light touch.

"Tod's right," Annie told Wolf Martyn, lowering her rifle. "Killing you ain't worth jail time." She glared at the outlaw. "But I'll be there in the front row to watch you dance at the end of a rope, you little squirt!"

She spat, point-blank, into Martyn's face. Then turned her back on him.

Thank God, Jessie thought, as she watched Tod lead Annie away.

All eyes were on the girl who'd come so close to committing murder. Perhaps that was why Wolf gained the opportunity he needed. One moment the little outlaw was standing there with Annie Slade's spittle dripping from his face; the next he was reaching beneath his frock coat with his cuffed hands and coming up with a twin-shot derringer!

"Squirt you called me!?!" Martyn roared in fury. "*Nobody* talks to the *Wolf* that way!"

Jessie clawed for the Colt tucked into her waistband. Out of the corners of her eyes she glimpsed Boyce going for his guns and Ki drawing back his arm, a glittering *shuriken* throwing blade having appeared in his hand as if by magic.

But none were so fast as Annie Slade. The girl spun around, at the same time stepping in front of Tod, as if she meant to protect him from stray bullets. Her sawed-off rifle barked twice, so quickly that the reports seemed to blend together into a long snarl of righteous rage.

The two .44-40 slugs doubled Wolf over. He let his derringer fall to the ground, unfired. The dying outlaw sagged to his knees, clutching at himself as he stared at Annie with stricken eyes.

"I-I'm s-shot?" he said in wonderment. "Y-you shot m-me . . ."

Annie showed him her rifle. "A midget gun, for a midget outlaw."

Wolf Martyn opened his mouth as if to say something more, but no sound came out. He coughed blood as he collapsed to the ground. His legs kicked feebly. Then he lay still.

"That wasn't murder," Tod said quickly, looking around. "You all saw it."

"We all saw it," Boyce agreed, holstering his guns. "It was self-defense, plain as day."

"It was a good thing Annie was so fast too," Jessie put in. "Else Wolf would have bitten one last time with that hideout gun of his."

Boyce shrugged apologetically. "We never did get a chance to do a thorough frisk on Martyn before that young lady took charge of the situation."

"Funny thing is," the army corporal said as some of his men lifted up Martyn's corpse, "he even *died* small."

That evening, a warm fire crackled in the great slate hearth back at the Circle Star spread. Jessie was glad to be home. And glad to have all of her friends—Ki, Dan Boyce, Annie Slade, and Tod Lane—seated around her massive mahogany dining table, enjoying dinner. Boyce was filling everyone in on what had taken place during the latter half of the payroll robbery.

" . . . So Ki had gone off to fetch his bow," Boyce continued. "And there I was hiding behind the station, watching through my spyglass at what was going on up the rise where Jessie, Tod, and Annie were being held. I saw Tod make his play against one of the outlaws, and Jessie snatch the other outlaw's gun. That's when I figured they had their situation well in hand." He paused. "Wolf Martyn was riding down to the station, and seeing my chance to nab him, I quickly decided to cut short the robbery."

"I saw that part," Ki said. "You removed your mask, pinned on your badge, and took Wolf prisoner."

"But what happened to the two ranch hands you said had been helping out?" Annie Slade asked.

"They got back here safe and sound, I know that much," Jessie said, glancing at Annie. Jessie had lent her a dress, a clinging, green velvet gown that allowed the girl to show off more curves than a mountain pass. With the auburn halo of curls framing her lovely face, Annie looked ravishing.

It's clear Tod thinks so as well, Jessie thought. He can't take his eyes off her . . .

"Mikey and Jimmy Flame got away easy as pie," Boyce assured Annie. "As soon as I decided to change the plan, I stepped out from behind the station, got their attention while the soldiers and cinder dicks were distracted by the gunfire that had gone on up on the rise, and gave them the signal to hightail it out of there. Later, I told that corporal that a couple of the Wolf Pack got away, but the kid agreed with me that with Wolf Martyn dead, his two surviving men were no threat, and not worth chasing. Jimmy Flame and Mikey are free and clear."

"But how did you explain *your* being there, and in outlaw garb?" Ki asked.

"That was easy," Boyce answered. "I just said that I'd been on the Wolf Pack's trail, caught up with a straggler, took him prisoner, and proceeded to interrogate him concerning the Wolf Pack's plan to rob the train at Goat Creek." He winked. "Unfortunately, the prisoner produced a hideout gun, just like Wolf's, and I was forced to shoot him dead. I buried him out on the prairie, but not before I calculated the plan to take his clothes and join in the robbery attempt in the hopes that I could foil it when the opportunity presented itself." Boyce looked proud. "Which I did. As I told that corporal, I waited for the rest of the gang to cover their faces, then I covered mine, and I blended right in . . ."

"Well, then, now it *really is* all over," Ki sighed. "I, for one, am very glad."

"Amen to that," Jessie said and laughed. It'll be nice to have some peace and quiet hereabouts, she thought. Now that Wolf Martyn is Lone Star history.

"Well, it isn't quite all over," Boyce announced. "There's still the matter of the reward for Wolf Martyn's capture. The Texas and Pacific was offering five hundred dollars for Wolf, dead or alive." He smiled at Annie. "That bounty goes to you, miss."

"What?" Annie exclaimed in happy surprise. "Oh, thank you!"

"You earned, it, Annie," Boyce said with a grin.

"I reckon that money will take you far," Tod murmured, his eyes downcast. "Far from me, that is."

"What do you mean, Tod?" Annie asked, sounding startled.

"I reckon you won't want to be near me now that you know I was a jailbird," Tod wistfully explained.

"Don't want to be near you?" Annie repeated, getting up from the table and moving to stand beside Tod's chair. "But if I wasn't near you, how could I do this?"

She tilted up his face in order to give him a passionate kiss. Everyone applauded.

"You and I are going to be married, just like you said, Tod Lane," Annie lectured the young wrangler. "And don't you figure on *ever* getting away from me, or you'll answer to Li'l Pete!"

179

"Yes, ma'am!" Tod said happily. "I reckon that's a life sentence any man would be tickled to get!" He sighed, clearly relieved. "And there I thought that my secret would drive you away."

"Not a chance," Annie said, stroking Tod's hair. "Of course, there are some secrets that are better left unsaid." She glanced across the table. "Right, Ki?"

"Indeed," the samurai agreed with a chuckle.

"What's going on here?" Jessie demanded. There's something up between these two, she thought.

"Nothing." Ki winked at Annie, who winked back. "Just warrior talk," he finished.

And when Ki had that mischievous tone, Jessie knew, there was no point in pursuing the matter further.

"Miss Jessie," Tod began, taking hold of Annie's hand, "I guess I'll have to resign as boss wrangler of the Circle Star." He glanced up at his bride-to-be. "With that reward we'll be able to buy a spread of our own, and start a family."

"And you'll have the wedding right here at the Circle Star, I hope," Jessie offered.

"Oh, yes! That would be grand!" Annie gushed. "Oh, thank you, for everything!"

"A toast!" Boyce exclaimed, getting to his feet. "A toast to the happy young couple!"

Everyone stood and raised their wineglasses.

"Here's to Annie and Tod," Jessie happily declared. "As long as they have each other, the 'wolf' will never again be at their door!"

Watch for

**LONE STAR AND THE CHICAGO
SHOWDOWN**

126th novel in the exciting LONE STAR series
from Jove

Coming in February!

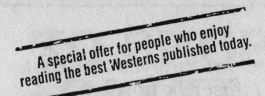